COMING HOME FOR CHRISTMAS

COMING HOME FOR CHRISTMAS

From the Editors
Of *True Story* And
True Confessions

Published by True Renditions, LLC

True Renditions, LLC
105 E. 34th Street, Suite 141
New York, NY 10016

ISBN: 978-1-938877-79-7

Visit us on the web at www.truerenditionsllc.com.

Contents

Beautiful Love Story!
PRETTY PAPER

Through the sound system's speakers perched who-knows-where in the store, Jose Feliciano was singing "Feliz Navidad."

Again.

That meant that the next song would be "The Little Drummer Boy," followed by "Jingle Bell Rock." I already knew the rotation by heart, having heard it every night at the department store ever since before most people stocked away their Thanksgiving leftovers.

A third time, I waved the wand over the barcode. Nothing. Biting back a cussword, I rang up the leather jacket manually.

"You have a gift box for that, right?" the customer, a guy in his midtwenties, asked.

"Sorry, we don't," I droned, sliding his credit card through the machine.

"You don't? Come on! No box? What am I supposed to do? Give my girlfriend the gift, no box?"

Quite a few suggestions came to mind, none of which I thought the guy would appreciate. Here's a clue, boyfriend: Don't wait till Christmas Eve to shop for your ladylove! Or you could always throw the leather jacket in the backseat of a sassy, little Maserati. I bet your special girlfriend would like that a whole lot more than a gift box.

"There's a dollar store down that way," I told him as he signed the slip, "right next to California Pizza. You can get gift boxes there."

"You mean I can buy gift boxes there," he muttered. "I'm spending a hundred and thirty on the jacket. You'd think the store would throw in a gift box for free."

Secretly, I couldn't blame him. Unfortunately, there's this little rule about not trashing your employer—especially not with your manager on another register, less than a stone's throw from the one you're working on.

And I needed that cheap, little, minimum-wage job.

Now more than ever.

"Sorry about that," I apologized. "Happy Holidays."

"Yeah. Happy Holidays." The customer didn't even look at me, just grabbed his receipt and purchase and shuffled through the crowd in the store toward the exit.

I didn't take it personally. Firstly, I try not to let a stranger's foul mood ruin my night; secondly, I didn't have the time to ruminate on it. Behind the next customer waited a long line of people, all last-minute shoppers. Some had one or two items; some came with entire cartfuls to be rung up.

"The Little Drummer Boy" was playing. Right on cue. I glanced at my watch just as my coworker on another register, Damien, spoke into the PA system.

"Attention, customers: We will be closing in ten minutes. Please bring your purchases to the registers as we will be closing . . . in ten minutes."

I sighed. As anyone in retail knows, that means ten minutes for the customers. Us poor employees are trapped there for at least another half-hour after that, vacuuming our section of the store and doing all of the final straightening up and refolding before at last punching out.

On my way to my car in the parking lot I realized that, between that job and working the front desk at the hotel earlier in the day, I'd been working for almost twelve hours straight.

That breakneck schedule wasn't new to me; I'd been working two jobs, trying hard to make up for the cut in salary I had to take when they outsourced my department at the insurance company seven months earlier.

I've never been one to whine or play the woe-is-me game. My parents were always the kind of people who rolled up their sleeves and got their hands dirty. Whatever they had to do to keep a roof over our heads, they did it—and with good nature and a lot of laughter, at that. Eventually, I knew I'd find another job—one as good as the one with the insurance company, maybe even better. For the time being, though, I was making ends meet—just barely.

Yet it was starting to wear on me after nearly a year. I know I felt a whole lot older than my twenty-six years. And the very last thing I felt—what I was totally numb to that night—was the Christmas spirit.

". . . It's just about a quarter to twelve here on this cold Christmas Eve," the DJ on the radio announced. "We hope your holiday's filled with lots of joy and fun! And here's our next Christmas tune—'Feliz Navidad!' "

I burst out laughing. Again, with the same song! Yet it hurt even to laugh.

This Christmas isn't even going to be a shadow of last year's holiday. Feeling my throat constrict, I pushed that thought away quickly.

I couldn't think of that night. If I let myself dwell on that painful thought—well, my heart just couldn't take it. Especially not tonight, of all nights of the year.

A light snow began to fall. Those of us who make our homes in the Northeast can tell which snows will stick and which won't, and that one certainly wouldn't. Still, it looked pretty through the windows of my used Camry.

I drove up my street, noticing how festive the other houses looked in comparison to mine. I bought the house when I was at the insurance company, when everything was going well for me—when it felt like I was on top of the world. When I bought it, it was a fixer-upper and it wasn't in the best of neighborhoods. The house was supposed to have been an investment; it would be someplace cozy to live in for a while and I'd fix it up slowly so I'd have a down payment on my future dream house.

Things don't always work out as planned, though. If I was learning anything from life, it was that lesson.

After parking in the driveway on the side of the house, I walked slowly to the front, admiring the homes across the street. The multicolored lights on the porches and windows glowed through the snowfall against the dark, starless sky behind the homes.

And then there was my house, looking like it was any other time of the year—

Wait a sec. What's that on the porch, leaning up alongside the door? Is that a Christmas tree?

"Hey, Nicki!"

Hearing my name called out initially startled me. It was almost midnight on the night before one of the biggest holidays of the year. The last thing I expected was a visitor.

And I recognized the voice, even if it didn't really seem possible.

"Ashton?" I asked incredulously, and stepped around the dying rosebush in the front yard and onto the porch steps.

Then I saw him standing there on my porch: Ashton Cutler. Although we hadn't laid eyes on each other in months, my heart still skipped a beat when I saw him. He was bundled up in a brown parka and hood, his hands clad in gloves and his feet in boots.

"What—what're you doing here?" I asked.

Ashton paused, then motioned to the tree. "Bringing you this."

"A Christmas tree?"

"Yep. A Scotch pine, to be exact. I remember you like that kind. Your mom told me you didn't put one up. I—I thought I'd bring you one."

My eyes widened in surprise. I had a sinking feeling that wasn't all my mom told my former boyfriend. In all likelihood, Mom probably bumped into Ashton at the card shop where she works part-time.

"That's very nice, but . . ." I giggled nervously. "It's been a long time."

He nodded. "Yeah. It has."

"How long you been out here?"

"A couple of hours. I parked over on that street." He waved a hand toward a side street. "I didn't want you to see the car; I wanted to surprise you."

"Oh, I'm surprised, all right!" I shared a smile with him as I fished my keys from my purse. "You look cold."

"Nah. I was cold the first hour I was here. Fortunately, I lost all feeling about an hour ago."

I made a face at him. Part of me wanted to greet him—really greet him, I mean—with a tight embrace and a deep, wet kiss: the works. The way we would've greeted each other back when we belonged to each other. But I held back, cautious with my heart, remembering, Those days are long gone.

"That was really nice of you," I said. Against my better judgment I added, "Come on in. Warm up a bit."

Deep down, I knew that inviting him in wasn't the smartest move on my part. But what was I supposed to do? Say, Thanks for the tree— now beat it? Besides, there was no way I'd be able to haul that big, old Scotch pine into the house by myself.

"You kept all those decorations, didn't you?" Ashton asked, bringing the tree in with him.

"Oh, yeah. The ornaments, the lights—everything. I think they're— uh—in the last place you saw them . . . when you were here."

When you lived here with me, I wanted to add. Remember? When we fell asleep in the same bed each night and woke up next to each other every morning. Because I haven't forgotten it.

Inside, I felt more than a twinge of pain. Funny, I thought, After all this time, I thought I was past this.

"In the basement?" Ashton clarified.

"Where else? Hang up your coat. Too late for a cup of hot cocoa for you?"

He unzipped his coat and pulled off his hood. Under the coat he wore a pair of faded blue jeans and a dark blue work shirt that bore his name embroidered on the front pocket. I guessed, correctly, that he was still working as a master mechanic at that commercial printing plant.

"Only if you're making some for yourself," he said. "Don't go to any trouble, Nicki."

"It's no trouble. It's the right kinda night for hot cocoa, you know?"

"I think so, too. And you don't need to worry—I won't stay long."

I watched him hang his parka on the coat rack in the foyer, right next to my coat. It was the little nuances like that—little pieces of the past—that threw me off slightly.

"You just got here," I reminded him lightly. "And—oh, I don't know. I thought you were helping me decorate the tree . . . ?"

All at once Ashton seemed to relax. The crooked smile he gave me was tender, hesitant—like he was treading carefully, perhaps afraid I'd be cold to him. Most likely he was as afraid as I was of making myself look silly by letting on about just how much I missed him.

"I'll light the fireplace, too," I told him, turning toward the living room.

"You mean the make-believe fireplace, right?"

4

Heartily, I laughed with him. That was an old inside joke of ours about how the house hadn't come with a fireplace, so Ashton bought me a good, artificial one—really just a fancy heater.

"Hey, it does the job!" I sang out.

"That, it does. It feels great in here already. Well—after standing outside in thirty degrees for hours."

While turning on the fireplace I heard the basement door open and his footsteps falling on the rickety, wooden staircase. I headed into the kitchen to put on some water for hot cocoa.

It's ironic how Ashton Cutler and I met. One Christmas four years earlier brought us together when one of his closest buddies married one of my roommates from college on the twenty-fourth of December.

Even though the church looked beautiful, decorated with all of those gorgeous poinsettias, I vowed that I, personally, would never get married so close to a major holiday. Weddings are rush-rush as it is and my former roommate was a total wreck by the end of it, a real bundle of nerves, snapping at everybody over every little thing. I understand none of the girls in her wedding party are speaking to her to this very day.

As for me, a regular guest, I had a great time! To top it off, the wedding planner seated me at the same table with the cutest, most rugged-looking blue-collar guy with eyes of clear blue that contrast dramatically with his dark brown hair. Plus, he has a fun sense of humor. Ashton took my number that night and promised he'd called me that week—and, unlike most guys—he kept his promise.

I poured the water into the cocoa mix in two mugs, added a little half-and-half to make it creamier, and gave each a dusting of cinnamon. I headed out to the living room, where Ashton had situated the tree in the stand from the basement and cut off the twine that bound it.

"That's a pretty tree," I marveled out loud.

He glanced at me, looking pleased. "You like it?"

"It's . . . maybe even nicer than the one we had last year. Fuller."

"Yeah? The one last year, though. That's hard to beat."

Ashton gazed at me with a look that was hard to read. I sat on the ottoman and started pulling boxes of ornaments from the large box.

"You had to wait a little longer than usual out there," I began, "because I'm working two jobs."

"I know. Your mom told me that, too."

"That woman should be on Eyewitness News!" He chuckled and reached for the lights. I waved a hand in the air and told him, "Aw, don't fiddle with those. It's too late."

"Sure? Ah, you're probably right. But back to your mom . . . she mentioned you're working at the mall. I'm sorry about your job—the one you were at for so long."

5

I shrugged. "That's what I get for not finishing college, I guess. But that was a bit ago. I'm doing okay now; I just don't have a lot of time to myself."

He helped himself to one of the mugs. "I know you're okay, but I'm sure it was tough. There's no company loyalty anymore."

"None at all. They do whatever they have to do for that bottom line." I held my mug in both hands, gingerly taking a sip of the piping hot, cinnamony brew. "How about you?"

"Ah, still at the print shop. But it's okay. I got a good raise about three months ago."

"Did you? Congratulations!" Our conversation was just too natural, too easy. That didn't seem right. So I had to ask then, "I would think you'd have something . . . more exciting to do than spending Christmas Eve decorating a tree with an old girlfriend."

Ashton shook his head. "No. I don't, in fact. Your mom told me you'd be spending Christmas with her and your dad tomorrow, but that you'd be working and just coming home tonight. And of course, that you had no tree. I couldn't think of anything that I wanted to do more tonight—or anyone who I wanted to be with more tonight—than you."

We were quiet for a few moments. Moments that felt surreal, but at the same time, sad. We sipped our hot cocoa and moved around the tree, placing gold and red ornaments on it.

Ornaments that we bought together.

No. I will not do this.

By then, it was clear to me that he had more in mind when he came to my house to surprise me. But I wasn't having any of it—

Not after it took me so long to get over breaking up with him.

As nonchalantly as possible, I murmured, "You're not going to see your folks this year?"

"No, not this year. I miss my mom, but my dad . . . well, you know."

I nodded. "You don't see eye to eye with him; I know. But it's been a hard year for all of you, I'm sure."

I noted that Ashton's hand shook slightly as he secured an ornament's hook on a strong branch. "It has been a hard year," he admitted without looking at me. "That—that had a lot to do with everything that happened between us—between you and me, I mean."

Oh, not this conversation, I thought, groaning inwardly. Not tonight. We can't get into this tonight.

To be honest, other than losing my job and my grandmother, who I was so close to, dying after years of being afflicted with Parkinson's, I've never been through much tragedy in my life. And that's exactly what Ashton and his parents went through when his brother died—tragedy. His older brother Matt, a cop, was shot and killed in the line of duty.

I looked him straight in the eye. "And how are you doing with everything that happened now?"

6

"With everything that happened to Matt?" He shrugged, like guys do. "I've been dealing with it. I think I'm finally coping."

"Good. I'm glad to hear that."

"Now, with how I handled it and how I let it destroy what we had—you and me? That, I'm still not really over. I'm not over the way I shut you out . . . the way I lost you. Especially when we needed each other the most."

"You know what? We need music. We can't do this without Christmas carols and stuff."

I tuned the radio to one of the Top 40 stations, which I knew was playing almost continuous Christmas songs. It was getting late, so I kept the volume low. I didn't want to disturb the neighbors; I just didn't want to get into that conversation. Not on Christmas Eve. Not when I'd worked twelve damn hours straight. Not when I was almost over Ashton Cutler. They could play "Feliz Navidad" for the thousandth time for all I cared, and "The Little Drummer Boy" and all of the other ones they'd been playing over and over again—anything to drown out that conversation.

But instead, ever so mysteriously, the Christmas song, "Pretty Paper," began flowing from the radio. It's an old song—one you didn't hear as much as the others. That particular song always seemed to play back in the day when Ashton and I were decorating "our" tree.

At first, no words passed between us. We listened to the beginning of the song, just looking at each other sadly.

"I imagine you're tired," he managed to rasp out. "I'll go after we're done here."

"All right. I am pretty tired, actually."

He nodded. "I understand. I really just wanted to see you, wish you a Merry Christmas. I didn't want to see you alone tonight. And this would've been my first Christmas without you since I've known you."

The rest of my cocoa sat getting cold in its mug on the coffee table. I found the little clown ornament—a very old one that belonged to Ashton when he was a little boy.

I held it out to him. "I guess you forgot this. You want it back?"

His eyes met mine. I looked at the ornament—that little thing, not nearly as fancy as the glittering things we bought together—and a tear betrayed me.

He didn't say anything, just reached to take my hand in his. Though it was difficult getting the words out, I confessed, "I don't really want you to go. And I don't want to talk about yesterday."

Ashton cleared his throat. "Okay."

Then he drew me in close, his hand closing around mine, the one that held the memory from his childhood. Softly, even a bit awkwardly, he pulled in closer. His lips brushed against mine at first, and then my lips parted to accept his kiss—a kiss that was warm and hungry and tasted like chocolate . . . and home.

We never finished decorating the tree that night because we ended up in my bed—the same bed we shared for so many nights—making love. We turned off the fireplace and fell asleep in each other's arms.

And we woke up that next morning to no presents waiting under the tree. But as Ashton and I had breakfast and finished decorating, we realized we had everything we could ever ask for.

THE END

TIFFANY'S CHRISTMAS TREE
I stopped being "Scrooge" for my daughter's sake.

"It's beautiful," I said to Tiffany, holding up the construction paper bell she'd made in her kindergarten class. "We can put it on Aunt Betsy's tree."

Tiffany's face fell. "Why can't we have a tree of our own?" she asked. "Like the one in the picture with the angel."

"Well . . .we'll see. Go wash up for dinner, honey."

"'We'll see' always means no," Tiffany muttered as she headed for the bathroom.

I sighed and thought, She's only five. How can I explain it to her?

I had a lump in my throat as I looked over at the picture on a side table. Tim, my husband, stood in front of a Christmas tree even taller than he was, holding Tiffany. She was just two years old. A beautiful angel topped the tree. It had belonged to Tim's grandmother, and it looked like it was hovering over his head like a warning that he belonged to heaven. Tim was a state trooper. Six months after that picture was taken, he stopped a car because the taillight was out. The driver had just committed a robbery and he shot and killed my husband.

I went into the kitchen to serve up dinner, thinking about a Christmas tree. The year after Tim's death, it had just been too painful to deal with Christmas. It was all I could do to deal with a toddler, a job, and my grief. Besides that, the mortgage on our house was too much for me to pay alone. We had to move from the house to this apartment. During the move, the box of heirloom ornaments—and the angel—got lost.

We always went to Aunt Betsy's for Christmas dinner. She called me the week before that first Christmas without Tim and said, "You can't be bothering with Christmas, Meg. It's too soon. Why don't you bring Tiffany over on Christmas Eve and we'll decorate the tree? You can help me cook Christmas dinner the next day."

Over the next few days, my mind kept returning to Tiffany and Christmas whenever it slowed a little at work. I work as a dispatcher for the county sheriff's department. Christmas is a busy time for us, even during the day shift. People drink more and have more car accidents. There were fires from Christmas trees, kids lost at the mall, and even the memorable incident when a father got into a fight with a Santa. We're located in the same building as the sheriff's department and the jail, so a day at work can feel hectic—especially during a hectic season.

Two different deputies asked me to Christmas parties that week, but they weren't surprised when I said no. Everybody knew that I wouldn't date a cop. I couldn't chance living through what had happened to Tim all over again. What everybody didn't know was that I didn't date anybody. I knew it was time to move on and to make a life without Tim; I just didn't know how. Tim and I had made so many plans. Now I just lived day to day.

Later in the week, Tiffany asked about a tree again when I dropped her off at school. After work, I went over to Drake's to look at Christmas tree decorations. It was three days before Christmas and there wasn't much left besides bedraggled-looking garlands and the ornaments nobody wanted. There were no treetop angels left, and certainly none like the beautiful one we'd inherited from Tim's grandmother. I felt discouraged.

Maybe next year, I thought. But on the way home, I saw Layton's vegetable stand all lit up in the early dark and surrounded by Christmas trees. On an impulse, I pulled into the parking lot. I wandered up and down the rows of cut trees, wondering how I could decorate one for Tiffany. The pine scent was wonderful.

"Those balsam firs look great," said a deep voice. "Still plenty of nice ones left."

I turned to see Mike Hustedt, the new deputy. He'd moved to town a couple of months ago. He had warm eyes with laugh lines and he looked like he'd been a football player in high school. The women at the station found him very sexy; I certainly had to agree with that.

"Yes. They smell good, too. I'm just looking; I don't think I'm going to buy one. Did you pick one out?"

"I was just looking, too. It doesn't seem like Christmas without a tree, but I can't bring myself to put one up just for me."

"No family?"

"Divorced. No kids and my parents live in Maryland."

"My little girl wants a tree, but our ornaments got lost when we moved. I'm thinking popcorn, beads, and ribbons, but it's just not the same."

"No, it's not. I have an idea, though." He tilted his head a little, looking down at me. "I got the ornaments after the divorce—I guess because I've been collecting them for years. I used to go to the stores earlier than everybody and pick a few of the best. I have lights, too. I'm not going to get a tree, so you could use them."

"Oh, but, I couldn't. . . ."

"Sure you could. It's just a loan. Next year, you can get your own ornaments earlier in the season."

Before I knew it, Mike had helped me pick out a tree. Then, when I realized my car trunk was full of presents for Tiffany, he threw it in the back of his truck and followed me home.

"Where's your little girl?" he asked as he pulled the tree out of the truck in my driveway.

"She goes to my aunt, Betsy, after school every day. I want to hide this until I can decorate it tomorrow evening. We can put it in the storage area in the basement of the apartment house."

"That sounds good. Lead the way."

I had to go upstairs to call Aunt Betsy to tell her I'd be late, so it only seemed polite to invite Mike in for coffee. As we sat down in the living room, I said, "Are you sure you don't want to use those ornaments?"

"I'm sure. I'm not working tomorrow, though, and I'm going out of town to see a buddy over in Brockton. I'll be back by five and I can bring the ornaments over then."

I searched for a nice way to tell him that I didn't date cops without sounding like I assumed he'd be interested.

He seemed to read my mind and grinned. "I know you don't date deputies. This is just a friendly favor."

I felt my face flush. "I guess everybody talks a lot."

He looked at the picture of Tim and Tiffany and his face turned serious. "I can understand how you feel. I hear he was a great guy."

Looking at the picture, too, I said, "Tiffany is going to be a little disappointed when that angel isn't on the top of the tree. I'll have to find her one next year."

By the time I got to Aunt Betsy's they were done with supper, but Aunt Betsy insisted on making up a plate for me. While Tiffany watched the end of a videotape in the other room, I ate and told Aunt Betsy about the Christmas tree.

"Good. I love having you here, but I have the other kids to help me. You and Tiffany need traditions of your own. Now tell me about Mike."

I flushed again. What was wrong with me? "I hardly know him."

"He sounds like a nice man."

"He is nice, Aunt Betsy. But I don't date deputies."

"Seems to me you don't date anybody. Meg, people are in harm's way all the time. It's dangerous just living. You can't hide your heart away because it might get broken again."

"I just can't take the chance that what happened to Tiffany and me could happen again. There are lots of nice men with safe occupations in the world."

"Except that you don't seem to be meeting them," Aunt Betsy said tartly.

The next evening, Christmas Eve, Mike was waiting for me when I got home from work. He had two big boxes with him and he carried them upstairs. Then he carried the tree up from the basement.

"I have a tree stand, too," he said. "Let me help."

"You've done too much already."

"This is the fun part."

11

I had to laugh at his enthusiasm. "Okay," I said. "Let's divide up the work. I'll cook dinner and you get the tree into the stand in that corner over there."

While we ate, Mike told me a little about himself. His ex-wife had wanted him to give up being a cop.

"She didn't like the danger?"

"In spite of all the rookies who watch television and think this is going to be an exciting job, it isn't all that dangerous outside the big cities." He saw the look on my face. "I'm sorry, Meg. I guess the chance is always there for trouble. No, she didn't want me to be a cop because she wanted me to make more money. She wanted me to work for her father in the insurance business, but it wasn't for me. We had a lot of other problems, though. She didn't want kids. I did. Stuff like that."

"So you're starting over here."

"That's it. I like it here." He glanced around the kitchen. "Right here." He gave me a smile that made my heart beat faster.

We got the lights on the tree and we put on the larger and more delicate ornaments. There was a tin star ornament for the top. As we worked together, I couldn't help but be aware of Mike physically. Down, girl, I told myself. Wrong guy.

"I think I'd like to leave the rest of the ornaments for Tiffany to help with," I said finally. "It will seem more like her tree, then." I went to get her construction paper bell from the other room and when I returned, Mike was putting his coat on. "I don't know how to thank you," I said.

"No need. One more thing." He picked up a bag he'd put to the side and pulled out a wrapped present. "It's for Tiffany," he said, putting it under the tree.

My heart melted. It didn't seem right that he would do all this for Tiffany and not get to see her face when she saw the tree, so I spoke on impulse. "Why don't you come with me to pick up Tiffany? We can all finish decorating the tree together."

"I'd like that a lot."

Aunt Betsy was all aflutter when I showed up with Mike. "He's very handsome," she said in a stage whisper. I found myself blushing again. She sent a pie home with us for later.

I thought Tiffany would be shy with a strange man, but she and Mike got along like old friends. She rode home in his truck, sitting between us and chattering away about her school day and what her surprise might be. She didn't guess.

The look on her face when she saw the tree was joyous. "My own tree!" she shouted. That's when Mike gave her the present to unwrap. It was a beautiful angel.

"Where in the world did you get it?" I asked him.

12

"There's one of those stores that sell Christmas decorations year-round over near Brockton. They don't run out because they're always reordering."

He lifted Tiffany up to help her put the angel on top. I felt close to tears. It was a wonderful evening. We ate pie and finished decorating the tree. When we said good night to Mike, Tiffany kissed his cheek. He looked very pleased.

I was tucking Tiffany in when she asked, "Can Mike come over for Christmas?"

How could I explain to her my rule about not dating deputies? I couldn't, but inviting Mike over would only be encouraging him. I already felt too attracted to him, as it was. "We'll see," I said.

As I turned out the light, I heard her whisper, "We'll see doesn't always mean 'no.' "

It was a very busy day at work. I didn't get out for lunch until late. When I came back, Diane, one of the other dispatchers, asked me, "Do you know Greg Harrison?"

"Yes. I went to high school with him."

"I hope he wasn't a good friend. He just got killed."

"But he's an accountant." Ignoring the puzzled look on Diane's face, I asked, "What happened?"

"He was up on a ladder, trying to get an outdoor Christmas decoration to stay up. He fell and he was dead when the ambulance got there."

My mind was on Greg Harrison all afternoon—but not because I'd known him well. I'd hardly known him at all and I only knew he was an accountant because somebody had told me at our last high school reunion. I couldn't stop thinking about him because he'd been a young man in a safe occupation. Aunt Betsy was right: Just living was dangerous. In my line of work, I should have known that.

Diane was working the swing shift so when I got up to go home, I asked her if Mike was still out on patrol. She said he was on his way in now.

"Tell him I'll meet him in the parking lot," I said.

Her eyes got big and round. I knew it would be all over the station in a couple of days, but I didn't care.

Half an hour later, Mike strolled over to my car. "Tiffany would like you to come over for Christmas Eve," I told him. "I'm making chicken stew with dumplings, if you like that. Tiffany will put up her stocking. You can even come over early the next morning, too, if you like. And Aunt Betsy has a big Christmas dinner . . ." I spoke in a rush and ran out of breath.

He leaned down and put his face close to mine. "I'm glad Tiffany wants me to come, but what about you?"

"I want you to come, too," I said. At that moment, something relaxed inside of me that I hadn't even known was tense.

He leaned over and kissed my lips briefly. "I'll see you in two hours," he said. "Merry Christmas."

I drove home with carols playing on the car radio and a new, bright hope in my heart.

THE END

A PICNIC . . . FOR CHRISTMAS!

His crazy idea was so romantic!

I looked up as my peppy roommate burst in the door. "Okay, don't say no. We're going for a ride to look at decorations."

"We—as in you, Don, a mysterious airman, and me?" I asked.

She nodded. "You've been mooning over that last jerk for too long. And Don's roommate is an absolute doll."

I grabbed my coat with a sigh. Everyone was a "doll" to Margie.

I climbed into the backseat and was introduced to a dark-haired, blue-eyed guy named Ike Burton. His blue uniform enhanced his blue eyes and he was really good- looking.

"Hi," he said, and offered me his hand.

I put my hand in his, which he held a little longer than necessary, and smiled back. "Caroline Bradshaw."

"Is it just me or are all you southern girls just this pretty?"

"Well, I don't know, but thank you, anyway," I replied, knowing right away that he must be from a northern state. Living in a town with an airbase, I had met people from everywhere.

"You're welcome, just making an honest observation."

Don turned around. "Let's show them the base decorations. They went all out this year."

"You see that Rudolph?" Ike pointed out when we reached the base. "That rascal keeps me awake all night with his nose going on and off. Don and I have the room right above him."

I laughed. "I think he's cute. Look at Santa. Someone must've tilted his sleigh."

"He had trouble landing, I guess." Ike got out of the car and straightened the sitting Santa.

I noticed how tall and well built he was. But one date was it; I wasn't going to get started with another guy—not even a good-looking airman.

Later, we stopped for something to eat and I found myself enjoying the evening, in spite of my reservations.

"Are you guys going home for Christmas?" Margie asked. "It's only two weeks away."

"Nope. Pennsylvania and South Carolina are too far away for us to make it this year," Ike answered.

"Oh, that's too awful. I can't imagine being away from home at Christmastime!" I exclaimed.

"I was in Korea last year," Ike said. "Coldest place I've ever been.

The South is much better." He moved closer and put his arm around me.

We drove up in front of Margie's house and got out. The wind was picking up and there were already a few snowflakes in the air.

"Oh, gosh, Margie—it's snowing! Can you believe it? I haven't seen snow this time of year in forever!" I ran, catching the snowflakes with Ike behind me.

"I guess you folks don't get much snow around here, do you?" He grabbed me and whirled me around and then pulled me close.

I knew he was really attractive, but when he gathered me up, I was surprised by how comfortable I felt in his arms. Almost immediately, I drew back. I wasn't about to lose my heart again.

"I guess we better get back to the base, girls," Don said after awhile, starting for his car.

Ike walked to the door with me. I had just started to tell him good-bye, I had a nice time, etc., when he turned me around to face him.

"I know, I know, first date—a blind date, even, and what-have-you—but. . . ." He leaned down and kissed me gently. "I'd like to see you again, Caroline."

I looked away. "I don't know, Ike. You'll be leaving soon and. . . ."

"And I know—you had a bad experience with another airman. Margie told me. Look, Caroline—I'll be here at the base for a year at least. A lot can happen in a year, you know."

I could hardly breathe. Ike was standing close and his kiss, gentle as it was, had simply bowled me over. "I . . ."

"Shhhh." He put his finger to my lips. "I tell you what—I'll pick you up tomorrow night and we'll discuss this then."

He left before I could answer.

When he arrived the next night, I had every intention of nipping it in the bud.

"Hello, Caroline! I thought we'd have a picnic out at the base picnic area."

"A picnic! In the snow?" I exclaimed. The snow had actually stuck and accumulated overnight and it was expected to stick around for at least a few days before it warmed up a little again.

"Sure. Why not? I have sandwiches I got at the mess hall and we'll stop along the way and pick up drinks and cookies."

I smiled. "Okay. Why not? Picnics aren't reserved for sunny, warm weather."

When we got to the base, Ike pulled me out of the car and we walked together over to a little picnic table in the snow. Ike cleaned the snow off the table and spread the food out and then gestured for me to sit down and eat. I giggled and tramped through the thin snow, rubbing my hands together.

"Cold?" he asked.

16

"Not much. I can't believe we're having a picnic in the snow! Are you always this impulsive?"

"Impulsive! I planned this for at least two hours," he said with mock indignation.

He dusted a bench off and motioned for me to sit down. Mother Nature decided to add her two cents' worth and snow started drifting down again.

"Isn't this just beautiful? Or maybe you're used to this kind of weather," I said, and laughed.

He pulled me closer. "Weather, yes, but not being in it with a beautiful woman." He lifted my chin and kissed me, this time with more passion. "Caroline, this is sudden, I know, but I think Santa has already brought me what I want for Christmas."

I was snuggled against his chest to keep warm and toasty so I answered him in a muffled voice. "I didn't even know what I wanted."

Ike laughed. "I did the moment I saw you," he said, and then his lips closed over mine.

THE END

HOW TO DECORATE
A CHRISTMAS TREE
My leading man always puts
the star on top.

December is my special month. It starts with my birthday and ends with Christmas and New Year's Eve—all wonderful, festive occasions. Everything seems brighter and more cheerful when colorful lights decorate the downtown streets and people smile more and call out, "Merry Christmas!" But after the way that December started out, I shouldn't have been surprised that the entire month was filled with highs and lows, ups and downs, and curves, just like a roller coaster ride.

I don't consider myself a material girl, but on my birthday I expected George, who I'd been dating for three months, to give me a gift. He did—a small toolbox for my car. It was very practical of him. My car is temperamental and has a history of minor breakdowns. I knew that his gift of pliers, wrenches, and a screwdriver in a lunchbox on which he'd painted my name would come in handy, but I would've preferred something more romantic. Flowers or perfume would've been nice.

After he gave me my present, he proceeded to give me a lesson in checking the little things that go wrong with a car. He showed me how to check the oil and the radiator levels and even how to make sure the hoses are on properly.

I could've cared less, but I pretended to be interested. After all, he was teaching me things that I should learn. Later on that night, he took me to a Mexican restaurant and we had a wonderful time. His good night kiss was special and I wanted it to last longer, but he pulled away and said he'd call me later.

George is good-looking. Tall with an athletic build, he has dark hair that's wavy in the front and he has a nice smile. Sometimes it's more of a boyish grin because he loves to tease me. He's the dependable type. If George says that he'll be at my apartment to pick me up at seven, he's there at seven on the dot—not a minute too early or a minute too late. He's predictable.

Three days later, George did call me and we arranged to go to a movie on Saturday night. We didn't end up going, though, because I broke the date.

I couldn't help it. When Claude walked into the bookstore at the mall where I work, I lost my senses. He looked like my idea of a

California surfer even though he had on jeans and a heavy sweater. His blond hair was longer in the back and his eyes were the bluest I'd ever seen. I didn't know how you could have such a tan in December, but he looked great.

I stood staring at him as he moved past me to the literature section. I made myself walk over to him. "Is there something I can help you find?" I asked. I hoped that I was using a husky voice, but I think it came out in a croak.

"Thanks. I'm looking for a gift for my sister. She likes pretty highbrow stuff. Hemingway or Faulkner."

"We have just that type of book right over here," I said, and led him to the special section we'd set up for the Christmas rush. "The leather-bound volumes are here and the less-expensive, but still very nice ones are over here."

"Thanks," he said, and smiled a hundred-watt smile.

I couldn't think of anything else to say, so I stood there for a moment and then decided I'd better move on. I did not want to look like a starstruck, thirteen-year-old kid.

Before I'd taken two steps he asked, "Which do you think she would like best?" He held a book in each hand.

I looked at each one. Although at the time I should've seen some sort of omen in Steinbeck's The Winter of Our Discontent, I didn't. "I think she might like Light in August," I told him. I hadn't read it, but the title seemed a bit more cheery and in his presence I was feeling pretty happy myself.

"You may be right," he said, and handed the book to me.

I walked with him to the cash register and rang up the sale. "Doing your Christmas shopping early?" I asked to make conversation. I wanted to say something extremely witty, but I couldn't think of anything.

He chuckled and it was a wonderful sound—sort of a husky, masculine laugh. "She mentioned something about a book last night, so I decided to act on it while I was thinking about it."

"Andrea," the manager said. She walked up behind the counter while I was giving him the change. "While there's a breather here, would you take your break?"

I glanced at my watch and saw that it was a half-hour before my scheduled time, but the store wasn't as full as it gets during our peak season. "Sure, Mrs. Brooks."

The guy was still standing there when I came around the counter. "Andrea, what a pretty name. Would you care to join me for a cup of coffee?" the California hunk asked.

I couldn't believe what he was asking me. I nodded and knew that I was smiling from ear to ear.

"How long do you have?" he asked.

"Fifteen minutes," I answered.

"Not long enough," he said. "What do you normally do?"

"I usually get a drink and just sit on one of the benches. I like watching the people walk by."

"Sounds good to me." He took my hand and placed it on his arm as if he were escorting me to some fancy ball. I felt goose bumps clear to my toes.

We picked up two cups of coffee and sat on my usual bench. He told me that his name was Claude and that he worked at the new art store that had just opened up at the mall.

"Are you working now?" I asked.

"Not yet. I don't go in until twelve thirty today. I work the evening shift on Friday nights. Tomorrow, I'm back on days."

He explained that he's an artist. Some of his works were for sale at the art store. We talked and talked until I realized that my break was over.

"I knew fifteen minutes wouldn't be long enough to get to know you," he said. "Let's have dinner together tomorrow night."

I said yes on the spot and it was only later that I realized that I already had a date with George. I knew the thing to do was walk to the art store during my afternoon break and tell Claude that I already had plans, but after the single rose arrived from the mall florist, I just couldn't do it.

The card read: Thanks for a fascinating fifteen minutes. Claude.

I used my next break to call George at work and tell him that I had to go home for the weekend and wouldn't be able to keep our date. He said that he understood the demands of family and he hoped that my mom would feel better soon.

I felt like a heel, but when Claude walked in on his afternoon break, my heart soared and I knew that there was nothing else I could've done.

To salve my conscience, I called home that night to see if everyone was all right. My younger sister and brother were fine and Dad was okay, but Mom had a slight cold. I felt better that at least that part was true. Mom really wasn't feeling well.

On Saturday morning I bustled around cleaning my apartment. I live in a great place above an architect's office on the corner of Main and Sixth Streets. On weekdays it's a bustling office area, but the weekends are fairly tame since a lot of the downtown merchants have moved out to the mall.

After I got my apartment sparkling clean, I drove to the Laundromat and got the week's laundry done. The rest of the afternoon I spent working on myself, washing my hair and giving myself a manicure. I wanted to look my best for Claude. Although he wasn't due to arrive until seven, I was dressed in my favorite red dress and waiting by six thirty.

I sat watching TV until seven and then put some music on. I had my rose sitting on the coffee table in a place of honor and picked it up and smelled that wonderful fragrance again as I waited. By seven thirty I was very nervous and wondered if Claude was going to stand me up. I couldn't believe that such a wonderful guy would do something like that, though.

Maybe he's ill, I thought. Or maybe he had a wreck driving to my apartment. I looked for his name in the phone book, but didn't find it.

I paced the floor, glancing out the windows that overlook Main and then walking to the windows that overlook Sixth. It didn't help. I didn't know what kind of car he drove, so I didn't know what to look for.

At ten of eight, I jumped at the sound of knocking. I was wound up as tight as a spring and I had to take several deep breaths before I opened the door.

"Hello, Claude," I said. "You're late." I hadn't meant to say that, but it came out of its own free will.

"Sorry," he said, and smiled that charming smile of his as he walked into my apartment. "I was thinking of you all afternoon and as soon as I got off work, I felt inspired. When the spirit moves me, I'm compelled to create. I painted an abstract of you with a rose. I'll show it to you as soon as it's finished."

His eloquent speech dissolved my anger over his late appearance. "Well, how nice," I said, once again grasping for something witty to say.

"This is a wonderful apartment," he said, walking over to look outside at the blinking Christmas lights. "It's your own little corner of the world. A window on Main Street."

"You have quite a way with words," I said, feeling a little awed to be with him.

He smiled again. "Are you ready to go? I know this quaint, little place you'll love."

"I'm ready," I said, and picked up the coat that I'd thrown over the back of the couch over an hour before.

We walked downstairs and out into the night air that was so cold that we could see our breath as we spoke. I don't mind the cold. Claude put his arm around my shoulders and I leaned into him. I wouldn't have known if it was twenty-two or eighty-two degrees outside.

The quaint, little place turned out to be a new Greek restaurant in town. I wasn't used to the strange spices and I don't like green olives, but I ate the odd concoction placed in front of me and acted like it was great. Claude ate his with a gusto that would've done a Greek proud.

Over dinner, I learned that he'd moved to town only six months before. That's why his number isn't in the phone book, I realized. He'd heard through his sister that the area fostered quite an artists'

21

and writers' colony and he wanted to meet the great and near-great and learn from them and maybe even make some contacts. So far, the closest he'd come to it was working at the art store, but he was meeting some people who buy art and that was a good start. He was very optimistic that his ship would come in soon. Already his luck was looking up because he'd met me, he told me.

As Claude drove me home, he kept me close beside him with one hand on the steering wheel and his other arm wrapped around me. It felt so cozy and so right until I saw George's car in the lane next to us. At the stoplight we pulled up right beside him and I burrowed down in the seat so that only the top of my head was visible.

"Comfortable?" Claude asked.

"Yes, and a bit tired," I added to explain why I'd settled down so low in the seat.

After two blocks of being within feet of George's car, we turned off on Main Street. George went straight, which isn't the way to his apartment. I wonder where he's going, I thought.

Claude walked me upstairs, but he didn't come inside because I'd mentioned how tired I was. I could've kicked myself for saying that. He did kiss me good night, though, and it was a powerful kiss.

"I'll call you," he promised before he turned around and went down the stairs.

That night I dreamed about Claude as a famous artist and me by his side, inspiring him. I really wanted to see his painting of me and the rose.

On Sunday I fooled around and waited for Claude to call. I even took the phone off the hook so he'd get a busy signal if he called while I was out at the grocery store buying food for my lunches and the usual staples. As soon as I got back, I put the receiver back in its cradle, but it didn't ring until around seven that night.

"Hello," I said breathlessly.

"Hi, Andrea," George said. "How were things at home? Your mom doing better?"

"Oh." I hesitated and bought time until I could think of a good line. I told part truth, part lie. "She's much better. I did some cleaning this weekend, picked up groceries—you know—that sort of thing so she can take it easy."

"Did you have a safe trip? No trouble with your car?"

I live fifty miles from the small town where my family lives. Again, I thought up a story to tell him.

"No problem, although it coughed a little when I started it today." It really had done that when I went to the store, so that was the honest truth.

"I'm glad you're back," George said, and continued to talk about his weekend. He didn't mention where he was the night before and I couldn't ask or he'd know I'd been in town.

"How about taking in the early movie on Tuesday?" he asked.

"I don't know if I'll be off in time. Mrs. Brooks has mentioned extending our work hours depending on the crowds at quitting time. Can I call you tomorrow night and let you know?"

By then I'd know if Claude had any plans for us to be together during the week. I felt confident that he'd come to the store during his break.

I was right. He came during both his morning and his afternoon breaks. I decided the matter of the evenings myself and asked him over for supper on Wednesday night. He accepted immediately and didn't mention getting together before then, so I called George and agreed to go to the movie with him on Tuesday.

I was glad that I had, too, because the movie had a scene where the leading lady prepared dinner for the leading man. Baked Cornish game hens and asparagus were the only two things I recognized, but it was a good start for my dinner with Claude.

After George took me home, I waited for him to pull out of the parking space below my window before I bundled up again and went to the all-night grocery store.

I'd planned on getting groceries on the way home from work on Wednesday, but the Cornish hens would have to thaw and besides, buying them sooner would give me extra time to get ready. I had a sexy caftan that I was going to wear that would knock his socks off. I wanted to look extra special.

On Wednesday after work I slipped into old jeans to work in the kitchen. I used a packaged mix for the dressing, stuffed the hens, and stuck them in the oven. Then I opened a package of asparagus and arranged the shoots in a dish for the microwave and placed the rolls in a basket to be warmed up later. Finally, I poured a can of applesauce into a bowl, sprinkled it with cinnamon and nutmeg, and stuck it in the refrigerator to cool.

I decided to set the table after I was dressed and I was just going into the bedroom when someone knocked on the door. Perhaps my neighbor next door needs to borrow sugar, I thought.

It was Claude. "Hi, Andrea," he greeted me as he closed the door behind him.

"You're early," I said, glancing down at my oldest jeans and ragged sweatshirt.

"I know. I just couldn't stay away from you for another minute," he said, and kissed me hard on the lips.

"Wow!" I exclaimed.

He laughed. "I wrote a poem for you," he told me, and proceeded to fish a piece of paper out of his pocket. He unfolded the crumbled paper and read the poem "To Andrea" out loud. In it, he compared me to a crimson rose and I nearly swooned at his feet. His poem was full of the bloom of love. Although he'd known me for only a short while, he was ready for a meaningful relationship and I was the special girl in his life. Claude was being so romantic that I forgot that I hadn't had time to comb my hair. He thought I was beautiful just the way I was.

"Do you believe in love at first sight?" he asked.

"I never have until now."

We talked before dinner and I asked him over on Saturday night to help me put up my Christmas tree. He thought that it would be fun and said he'd bring a pizza.

Dinner was a grand success. The Cornish hens looked like a picture in a cookbook. When Claude praised my cooking ability, I made a mental note to add Cornish hens to my regular shopping list.

He told me more about his background. He's from the Midwest, I discovered. The great tan was from a tanning salon. He told me that it's important for him to look good to get people interested in becoming a patron and sponsoring him. I supposed he had a point. He sure looked good to me.

Instead of giving me the poem he'd written for me, Claude decided that he wanted it and would make a neat copy for me. His thoughtfulness truly touched me.

Again, though, he left after only one good night kiss. If I'd had the time to change into my caftan, I might've gotten three or four of his fantastic kisses.

I saw Claude every day after that during work breaks, but not in the evenings since he was coming over on Saturday night.

I asked George over for dinner on Friday night to ease my guilty conscience. I didn't like deceiving him. I thought about breaking up with him, but decided that we weren't really going out together that much—just a couple of times a week. I even rehearsed a little speech about not seeing him again, but something kept me from saying those final words.

I fixed the same meal I'd fixed for Claude on Wednesday night and George ate every bite and said it was good. He talked a lot about his ambition to own his own sporting goods store someday. He was getting lots of experience working at The Dugout, but he didn't want to always depend on someone else for a livelihood. It was the first time he'd talked to me about his future. He's intelligent, thoughtful, and honest and my lies weighed heavily on my shoulders.

I'd had plenty of time to change into my caftan since he didn't arrive until the stroke of seven. And that night the sexy outfit worked. We cuddled together on the couch and watched the late movie, exchanging kisses from time to time. It was really quite a pleasant evening, but it paled in significance the next morning when I thought about seeing Claude again.

I searched through two Christmas tree lots before I found the perfect tree to go in my front window. At home, I brought the Christmas decorations down from a high shelf in the big closet. I don't have many—most are hand-me-down decorations from Mom—but I was proud of the ones I'd added during the two years that I lived on my own. Again, Claude was supposed to arrive at seven. This time, I was prepared and had my long caftan on by five thirty. However, when he didn't arrive by seven thirty, I began getting worried—just like the time before when he was late. By eight thirty I was angry, but figured he was working on another painting. I went ahead and put the Christmas tree in the stand and placed it by the window.

Next I checked each strand of lights for burned-out bulbs and strung them around the tree. Hunger pains reminded me that I hadn't eaten since lunch and even then I'd only had a sandwich. Since I figured Claude would eventually show up with the pizza, I fixed only popcorn and had a Coke with it.

By nine o'clock I'd finished my snack and was ready to put the ornaments on the tree. I fluctuated between wanting to call him and wanting to leave him alone to finish his painting, if that was what he was doing. Although I called information and got his phone number, I decided that I wouldn't lower myself and call him. If he didn't want to show up, I certainly wouldn't beg him.

I hung the ornaments and played my only Christmas album. Decorating the tree has always been a wonderful activity for me and I refused to let Claude spoil it.

At a quarter to ten, he finally showed up.

I let him in without a word.

"Sorry I'm late," he said. Instead of a pizza box, he had a poinsettia plant in his hand. "For you," he said, and handed me the plant. "Merry Christmas."

"Thanks. Why are you late?"

"A patron came into the art store right before my shift ended and wanted to buy one of my paintings. One thing led to another and I ended up taking the patron to my apartment to look at other paintings. I sold two more!" he said proudly.

"That's wonderful," I said, softening. "But you could've called me."

"There wasn't really an opportunity. Aren't you excited for me? This is important for the future."

"Of course I'm excited," I said, and kissed him.

He kissed me back and held me against his hard length for a long time. "Your tree looks great! Anything I can do to help?"

He didn't mention the pizza, so I figured he'd eaten with his patron. I was still annoyed, but I didn't want to push the issue since having patrons is crucial to his success as an artist.

"I have the star left to put on top." In my family, the star is placed on top of the tree by my dad. It's sort of symbolic of the head of the family. Letting Claude do that instead of doing it myself in my own apartment was giving him a special gift.

"Here, that's no trouble. I can reach it easily." He picked up the star and placed it on the very top of the tree.

"Beautiful," he said. "Just like you." He swept me into his arms and it was then that I smelled the perfume. It was one I'd wanted for the longest time, but at thirty-five dollars an ounce I was still waiting for a fairy godmother to get it for me.

I pulled back. "Was your patron by any chance a woman?"

"Yes, she was," he said. "And she loved my paintings. She bought one for her husband as a Christmas present."

"Oh," I said. That would explain the fragrance. She was probably floating in money and a heavy dose of perfume.

"I feel inspired tonight," Claude said. "I want to go back to my studio and paint."

"Don't you need sunlight for that?"

"It's best, but I have special lights that work just fine. Thanks for being so understanding, darling," he said and held me in his arms again.

I could've stayed like that forever, but he broke the embrace. "Oh, and here's the poem I wrote for you." He fished a folded piece of paper out of his shirt pocket.

"Thanks, Claude," I told him and kissed him again.

He kissed me back and then disappeared out the door with a wave.

Afterward, I read my poem again and again, memorizing each word. Claude was the most romantic guy I'd ever known.

Finally, I put away the boxes and straightened up the room. We hadn't plugged in the lights. That's what we did at home when Dad put the star on top.

I plugged them in and admired the tree. All it needed now were presents. I sat down and made a list of the gifts I wanted to get for my family, for Claude, and for George, I finally added.

I decided that I'd start seeing George just once a week and then gradually fade to not seeing him at all. That would be better than having to explain anything about Claude.

On Sunday afternoon I went out to the mall. It was sort of a busman's holiday to go there on my day off, but I wanted to do some serious shopping and even if Claude didn't monopolize my break time, fifteen minutes isn't long enough to look for the special present I wanted to find for him.

I'd located just the right scarf for my sister and a new wallet for Dad when I bought a Coke and sat down to rest my feet. Instead of my usual break bench, I chose a place close to Santa's chair where he listened to the children tell him their Christmas wishes.

I was sitting behind a mountain of poinsettia plants that formed a Christmas tree when I heard a familiar voice.

"Darling, I've been looking for you!"

I smiled. Claude had found me! I looked around, but I still couldn't see him.

"Hi, Claude," a sultry voice answered. "Thank you for the rose."

I was stunned into silence when I realized that the voice was coming from the other side of the poinsettias. My heart stopped as I heard the sound of a quick kiss.

"Are you on break?" she asked.

"Yes. I only have a couple of minutes left, but I wanted to give you this. I wrote a poem for you. To Bianca," he said, and then he started reading my poem!

I jumped to my feet, circled around the poinsettia tree, and stood directly behind Claude. Although my voice quavered, I began reciting the poem in unison with him.

Claude stopped in the middle of his sentence—the one about how we've only known each other for a short while, but you're someone special. Bianca, who's from the dress boutique only two shops down from the bookstore, stared at me.

I grabbed the poem from Claude, handed it to Bianca, and continued reciting.

"Claude?" Bianca asked with a gleam of anger in her eyes.

"Claude?" I echoed, waiting for an explanation.

"Well," he said, his face bright red. "I've got to get back to work." He turned and fled down the mall.

"Do you believe that guy?" Bianca asked. "He probably has girlfriends in every store out here."

I nodded and walked off before I could embarrass myself by crying in front of a crowd of holiday shoppers.

By the time I reached my car, tears were streaming down my cheeks. Somehow, I made it home. I threw myself onto the couch and sobbed.

When I'd finally gained control of myself, I washed my face and fixed a cup of tea. It wasn't as if a long relationship was over; I'd only known Claude for a little over a week. But still, he was my golden boy—a dream of romance and love. I realized that it was the dream I missed and not him.

A noise startled me and I looked up in time to see the star slide off the top of the Christmas tree and fall to the floor, knocking two other decorations off along the way. I walked over, hung the two ornaments back up, and then picked up the star. One of its points was bent.

A knock on the door caught my attention. Could it be Claude here to apologize? I wondered.

I opened the door and found George.

"Hi, Andrea. I was driving by and, just on a whim, I decided to see if you were home. Do you mind?"

"Of course not, George. Come in."

"What's that?" he asked, motioning at my hand.

"The star fell off of the Christmas tree and one of the points is bent."

"Let me see," he said, and took it from me. "I can fix this." With his pocket knife, he molded the shiny metal back into shape. "What was holding it in place?" he asked.

"I don't know," I answered.

"It really needs a little piece of wire running from here to here. Then it won't fall again. Do you have wire? Of course not," he answered his own question. "I'll find something in the car and be right back." He disappeared out the door and returned a moment later.

I turned the kettle on so he could join me in a cup of tea while he fiddled with the star.

"Okay. Good as new! Do you want to put it on top?" he asked.

I hesitated. "No, would you put it up there, George?"

"Sure." He stepped over to the Christmas tree.

"Wait," I said. I moved over to the electrical outlet. "I'll turn on the lights at the exact moment that you put the star on. It's tradition," I explained.

"Traditions are important," he agreed, and secured the star in place as I plugged in the lights.

"It's beautiful!" he exclaimed, stepping back to admire the tree.

"Christmas is a special season." I walked over and joined him.

He slipped his arms around me and gave me a thrilling kiss. The little kisses we'd shared before that were nothing compared to the combining of our souls and hearts and minds that happened at that moment. I felt tingles all over and my knees would've given way if George hadn't been holding me so tightly.

I couldn't believe what I'd almost thrown away. George is as romantic in his own way as Claude is in his phony way. George is genuine, he's honest, and he's true. I was blind not to have seen it all before and to have been deceived by a blond-headed Romeo. What's in the heart is more important than what is on the surface.

George may not bring me roses or poems, but he knows the worth of traditions and family and caring. I can't wait to see what he gives me for Christmas!

THE END

THE GIFT
A heartwarming Christmas tale
about a special present.

It was four days until Christmas, and I was being assaulted with requests from my children. Adrienne and Karyn were three and four, respectively, and Gabriel and Graham were six and seven. They were driving me crazy with their lists—almost demands—for their holiday gifts.

"I want this doll, and the doll house that goes with it!" Adrienne screamed as they looked through the ads in the Sunday newspaper.

"Yeah, Mom. I really want that bike with the helmet and skates and . . . and . . ." Karyn went on and on and on.

Then Graham chimed in. "Ma, I need a new bike, too. And I need skates and a soccer ball."

Gabriel gave me his list of about twelve things he absolutely had to have.

"Where is all this money going to come from?" I asked all four of my beautiful children. "Do you think money grows on trees?" I asked them in a huff.

I loved them, but I just couldn't afford everything they wanted with my small paycheck from the nearby plant where I packed meat part time. My husband, Andrew, worked at the same plant as a butcher. It was hard work for us, but we did our best with our small home and our family. I was slowly getting into a bad mood when I looked at the amount of money I had in my wallet to spend.

"Santa is going to have to look at the lists and see what he can afford to ask the elves to make," I said as I looked at their cute little faces eating cookies and milk at the kitchen table. "I am going to go do some Christmas shopping now. You be good for Daddy. He worked all day and is tired . . . I'll go see if I can get a present for Daddy. If I see Santa at the department store, I'll ask what he can afford to pay his elves to make all the presents you all want.

"But you cannot 'want' all the time. You should learn to be happy with what you get and to be thankful for it—all of you."

I put on my coat and got my car keys off the kitchen desk, "Andrew, I am going to the store. I will be back in about an hour or so. Please watch the kids."

I grabbed for the door as I heard my husband call out from in front of the television. He was watching the football game. "Okay, honey. Don't spend too much. See ya."

I hurried into the local department store to grab some last-minute

Christmas gifts for Andrew but mostly for the four little people in our lives. I looked at all the people and grumbled to myself. I would be in here forever, and I just had so much to do. Christmas was beginning to become such a drag. I wished that I could just sleep through Christmas. But I hurried the best I could through all the people to the toy department. Once again, I kind of mumbled to myself about the prices of all the toys. I wondered if the kids would even play with them after the initial frenzy of Christmas disappeared. Would they throw them in their closets because they were tired of playing with them a week later?

I found myself in the doll aisle. Out of the corner of my eye, I saw a little girl about six holding a lovely doll. She kept touching the doll's hair as she held her so gently. I could not seem to help myself. I just kept looking over at the little girl and wondered whom the doll was for.

I watched her turn to a woman and say "Aunt Helen, are you sure I don't have enough money?"

She replied a bit impatiently, "You know that you don't have enough money for it."

The woman told the little girl not to go anywhere that she had to go get some other things and would be back in a few minutes. And then she left the aisle. The little girl continued to hold the doll.

After a bit, I asked the girl, "Is the doll for you, sweetie? Is that what you want for Christmas?" She was so cute with rings of brown curls and a light in her sweet shining eyes.

She said, "It is the doll for my sister, Imani. She wanted it so badly for Christmas. She just knew that Santa would bring it."

I told her that maybe Santa was going to bring it.

She said, "No, Santa can't go where my sister is. I have to give the doll to my mama to take to her."

I asked her where her sister was. She looked at me with the saddest eyes and said, "She has gone to be with Jesus. My daddy says that Mama is going to have to go be with Imani now, too. My mama is leaving maybe today to be with Jesus and with Imani. Mama is leaving to go be with Imani in heaven."

My heart nearly stopped beating. Then the little girl looked at me again and said, "I told Daddy to tell Mama not to go yet. I told him to tell her to wait till I got back from the store. My mama is in the hospital."

Then she asked me if I wanted to see her new pictures. "Aunt Helen just took these pictures of me a few minutes ago. Do you like them? Do you think they are okay? Do I look pretty?" She handed me a couple of pictures from an instant shot-taking camera. I told her that I would love to look at them. She pulled out some pictures she had taken near the big Christmas tree in the store. Obviously, she had put on her aunt's shoes in some of the photos.

"I want my mama to take these pictures with her in heaven so she doesn't ever forget me. I love her so much, and I wish she did not have to leave me. But Daddy says she will need to be with Imani, and my sister can see these pictures, too."

I saw that the little girl had lowered her head and had grown so very quiet. While she was not looking, I quietly reached into my big purse and pulled out a handful of bills.

I asked the little girl, "Shall we count that money one more time?" I gave her five dollars. It had been a very small and inexpensive rag doll, but it seemed to be the one she really wanted to give her mother to take to her little sister in heaven.

She grew excited and said, "Yes! I just know it has to be enough."

So I slipped my money in her hands, and we began to count it. And, of course, it was plenty for the doll. She softly said as she looked up toward the sky, "Thank you Jesus for giving me enough money."

She smiled at me and said, "Thank you lady for helping me. I said a prayer to help me get this doll for my sister and to be able to give it to Mama in time to take it with her to heaven."

A tear came to my eyes as I looked at her. "What is your name?" I asked her.

"My name is Takesha," she said, smiling at me.

Little Takesha continued, "God sent you to help me. He heard my prayer. I wanted to ask God for enough to buy Mama a red rose. But God sent you, so now I have enough for the doll and a rose. She loves red roses so very, very much."

A few minutes later, her aunt came back. I wheeled my cart away. I could not keep from thinking about little Takesha. My heart was breaking for this poor little girl. First, she had lost her baby sister, and now, it seemed she was losing her mother. It all seemed so very cruel. I thought about how lucky I was to have my wonderful family. I thanked God, at that moment, for what I had and promised I would never ever complain about shopping for my wonderful family again. Then I happily returned to doing my Christmas shopping.

I finished my shopping in a totally different spirit than when I had started. And I kept remembering a story I had seen in the newspaper several days earlier about a drunk driver hitting a car and killing a little girl and seriously injuring her mother. The last report I saw was that she was in a critical care unit in the hospital, and the family was deciding whether to remove the life support. Now surely, that's not Takesha's family? I wondered.

Two days later, I read in the local paper that Mr. Maxwell had been interviewed about why he had okayed his wife, Jeralyn, being taken off her respirator. They were making a huge deal about it in the papers. He was even interviewed on the local television.

When I was watching the news, I heard him say he did it because she had a living will and had said she never wanted to be on machines and had a "Do Not Resuscitate" clause in her will. She had been brain dead after the crash that killed her daughter, Imani. She also had a clause in her living will to donate any and all organs. Her organs and Imani's organs were going to be donated as Christmas gifts to others who needed them. It was such a heartwarming and wrenching story. I watched it and cried knowing I had met the little girl who wanted her mother to have a rose and her sister to have a doll in heaven. Her father had waited until Takesha gave him the rose and the doll to give her mother before he disconnected the life support. Then the young woman had died. I could not forget Takesha.

Later that day, I went out and bought some red roses and took them to the funeral home where the young woman was. And there she was holding a lovely red rose. The beautiful doll and photos of Takesha were right below the red rose.

I left there in tears, my life changed forever. The love that little girl had for her little sister and her mother was overwhelming.

I saw little Takesha about six years later. Her father had remarried, and she was with her new mother at the mall. She ran up to me and remembered that I helped her that Christmas years ago to buy her sister a doll and her mother a rose. She thanked me once again and I thanked her. I cherish my four children and my husband. Takesha taught me that material possessions and money mean nothing without love. Love is what really counts.

THE END

GRANNY GOT TIPSY, MY DAUGHTER'S GOT A "SURPRISE," AND THEN THERE'S THE TATTOO . . .
Just another Christmas at our house!

I've always loved Christmas. Ever since I was a little girl I've loved everything about it—the gifts, the food, and especially having the whole family together under one roof makes it the most special time of the year for me. I was really looking forward to it that year since my twin daughters had left for college that fall. Audrey and Sara are my babies and I'd been suffering from a bad case of empty nest syndrome ever since they left.

"Did you remember to get the oysters?" I asked my husband, Oliver, as he carried in groceries from the car.

"Yes, of course. I didn't forget that oyster dressing is Audrey's favorite."

"And pumpkin pie is Sara's favorite. I also made a mincemeat pie because Father Wyck told me how much he loves it."

Oliver wrinkled his nose. "He's the only one."

I grabbed a bag from him and started putting things away. "Honey, why did you buy all this beer?" Neither of us are big drinkers.

"It's for Jud," he answered shortly. His brother does love his beer—a little too much if you ask me.

"You shouldn't encourage him, Oliver," I said. "You know how he gets when he's drunk."

"Don't worry about it, Marla. He'll be fine. What time do you want me to go get your mother?"

"Oh, pretty soon, I guess." My mother lives in a seniors-only apartment complex across town. She's in good health, but I worry about her mental state. Ever since my father died a few years ago, Mom's stopped censoring herself and nowadays she says pretty much whatever she thinks. Which is fine when it's just the two of us, but can get pretty embarrassing around company. I made a mental note to warn her to watch her tongue around the pastor.

"Hey, Mom." My son, Donovan, walked into the kitchen leading Father Wyck, who is blind.

"Hello, Marla. It smells wonderful in here." He patted my shoulder. Father Wyck was new to our church, but his warm personality endeared him to his flock.

Greetings were exchanged and we sat down to make small talk as Oliver left to get my mother. I brought out the relish tray for everyone to nibble on and then started on the dressing.

"Need any help, Mom?" Donovan asked.

I smiled at my son, musing, He's so grown up now at twenty-two. I miss having little children around, but I'm very proud of the man he's become.

Just then the doorbell rang. "You can get the door," I told him.

Oliver's brother, Jud, and his wife, Harmony, came in, apparently in the middle of an argument.

"It is, too," Jud was saying as Harmony vehemently shook her head. Oliver and my mother followed them.

"You are so wrong," Harmony replied.

Jud gave her a thunderous look. "Hello, everybody," he greeted, immediately heading for the refrigerator and taking out a beer. Jud drinks way too much, but secretly, I don't blame him. My sister-in-law, Harmony, recently earned her master's in English and she likes to remind people of her education constantly. Of course, she's always been that way. She often gets on my nerves.

Mother pecked me on the cheek. "Yuck! It reeks of oysters in here!"

"Nice to see you, too, Mother," I muttered.

"It's always nice to see you, dear. I thought you knew that." She sat down at the table next to Father Wyck. "Hello, Jud. Pass me one of those beers, won't you?"

"Mother," I said. "It's only two o'clock in the afternoon."

"So what? At least it's not morning."

I can't remember her ever drinking when I was a kid, but recently she'd acquired a taste for it. It worries me, among other things.

"Why are you wearing dark glasses? Are you blind or something?" I heard her ask Father Wyck as my daughter, Audrey, burst into the kitchen trailed by a scraggly looking young man.

"Hey, Mom!" she greeted, enveloping me in a big hug.

"Oh, sweetie—I missed you so much!" I gasped, hugging her back tightly, then drawing back to look at her.

What I saw was a shock. She was wearing ragged clothes that looked as though she'd pulled them out of the trash and her pretty hair was coiled up into messy, matted spirals. The young man with her wore the exact same hairstyle. Both of them looked like they hadn't bathed in a month—at least.

"Mom, this is River." Audrey pulled him over to me.

"Nice to meet you," I said, peering at his eyes. They were red like he'd just finished crying, or swimming in a heavily chlorinated pool.

He shook my hand. "Thank you for bringing Audrey into this world," he said solemnly. "She's like an angel, just a totally pure human being. Seriously."

34

"Ummm, okay." I said, not sure about how to respond. Is he joking? I wondered. But his face was serious. Seriously. "Oh, Aud—I'm making your favorite oyster dressing," I told her, knowing she'd be happy.

"Ugh! Sorry, Mom, I forgot to tell you but we're vegans now. I like, totally can't eat that."

"What?" I asked, bewildered. "What on earth is a vegan? Is that the same as a vegetarian?"

"Oh, it's much more hardcore than vegetarianism," she said, flipping her matted hair over her shoulder. "No meat and no dairy."

"No animal products of any kind," River explained in a monotone. "We're very much against the exploitation of animals."

"Well, I guess you'll have to stick to the mashed potatoes and pumpkin pie, then," I said, shrugging glumly.

"No, Mom—you put milk in the potatoes and pie, remember?"

"Well . . ." My mind was drawing a blank. Her brand-new and totally unprecedented dietary restrictions made my head spin.

"No worries. I brought some stuff for us to eat." River produced a plastic bag and began pulling various foodstuffs out of it and stacking them on the counter.

"Are those brownies I spy?" my mother asked him, pointing to a small pan. She's always been something of a chocoholic; you can't hide dessert from her.

"Oh, uh—those are vegan brownies," he stammered, putting them back in the plastic bag. "You probably wouldn't like them."

"Phooey. Let me see them." She grabbed the pan from him and sniffed. "These things smell funny . . . sort of like they've been sprayed by a skunk or something."

"Grandma!" Audrey pulled the pan from her grandmother's hands. "They have special vegan herbs in them. They're for River and me only."

Donovan began to shake with laughter.

"What's so funny?" I asked. Something about the brownies was alerting my suspicions, but I couldn't quite put my finger on it.

"Well, I certainly hope they taste better than they smell!" Mother declared.

"Oh, er . . . they're an acquired taste, actually," River replied.

I was looking hard at Audrey, intending to get to the bottom of this, when I heard my husband calling me into the living room. Our other daughter, Sara, had arrived.

"Sara's here!" I told Audrey, and ran out to greet her.

"Hi, darling!" I said—and stopped to stare at her. She'd dramatically changed her look, as well. Her lovely, red hair had been dyed jet black and she'd gotten a peculiar cut—very short in the front and sides and long in the back. She was wearing black jeans, black boots, and a black sweater.

"Nice mullet," Donovan said, punching her in the arm.

She scowled at him. "Mom, this is my friend, Ellen." She gestured at a girl I had not noticed until then. She was very tall and dressed sort of like a lumberjack, with the same kind of hairstyle as Sara's.

I shook Ellen's hand and thought about how pretty she'd look with a bit of makeup. What is it with today's generation? I wondered. Nobody wants to dress up or put out the slightest bit of effort.

Audrey and River joined us and introductions were made.

"How do you like college, Sara?" Harmony asked. "I know when I was getting my master's . . ." She started in on a long, long story without even letting Sara answer the question. I went back to the kitchen to check on my dressing and the turkey.

"You know, these things aren't half bad." My mother held River's pan of brownies in her lap as she gobbled one down. "They could use a little more sugar, though."

"Mother, leave those alone!" I scolded. I bustled around the kitchen, tending to the food. Having so much company all at once had made me neglect my cooking, but I still wished I were a better hostess. As it was, I realized we'd been neglecting Father Wyck. "So, Father," I said, trying to make small talk, "have you seen any good movies lately?" Right after I said it I wished I could have the words back. What a dumb thing to say to a blind man!

"No, not lately, Marla," he answered, good-naturedly.

River entered the kitchen and blanched when he saw Mother scarfing down another brownie. "I think I've acquired a taste for these," she told him.

He blanched further. "Oh, ummm . . . cool."

"Sorry," I said, pulling the pan away from her and handing it to him. "Why don't you put these away somewhere?"

He scurried out of the kitchen.

Mother smacked her lips and took a sip of her beer. "So, Father," she said, "what do you know about all of those Catholic priests having sex with young boys? Has that ever happened in the Episcopalian church?"

Father Wyck spit out the soda he'd been sipping. Donovan, who'd just entered the warm kitchen, burst out laughing.

"Mother!" I felt a blush creeping up my cheeks. It's comments like that that have me seriously wondering if my mother's in the early stages of Alzheimer's!

"Dinner is almost ready," I announced, desperate to change the subject. "Donovan, why don't you help Father Wyck to the dining room table? Tell the girls I could use a hand in here, too." I pulled the turkey out of the oven for a final basting.

Audrey appeared behind me. "Um, Mom?" she whispered. "Is it true that Granny ate some of my brownies?"

"Yes, she did. I'm sorry, honey. You know you can't leave anything chocolate around her."

She turned pale and then left the room.

"Hey—a little help here?" I called after her.

Sara stalked into the room looking angry. "God! Uncle Jud is so sexist! He just told Ellen that women should stay out of the construction business! She worked construction all this summer! He's so gross!"

"Sorry, hon." I pushed the newly dark hair out of her eyes. "You know how he is. Let's all just try to get along today, okay?"

"Why are you dressed so butch?" Mother asked Sara as she reached into the refrigerator for another beer. "You look like Johnny Cash."

Just ignore her, I mouthed to Sara. I pulled the steaming turkey out of the oven and set it on a platter. It smelled wonderful and looked to be nicely juicy as I cut into it.

"Come on, everyone—let's gather 'round the table!" I said as I proudly presented the turkey in the dining room. "Oliver—carve, please."

The kids helped me make several trips to and from the kitchen to bring in all of the food. Harmony was in the middle of arguing with Oliver about the state of education and didn't help at all—not that I expected her to. Jud just rolled his eyes and chugged another beer. Ellen and River sat stiffly on either side of Mother at the table and Father Wyck smiled benignly at us all.

"Okay," I said, sitting down. "I think we're ready. Father, would you please say grace for us?"

"I would be honored," he answered.

We all bowed our heads. Suddenly, a scent so foul that I nearly gagged from the stench filled the room. Everyone looked up, scrunching their noses and looking around in disgusted horror.

"I didn't do it," Mother announced.

I knew immediately what it was. "Oh, dear. Bunny must be under the table."

Bunny, our ancient basset hound, was sitting by Oliver, hoping for a piece of turkey. She's always been a somewhat . . . fragrant dog, but just lately her emissions could clear a room. I'd been trying different brands of dog food in vain hope of curing her gas problem, but nothing had worked so far. In fact, if anything, she was worse!

"I'm so sorry," I said, grabbing Bunny by the collar and dragging her out of the dining room.

Oliver just grunted and continued carving and piling turkey on the plate in front of him. Father Wyck finally said grace and we all began to help ourselves. The stench wasn't clearing out as quickly as I hoped so I resorted to opening a window.

Mother piled her plate high. "Don't know why, but I'm really feeling hungry!"

Donovan snickered.

"Is that going to be enough food for the two of you?" I asked Audrey. She and River had piled their plates with nothing but rice and salad.

"It's fine, Mom." She cleared her throat. "I actually have an announcement to make. I thought I'd wait until everyone was together. . . ."

We all looked at her expectantly—except for Oliver, who continued to shovel in turkey.

"Well, when River and I met it was like, love at first sight. We're crazy about each other and, well—" She gave us a radiant smile. "—I'm going to have a baby."

"What?" I cried. I looked over at Oliver.

A piece of turkey fell out of his mouth.

"Way to use birth control, dummy." Sara curled her lip contemptuously at her twin.

"Audrey, you can't be serious! You're only eighteen years old! What in the world were you thinking?"

"Women need an education before they start having babies," Harmony threw in.

"I don't know about that," Jud said, glaring at her. "You've been getting an 'education' for the past eighteen years. When are you ever going to spit out a kid?"

"Oliver?" I looked to him for help.

He got up, walked over to the breakfront, pulled out a bottle of Wild Turkey, and poured himself a healthy shot.

"Pour me one of those, too, will you?" Mother asked.

"One for me, too," Jud said.

"If you're having a spirit, I wouldn't mind a wee drop myself," Father Wyck put in.

I turned to Audrey. "We need to talk about this, young lady. You are much too young to be having a baby! You're still just a child yourself!"

River put his arm around Audrey. "Dude, she's like, 'the one.' We are sooo totally in love. We want to get married, like, right away and stuff."

"And just how are you planning to support her, you scrawny, little turd?" Oliver growled at River, who instantly had at least enough sense to look frightened.

"Daddy!" Audrey grabbed River protectively by the arm. "If you can't be happy for us then we're leaving!"

"No—don't go!" I pleaded. "You haven't even eaten anything yet!"

She ignored me and stormed out of the room, pulling the sheepish-looking River behind her.

I jumped up to follow them.

"Sit down, Marla!" Oliver thundered. He poured himself another stiff shot. "Eat your food. There's plenty of time to talk her out of this nonsense."

38

"You were only twenty when you had me, Mom," Donovan said quietly.

"Well, it was a different time." I sat down and took a long drink of my iced tea. "How is the turkey? Not too dry?" I asked. I was trying to be a good hostess even as I fretted about my daughter's future.

"It's delicious," said Father Wyck politely.

"I'm kind of surprised that boy knocked her up," Mother said, helping herself to some more mashed potatoes. "I thought he might be gay."

"Grandma!" Sara jumped up. "I was going to wait to tell you all this, but since Audrey's already ruined dinner I might as well get it out in the open right now. I'm gay and Ellen and I are more than just friends!" She grabbed Ellen's hand and kissed it. "She's my girlfriend," she declared proudly.

There was silence as we all stared at the two of them in shock.

"Which one of you is the man?" Mother suddenly asked.

I grabbed the Wild Turkey bottle and poured the rest of it into my iced tea. Unfortunately, there was only a little left.

"Well?" asked Sara. "Mom? Aren't you going to say anything?"

"What can I say?" I moaned. "Oliver?"

Oliver wiped his mouth carefully with his napkin. Then he got up and walked out of the room.

"It's not that big a deal," Harmony began. "Plenty of the women in my master's program were gay."

"Shut up, Harmony!" Jud roared. He picked up his beer and went off to join Oliver.

Harmony bit her lip. "The food was lovely," she said to me, tears beginning to leak out of her eyes. She picked up her plate and left for the kitchen.

Sara just continued to glare at me, waiting for a response from me. I cradled my head in my hands. It was starting to throb. "Sara, I don't know what you want me to say. If you're happy, then I'm happy for you, okay? But I do think you're a little young to decide this sort of thing."

Apparently, that was the wrong thing to say.

"See? I knew you wouldn't accept it!" she yelled. "Come on, Ellen—let's go!" She and Ellen stormed out of the room, hand in hand.

"Well," said Donovan, "at least you won't have to worry about Sara getting pregnant." He patted me on the shoulder. "Would you like a beer, Mom?"

I sighed. "Yes, please. And get one for Father Wyck while you're at it."

"Me, too!" Mother yelled.

Father Wyck patted my arm. "Don't worry about your family,

Marla. Both your girls have good heads on their shoulders. I think everything will turn out just fine."

"Thank you, Father." I accepted the ice-cold beer from Donovan and put the can to my forehead, thinking, Some holiday this turned out to be.

"Good food, hon," Mother said to me. "I wish Audrey and her fella had left those brownies, though. I could go for a few more of them. Or maybe some ice cream."

Donovan snickered.

I'd finally lost my patience. "Donovan, why do you keep laughing? What on earth is so funny?"

He looked at me kindly. Then he sat down next to me and whispered in my ear, "I'm sorry, Mom, but Grandma is stoned."

"What do you mean?"

"Those brownies had pot in them. You know—marijuana."

I stared at him blankly. By this point I was beyond surprise.

"Don't worry; she'll be okay."

I sipped my iced tea, thinking, One of my daughters is pregnant, and apparently a drug addict. The other is a lesbian. My mother's stoned and probably has Alzheimer's. My husband's turning to drink just like his brother and all of this has happened in front of Father Wyck.

"Are there any potato chips around here, hon?" my mother asked.

"In the pantry," I said with a sigh.

Mother got to her feet. "I'm going to see what's on TV. Why don't you join me, Father?"

"I'd love to," he answered, putting his arm through hers.

"So, have you seen that new wrestling show?" Mother began asking him as they left.

I winced. Maybe I'm just being overly sensitive about the whole blind thing, I thought. He probably thinks we're all raving nuts, anyway.

Donovan and I were the only ones left at the table.

"So? What about you?" I asked, glaring at my son. "Do you have any announcements you'd like to make? Got anything pierced that I should know about?"

"Nope." He grinned and put his arm around me. "The only thing I have to say is that I love you very much. Merry Christmas, Mom."

"I love you, too, honey. Merry Christmas," I said, patting his hand.

Then I noticed a strange mark on the arm poking out of his sleeve.

"What's that?" I asked, pulling up his shirtsleeve.

A very detailed and elaborate tattoo of a dragon covers his forearm from elbow to wrist.

Next year, I think Oliver and I will be going on a cruise.

THE END

CHRISTMAS TRAIN
OUT OF THE CITY
We connected during the chaotic commute.

It was five-fifteen p.m. on December twenty-third and the Nutcracker commute was in full swing at New York's Penn Station. Crowds of people were staring intently at the schedule board suspended above the plaza and they made a human obstacle course to those running desperately around them to catch departing trains. Crackling from the intercom was, "Have Yourself A Merry Little Christmas," which partially succeeded in drowning out the cacophony of noise below.

New Jersey Transit and Amtrak share the same concourse at Penn Station and it results in a curious convergence of travelers during the holidays. Daily commuters from New Jersey hardened to the rigors of commuting wait impatiently for their trains home with others who are returning home from a rare trip to the city to catch a glimpse of the tree at Rockefeller Center or do some shopping. And still for others, it's the end of a long journey home to be with loved ones. A small group of travelers, me included, do not fall into any of these groups. Living just far enough outside of the city to occasionally travel in for business or a shopping trip, many of us experience our trips to New York with just enough familiarity to be slightly jaded.

Like many of my fellow travelers, I found myself anxiously looking up at the board, awaiting the posting of the gate number for the five thirty p.m. Empire Service train to Rensselaer. I'd taken an early-morning train into the city for a ten o'clock meeting and would've comfortably made the one forty-five p.m. train home, but I decided to do some Christmas shopping, instead. Judging by the crowded station, many others had the same idea. As the board clicked off Gate 5A, we all raced to the gate while at the same time attempting to appear nonchalant about it.

I headed for a window seat on the left side of the train which would afford a view of the Hudson River for the two-hour-and-fifty-minute ride home. Although it was dark outside, most commuters prefer that side of the train out of habit. I spread my things out on the adjoining empty seat and hoped that nobody would sit beside me.

The announcement by the conductor that it would be a full train ended any thoughts of spreading out and everyone dutifully placed their Christmas gifts, briefcases, luggage, and packages on the overhead rack. Settling into my seat, I sipped my Starbucks eggnog latte and alternately began looking out the window and glancing down the aisle to see if any of my business colleagues were taking the same train. Although usually not anti-social, I was in a somewhat pensive mood and was looking forward to the solitude of the long ride home.

Usually the faces that file by on an average trip express a sense of fatigue and resignation. People are returning from a long day at work and there's the shared perception that the trip home takes much longer than the trip down. However, since most people were looking forward to a long holiday weekend, the usual malaise was replaced by a buzz of expectation and excitement. Although I tried my hardest to get caught up in the mood, I found it difficult. This was to be my fourth Christmas alone.

Theresa and I were married for twenty years and they were years filled with an ever-evolving and deepening love. We were best friends and losing her is as surreal today as it was that evening when two police officers appeared at my door. At age forty-five, I was about to spend my fourth Christmas alone.

That first Christmas alone was almost unbearable. For over a year, I barely ate or slept. I often felt like Jacob Marley because I observed life with a self-imposed detachment. I was unable to feel and experience life swirling around me. Just a month before Theresa's death, I remember how blessed we felt. I was scheduled to attend a meeting on the sixtieth floor of the World Trade Center's north tower at eight thirty a.m. on September eleventh, but the meeting was canceled at the last minute. As I watched the horror on TV like everyone else, I shuddered at the thought of what might've been. I kept telling myself how lucky I was, only to learn a short month later about the arbitrariness of luck.

After Theresa's death, well-meaning relatives and a few good friends extended invitations to spend the holidays with them but, instead, I flew to London. I walked the streets day after day until sheer exhaustion set in. When walking failed to kill the pain, I headed to the nearest pub and let several pints of beer finish the job. But there was really no escape and no way to numb the pain.

The next few holiday seasons after that were a perfunctory sojourn of parties and get-togethers for the sake of family and friends. Shortly after Thanksgiving, though, I began to feel that this holiday season might be different. I started to sense that I was beginning to emerge from the persistent veil of sadness and for the first time in years I experienced the slightest twinge of holiday spirit. As I waited for the train to depart, I remembered when I worked in the city in the mideighties and Theresa would meet me after work. We'd usually head down to Little Italy and then head uptown to B. Altman's, our favorite department store, where Christmas carolers serenaded the shoppers.

42

We'd feel like kids again at F.A.O. Schwartz where we'd buy toys for our nieces and nephews.

Reflecting on those New York landmarks that no longer exist, I found myself longing for Christmases of the past. Mostly, though, I longed for the time when the holidays meant being with Theresa. As I found myself playing this all too familiar game, I caught myself and forced the thoughts out of my mind. It was Christmas 2004 and it was the only Christmas I had.

As the train started to pull away from the platform, I began to relax, confident that everyone had found their seats. Then a figure in the semi darkened car began sizing up the few remaining empty seats. As the figure moved up the aisle, I could see that it was a woman carrying an oversized, canvas gym bag. Her dark-brown, shoulder-length hair fell across her face and every few steps she swung her head from side to side to get the hair out of her eyes. She had on an ankle-length, dark-green dress with a turtleneck and a modest slit running up her right leg. The effect was one of casual elegance and it contrasted with the formal business attire that many of the women on the train were wearing. She appeared to possess no Christmas gifts—only a book clutched to her body. I guessed that she was in her late thirties or early forties and with just the lone bulky, Nike bag, she didn't seem to fit in with the typical upstate Christmas traveler.

I watched as she walked up the aisle, curious to see which of the few remaining seats she'd sit in. Usually there's a deliberateness to where a person chooses to sit, but in this case it appeared more like the out-of-control randomness of a roulette ball. She appeared to bounce through the car without any thought as to where or what she was doing. And like those roulette balls that spin at breakneck speed and then suddenly settle on a number, she abruptly stopped, threw her bag on the overhead rack, and flopped onto the seat beside me.

As she sat down, I glanced over and nodded. She didn't respond, but stared straight ahead, slightly breathless with her eyes boring into the seat in front of her. I turned away and looked out the window into the darkness as the train passed under the George Washington Bridge, its majestic lights extending across the Hudson River. As I observed the cars that were traveling across the bridge heading home for the holidays, my thoughts returned again to the past.

Theresa and I met in college and spent most of our life together in New Jersey, a few miles from the bridge that we were passing under. Memories of our families getting together for the holidays flooded my mind. For a second, I was brought back to those days when Theresa would make me hold up dozens of Christmas trees while she'd circle each one, observing it from all possible angles until we had the perfect tree to fit our twelve-foot high living room ceiling.

Christmas Eve was special because both of our families lived nearby and we'd all come together to exchange gifts, eat, drink, and laugh late into the night. The next morning was always reserved for the two of us. We'd exchange gifts over brunch and then watch It's a Wonderful Life. As the lights on the bridge faded behind me, I realized once again how much I cherished those past holidays, even though those days were starting to seem like they never existed.

My thoughts were interrupted by the sound of soft weeping. I slowly turned away from the window in trepidation. I thought "Are you alright?" would be a silly question, but I wasn't really quite sure what else to say. Finally, I said, "Albany can't be all that bad."

She looked at me first with mild irritation, but then the outer edges of her lips began to turn upward. While I thought about pulling out a book and leaving my troubled neighbor alone with her thoughts, my general nature to make those around me feel better won out. "Where are you heading?" I asked.

She hesitated. Then, in a barely audible voice, she said, "Columbia County." Fully expecting her to retreat into her sadness, I was surprised to hear her ask, "What about you? Don't tell me your heading to Albany."

"Well, actually, I have to. You see, I'm the mayor." This actually produced a laugh—a grudging laugh, but a laugh, nonetheless. There was a profound sadness in her eyes, and as I was contemplating it she got up and started walking toward the café car.

She returned five minutes later with a bottle of Sam Adams, a glass, and a bag of pretzels. Sipping my latte, I found myself sneaking glances at her. As I tried to discreetly observe her face, I was struck not so much by her attractiveness—though she certainly was attractive—but more by her dignity that stubbornly refused to be extinguished by the sadness and tears. Despite what was troubling her, there was an air of self-assuredness about her.

My intuition told me that she wanted to talk, so I asked her if she was going to be spending the holidays with family. She continued to stare straight ahead and gently shook her head. After what seemed like a long time, her words emerged haltingly, "I'm heading up to my weekend home and I might get together with some friends, but I'm looking forward to some solitude."

I simply nodded, not wanting to push for any more than she was prepared to offer. After a few more minutes of silence, she began to slowly open up. She told me that she lives in New York City, is a freelance writer, and has a weekend home in Chatham. Still, her answers to my questions were guarded and she didn't reciprocate with questions of her own.

After an awkward silence, I thought, What the hell? I extended my hand. "By the way, my name is Barry," I said.

"Ellen."

44

Not being able to think of anything else to say, I said, "Happy holidays."

Ellen looked at me, an ever-so-slight smile starting to form. "Well, happy holidays to you, too. Are you leaving?"

Realizing how it must've sounded, I started to laugh at myself—a quality that Theresa always found endearing. We were both laughing and Ellen apologized for giving me a hard time. "Forget it," I said. "I'm used to it."

Looking out the window, I noticed for the first time that it was snowing. Across the Hudson, you could see houses with single candles in their windows and many with smoke billowing out of their chimneys. As I returned to my latte, Ellen asked if I wanted some pretzels. I grabbed a few out of her bag and noticed that she was beginning to tear up again.

Turning toward me, the look on her face belied the seriousness of what she was about to say. With great difficulty, she explained the reason behind the sadness in her large, brown eyes. "I lost my husband on 9/11." This caused a cold shiver to run down my back. "He was a commodities trader and worked on the ninety-second floor of the north tower." She took a long drink of her beer and with tears welling up in her eyes she looked down at her feet. What she said next caught me equally off-guard. "I didn't love him. I knew for a long time that he was cheating on me and at the time of his death we were barely on speaking terms. I hated his job and the type of people it tended to attract. I had an appointment that morning to meet with a lawyer to file for divorce.

"My parents and friends thought that we had a great marriage, and after he died I saw no reason to change their perceptions. Whether it was out of a sense of guilt or to convince myself that I hadn't spent so many years in a bad marriage, I don't know. After a lot of soul searching, I realized that my marriage was a lie, both to myself and to everyone around me." After reflecting briefly on her admission that came across more as a confession, Ellen apologized for "laying so much" on a stranger. She then let out a chuckle of surprise and resignation. "I have no idea why I'm telling you this. Until now, I've only shared these thoughts with a few trusted friends."

"Poughkeepsie is the next stop," the conductor announced, and it reverberated throughout the train. We both sat in silence, alone with our thoughts. She started to quietly sob, her body convulsing more and more with each passing moment. She buried her face in my shoulder and shook violently for a number of minutes. I was slightly embarrassed and unsure about what to do, so the semidarkness of the train and noise of the engine as it left the station were a godsend.

After what seemed like a long time, she managed to regain her composure. "I'm so sorry. I have no idea why this is happening—not to mention with a total stranger."

45

I suggested that perhaps it was safer to let loose with a stranger or maybe the time was simply right for her to get this burden off of her shoulders. She just shrugged.

Observing my uneasiness, Ellen attempted to deflect the awkwardness of the situation by asking me about myself. I thought about telling her about Theresa, how deep my love was for her, and how profound a sense of loss I continued to feel. Instead, though, I told her that I also lost my spouse in 2001, only in my case because of a drunk driver.

Upon absorbing the irony of our similar situations, she hesitantly asked, "Do you have children?"

"No. We tried for many years, but without success." Despite the pain that not having had children brought to the surface, I managed to ask, "And what about you?"

Ellen stared at me intently and tears again started to well up in her eyes. "My husband never wanted children. His career was his life and pretty much everything else was an afterthought." For a second we made eye contact, conveying silently what was becoming apparent— that we were drawn to each other. Whether it was through tragedy or simply because we were both alone for the holidays, I didn't know.

The train pulled into Rhinebeck, the next stop along the line, and people started getting off. We both watched as the people waiting on the platform anxiously looked for friends and family members. In the distance, the town was adorned in white lights. The streets were full of people doing last-minute shopping. As we observed the happy reunions taking place, I felt like we were both sharing many of the same feelings. I asked Ellen if she'd be getting off at Hudson, twenty minutes up the line. Without turning toward me, she slowly nodded.

We sat in silence as the train pulled out of the station. Looking outside, the snow was getting much deeper as a blizzard began to take hold of the area.

While watching the snow intensify, I found myself overcome with conflicting emotions. I felt a strong attraction to Ellen, but at the same time I felt vaguely guilty. As the train pulled out of the station, I said, "Ellen, I don't know what your plans are for the holidays, but I'd like to see you before you head back to the city. Could we have dinner one night?"

She sat silently for a moment and I sensed that she felt equally conflicted. After a few seconds, she looked at me and said, "Barry, I feel we have a definite connection, but I came up here to simplify my life, not to complicate it. I planned on putting the upstate house up for sale, returning to New York City, and finally moving on with my life."

Though I didn't want to dismiss the significance of what she'd said, my nature to diffuse situations with sarcasm got the best of me. "Ellen, we're just talking dinner here," I said.

46

She let out a genuine belly laugh that was totally unlike her previous guarded responses. The effect on her face was magical as her eyes brightened and her whole face lit up. Once she stopped laughing, she responded, "Okay. I get it." She then asked me to write down my phone number and said she'd call.

Immediately this brought up a slightly uneasy feeling. I had to consider that for any number of reasons I might never hear from this woman who was rekindling strong feelings and emotions inside of me. With little choice in the matter, however, I wrote my number down and took a leap of faith.

"Hudson will be the next station," the conductor announced. As the train pulled into the station, Ellen started to collect her bag. As she did, she grasped my hand and said, "I'll call you."

With that, she got off the train and went off into the winter darkness.

THE END

Short Holiday Tearjerker!
"YES, SHANNON—THERE IS A SANTA CLAUS"
I helped my saddest little student believe.

The sound of "I Saw Mommy Kissing Santa Claus" drifted through the Victorian house that's home to The Happy Village Nursery School. My class was practicing for the Christmas program that was coming up in two weeks. They might've been off-key, but they were singing with the enthusiasm that all children have for Christmas.

As the last notes of the song trembled in the air I told the class, "We're going outside now! It's playtime!"

I neatly sidestepped their scurrying little feet as the kids formed a straggly line to march outside. I opened the door and led them out into the bright, winter sunshine, thankful for the unseasonably warm weather that made cumbersome coats and hats unnecessary. "We're a bunch of little ducks, waddling in a row," I sang, putting my hands in my armpits and waggling my arms with a flapping motion. The kids all fell in line behind me, cheerfully mimicking me.

I felt like a fool the first few times I had to pretend I was a duck. Lila, my longtime friend and the owner of Happy Village Nursery School, didn't help by laughing uproariously at my efforts. "Loosen up, Kristin," she said. "You're as tight as a drum. Don't you ever do anything silly or nonsensical?"

I shook my head, lamenting the fact that I was such a stick-in-the-mud. "Never."

"Well, you can't be inhibited at Happy Village. You have to get down to their level or you'll scare the devil out of them." She put her hands in her armpits, flapping her arms frantically and quacking like a fool. I collapsed with laughter and followed suit. Now it's second nature to do all of the silly things the children love.

Outside, the children made a mad dash for the swings and the slide. I stood there watching them, the warm sun making me feel drowsily contented. I felt a little hand slip into mine and looked down to see the anxious face of Shannon Roberts looking up at me. I dropped to my knees beside the child and asked, "What is it, Shannon? Do you need to go to the bathroom?'"

Her little, auburn head shook from side to side and her mouth formed a silent, No. Her damp, little hand then tightened in mine and a fine film of perspiration dewed the flawless skin of her face.

"Then what is it, honey?" I asked, watching the way the light caught her auburn hair and made it shine with reddish highlights. Since going to work for Lila, I'd found that I love children and this little girl seemed to tug at my heart in a way that none of the others did. I often had to struggle not to show my partiality. I wanted to take her on my lap and hug her as Lila had advised doing as a panacea for most of the ills that befall the children. I wanted to make the worry that was so plainly etched on her solemn, little face go away. "Want to tell me what's wrong, honey?" I asked, brushing the fine hair away from her forehead.

She needs a haircut, I thought. These wispy, little bangs are beginning to get in her eyes.

Shannon leaned against my knee and whispered worriedly, "I don't think I should sing about Santa."

"Why not, darling?" I asked, thinking it was an odd thing for a child to say.

"Because there isn't a Santa," she said. Her voice rose ever so slightly at the end, making it sound like a question, and her little mouth started to quiver.

"Oh, honey, sure there's a Santa!" I said, shocked by the bald statement from that tiny thing. That's a statement you normally hear from worldly eight-year-olds. "What makes you think there's no Santa?"

"Because," Shannon confided in a whisper, "Daddy says there's no Santa and no Easter Bunny and no Tooth Fairy."

Oh, he does, does he? I fumed inside. What kind of unfeeling brute tells a four-year-old something like that? It's terrible, unfeeling, and stupid. "And what do you think, Shannon?"

"My daddy's always right," Shannon said, sniffing quietly.

"And your mother, darling? What does she say?"

Shannon inched closer. "My mommy went away."

Oh, Lord, I thought. Poor child. Divorce can be such a nasty business. I gave the child a fierce hug, feeling protective. "Well, why don't I have a talk with your daddy about Santa Claus?" Silently I added, And later I'll tackle him about the Easter Bunny and the Tooth Fairy.

Her chocolate eyes rounded and her fine eyelashes fluttered. "Daddy doesn't like to talk about Christmas."

"Does he get mad?" I asked, beginning to get mad myself.

Shannon shook her head. "Daddy never gets mad at me."

Well, that's something in the wretched man's favor, I thought. "What does he do when you talk about Christmas?"

Shannon's little mouth trembled. "He looks so very sad."

"Well, I'll tell you what. When your daddy comes to pick you up this evening maybe I can change his mind," I said, adding silently, At the very least I can give him a piece of mine. "Now you run along and play."

I watched Shannon run off and join the other children. Then I went inside to my little office and picked up the phone, all the while keeping a watchful eye on the children from the window.

Lila was home with the flu and I had to watch her class in addition to mine. Shannon Roberts had been Lila's pupil for almost four months. She would've met Shannon's father and perhaps she'd have some pointers on how to handle him.

"Oh, Lord, Kristin," Lila moaned when I related my conversation with Shannon. "Leave it alone. You can't talk to that man. Well, you can talk, but he's not going to listen. The man's a chunk of ice—as frozen as an iceberg. He gives me the shivers. And it's too darned bad. He's quite a hunk—the tall, dark, handsome, brooding type. He has quite a body, too. He has bi, tri, and quadriceps to spare."

I laughed. "I certainly trust you to notice."

"Well, my girl, you'd be better off if you started noticing things like that again. That broken engagement of yours was nearly two years ago. Just because that philandering jerk dumped you is no reason to stop living. It's about time you had another man in your life. If you're not careful, you'll end up an old maid."

"Lord, Lila! They don't have old maids these days," I told her quickly, my heart losing a couple of beats at the mention of Richard and the way he betrayed me.

"My mother says that we do and that's good enough for me. She gives me the same advice I'm giving you. That's why I'm always out there beating the bushes looking for Mr. Right. And you'd better start looking, too. After all, you're pushing thirty."

"About this Mr. Roberts," I said, not wanting to discuss my single status. I was still smarting over being dumped just two weeks before my wedding and I couldn't bear to talk about Richard—not even with Lila.

"Honey, don't even think about him. He was crossed off my list months ago. I'd just as soon cozy up to the Rock of Gibraltar."

"I wasn't planning on cozying up to him, Lila," I snapped. "I just want to talk with him."

Lila sighed. "Okay, but it's on your head. He picks her up about five thirty. He drives a black pickup with 'Roberts Construction' printed on the door. You'll know him when you see him because of all the muscles."

I hung up, laughing, and went out onto the playground to break up a fistfight between two five-year-olds.

At five thirty I was out front herding the children through the gate into waiting cars. When the black pickup pulled up, I was ready. My little speech to Mr. Roberts had been rehearsed and I had it down pat.

"Mr. Roberts," I was going to say, "Shannon seems to be laboring under some misconception regarding Santa Claus and she's clearly unhappy about it. Since she's only four, perhaps she misunderstood something you said. Could we talk about it?" I figured that cool, calm, practical statements like that would make a sensible man see the error of his ways—or at least prompt a rational discussion.

The pickup came to a halt and he unfolded his long length and got out. I gulped audibly. He was indeed tall, dark, and handsome and the smile that he gave his daughter was one that probably charmed a lot of females. "Hi, honey!" he called. "Ready to go?"

I watched, fascinated, as his arm muscles flexed under the white T-shirt when he bent down to swing a giggling Shannon high into the air. Lila must be wrong, I thought. He doesn't look cold. In fact, he looks warm and approachable.

"Er . . . Mr. Roberts!" I called, moving toward the truck. My mouth was suddenly dry and my carefully rehearsed little speech was evaporating.

He swung around to look at me, his dark eyebrows rising in question. "Yes?" He swung Shannon down, opened the truck door, and put her inside. When I continued to stand there at a loss for words, he asked, "Do you want to talk to me?"

"Yes, Mr. Roberts," I said. "I want to talk with you about Santa Claus."

"Santa Claus?" he repeated, staring at me as if I'd sprouted another head. "Did you say Santa Claus?"

"Do you believe in Santa?" I blurted out, and then cursed myself for losing control of the situation and sounding like an idiot.

He snapped Shannon's seat belt into place and shut the truck door. He then turned toward me, his expression a cross between exasperation and amusement. "I'm thirty-three years old. Should I believe in Santa?"

"No, no," I said, stifling a groan. I was ruining everything. "It's Shannon. You told her there's no Santa and it's making her unhappy."

"Life's full of unhappiness, miss. Just who are you, anyway? Where's Miss Barone? Surely you haven't been left in charge here. Miss Barone is sensible and responsible, but I'm beginning to wonder about you," he said, running his eyes over my mussed hair and shirt covered with finger paint.

"Kristin," I mumbled. "I'm Kristin Weeks and I'm in charge while Miss Barone is home with the flu. I'm also sensible and responsible. Just because you don't believe in Santa doesn't mean I—"

He held up his hand and stopped me midsentence. "Wait just a minute. This is an asinine conversation. There is no Santa. I know it. You know it. And Shannon knows it. Let's drop it." He turned on his heel and walked around to the driver's side of the truck. "If Miss Barone doesn't return soon, I may have to consider taking Shannon somewhere else. I don't care for your attitude."

51

"Mr. Roberts!" I yelled, following him. Anger was overcoming my natural reserve and making me want to say something unforgivable. "Mr. Roberts, just because your wife left you doesn't mean that you have to make that darling, little girl unhappy. Would it hurt you to let her hang onto her illusions for a little while? Just because you're disillusioned with life doesn't mean that the rest of us have to be."

He paled and I watched a muscle twitch spasmodically in his jaw. He walked around the front of the truck and then stopped with obvious effort. He slapped his hand down on the hood of the truck, making me jump. "Not that it's any of your business," he said in a flat, unemotional voice, "but my wife didn't leave me. She died. Now, as far as I'm concerned, this subject is closed. I'll call Miss Barone at home regarding your attitude. Good day."

Oh, good grief, I thought. I stood there, dismayed, as I watched the truck pull away from the curb with an angry gnashing of gears. What have I done?

I've probably cost The Happy Village Nursery a good customer, that's what I've done.

Lila struggled to get to work the next day. She looked tired and washed out, but ready to take over again. Her expression clearly said that it was not a minute too soon. "Max Roberts called me last night," she told me hoarsely, clutching her box of tissues and wiping her reddened nose.

"You should've stayed home another day," I told her.

She snorted. "I didn't want to come back to find that he'd strangled you for meddling. He told me that unless I came back here today and took care of his daughter, he was removing her from the school. What the heck did you say to him, anyway?" Her frown turned into a look of amusement. "You're such a shy person, Kristin. For the life of me, I can't imagine what you could've said that offended him."

"I'm sorry," I told her. "He just made me so angry. I forgot to be sensible and responsible."

"His very words," Lila said, heading for the coffeepot.

"Are you upset with me?" I asked.

Lila shook her head and took a sip of coffee. "No, hon. I understand and I'm prepared to be philosophical about it. After all, when I got my first look at the man I couldn't say anything sensible or responsible, either. I think I talked nonstop about the delightful weather we were having and it was raining cats and dogs!" She sighed and stared dreamily out the window. "A man like that could make a female forget a lot of things."

"That wasn't the reason," I denied hotly. "I hardly noticed."

"Hardly noticed what?" Lila asked, with a big grin on her face.

"The muscles," I said without thinking.

Lila choked on her coffee. "And pigs fly!" she said, waving me out

52

of the room. "Let's get busy. I hear the patter of Happy Village feet."

I didn't come in contact with Max Roberts for a while after our encounter, but I have to confess that I found myself looking for his pickup truck every evening. I'd watch him swing Shannon into the truck, tickling her, nuzzling her neck, and making her squeal with delight.

I was also surprised one day to wake up and find that my first thoughts were of Max Roberts—not Richard. I'd loved Richard. We were just days away from our wedding where we were going to promise to love each other for the rest of our lives. Where did that love go?

"Forget men," I muttered. "Forget love. You can't trust either of them. And stop mooning over a contrary man like Max Roberts."

One snowy evening he was late picking Shannon up. Lila had left early to finish her Christmas shopping and left Shannon in my care. "When he gets here to pick her up, play nice, all right?"

"Don't worry. I learned my lesson."

All of the children had been picked up except for Shannon. She followed me around and finally ended up clutching my hand in a death grip. She gnawed on her lower lip, but I still saw it tremble.

The phone rang at five forty-five and I went to answer it. "Miss Barone," a deep, male voice said without preamble. "This is Max Roberts. I've got an emergency here at work and I can't pick Shannon up right now. What's your normal procedure when something like this happens?"

"This is Kristin Weeks," I told him uneasily. "Miss Barone is gone for the day. I can wait here with Shannon until you come or I can take her home with me. I'll do whatever is convenient for you," I told him, being very careful to sound sensible and responsible.

There was a lengthy silence on the other end of the line and then came a heavy sigh. "All right, Miss Weeks. I know this is asking a lot, but could you take Shannon home? I don't know when I'll get out of here and Shannon will be better off in her own house. She could go to bed and I won't have to worry about her."

"I'd be glad to drive her home. Give me the address," I said. "And what do I do about a key?"

"Mrs. Hill is there. She takes care of the house and Shannon when I'm not around. You can just leave Shannon with her."

I bundled Shannon into her coat and wool cap and got my own coat from the closet.

"Where's Daddy?" Shannon asked, looking worried. Her little voice was trembling.

"He's still at work and can't get here to pick you up. I'm going to drive you home in my car. How about that?"

Shannon looked relieved. "Good," she whispered.

"Were you worried, darling?" I asked, hugging the tiny figure to me. "Did you think he forgot you?"

Shannon nodded and then shook her head. Her silky hair swirled about her face. "Daddy wouldn't forget me, but it's snowing. I thought he might've been in a car wreck. My mommy had a car wreck in the snow."

Oh, Lord, I thought. I hugged her again for good measure. "Well, your daddy is just fine. You don't have to worry about him."

The snow was coming down rapidly from the sky when we went outside. Huge, starry flakes were piling up at an alarming rate on streets and lawns. I eyed it warily. Driving in snow isn't something I like doing.

Shannon Roberts's home is a two-story Victorian that sits well back from the street on a heavily wooded lot. Although it's a lovely house, I noticed there was no Christmas wreath on the door and no lights in the windows. "Figures," I muttered as I helped Shannon out of the car.

I rang the doorbell and a slightly overweight woman opened it. "Hi, darlin'!" she said to Shannon. "You're Miss Weeks, I take it. Mr. Roberts called me and told me you'd be bringing her home." She frowned. "He was in such a hurry, though, that I didn't get the chance to remind him that Mr. Hill and I were planning to go out to dinner tonight."

"You run along," I told her. "I'll stay with Shannon until Mr. Roberts gets here."

She looked relieved. "Well, if you're sure," she said, sounding unsure. "I can stay if there's a problem. I sort of hate to, though. It's our anniversary."

"You go right ahead. Shannon and I will be fine, won't we, Shannon?" I asked, stroking Shannon's head.

Mrs. Hill reached for her coat and slipped her arms into it. "My husband should be here in a few minutes to pick me up." She glanced worriedly out the window where the snow could be seen drifting down in the glow of the porch light. "Let's hope this snow lets up. I get nervous driving in the snow."

Me, too, I thought. I wondered how I'd summon up the nerve to drive home in the mess that was accumulating out there.

After the housekeeper left, I looked around. It's nice, I thought. The place was homey and neat and it had hardwood floors and beautiful, old furniture polished to a face-reflecting shine.

I fixed grilled cheese sandwiches and chicken noodle soup for Shannon in the modern kitchen and carried it into the living room to the coffee table. I put a match to the firewood in the fireplace and we soon had a cheery fire going.

Shannon ate every crumb of her dinner and asked for more milk.

54

Good, I thought. I often worried about Shannon's slight, little body. I wondered if she needed to gain some weight. Maybe she needs vitamins or something, I thought vaguely, watching Shannon finish her glass of milk.

"Let's sing some Christmas songs, all right?" I asked.

"Can we sing some songs about the baby Jesus?" Shannon asked. "I don't think Daddy minds the baby Jesus. He just doesn't like Santa Claus. I asked him why and he said that we have to be r-realis—oh, I forget."

"Realistic," I supplied angrily. Damn that man! I wanted to knock some sense into his head for telling a four-year-old to be realistic.

We were doing a loud, if amateurish, version of "Frosty the Snowman" a half-hour later when I heard the front door open and close. Moments later a harsh voice asked, "What's going on in here? And where's Mrs. Hill?"

Max Roberts was standing in the doorway. His head and shoulders were covered with snow and he looked mad enough to chew nails— and delicious enough to eat with a spoon.

"We're singing Christmas songs, Mr. Roberts." I managed to say it calmly even though my heart was trying to pound its way out of my chest. "Mrs. Hill went out to dinner with her husband. It's their anniversary." Before I could bite my tongue, I asked, "Are you against anniversaries, too?"

Now why did I say that? I wondered in dismay as I saw his face darken with anger and his well-chiseled mouth pull into a thin, uncompromising line. The man positively brought out the worst in me. He turned me into a rude shrew!

"I have nothing against anniversaries," he told me. "Thank you for staying with Shannon. I appreciate it."

"You're welcome. I enjoyed it."

"I like Miss Weeks," Shannon told him, smiling at her father. "She's nice."

"I'm sure she is," he said. "Now, isn't it just about your bedtime?"

Shannon made a face, but nodded, and her father bent down to pick her up. "I want Miss Weeks to come up and tuck me in," Shannon said as he swung her high onto his shoulders.

I took a small step back. "Oh, Shannon, honey, I don't think . . ."

"That's a relief," he said under his breath for my ears only. "Because I have a feeling that when you think, you create problems for me." He started up the steps and turned to me as I stayed rooted at the bottom of the staircase. "Well, come on. Shannon wants you to tuck her in."

My face burned as I trailed up the steps after them. I stood in the hallway and watched his uninhibited and loving teasing as he made Shannon brush her teeth.

"Will you tuck me in, Miss Weeks?" Shannon asked after her

55

father had helped her into pink pajamas, put her in bed, and kissed her.

I moved over to the bed and tucked the pink blanket under Shannon's dimpled chin. "Sleep tight, honey," I said. I was tempted to kiss her on the cheek, but I was also aware of Max Roberts's watchful eyes on me. "Don't let the bedbugs bite!"

Shannon smiled drowsily at me. "That's what my mommy always said when she tucked me in."

I heard Max's sharp intake of breath behind me and I slipped from the room, dismayed at having done something that might've caused him and Shannon pain.

He followed me down the steps, neither of us speaking. I was very conscious of his eyes boring into my back. At the bottom I turned around and before I could change my mind I blurted out, "She's such a darling girl. Why are you forcing your pain and anguish and disillusionment onto her? Why would you object to fairy tales and Santa Claus and the Easter Bunny? Let her live in a make-believe world for a little while."

"Are you finished?" he snapped, his handsome face a mask of anger. "Listen carefully because I will not repeat myself: Shannon is my daughter, Miss Weeks. I will decide what's best for her and I do not want or need your unsolicited advice." His dark eyes were snapping fire in his stern face.

I didn't have the good sense to leave it alone. "But little things like Santa Claus, the Easter Bunny, and the Tooth Fairy—how did they get to be so important? Are you simply using them as symbols of this sometimes harsh, sometimes cruel world? Are you trying to teach Shannon not to believe, not to have faith, and not to pretend because life's just a house of cards and if she isn't cold and calculating and realistic it'll all come tumbling down on her?"

"Miss Weeks, are you deaf?" he shouted. "I told you what my views are on this Santa nonsense. He does not exist. Neither does the Easter Bunny nor the Tooth Fairy. There was never a Rapunzel or a Snow White or a Cinderella. Shannon has to realize that and the sooner the better. She needs to know that the happily-ever-after ending simply doesn't exist. There are no happy endings."

"Did you get this bitter just over the unfortunate death of your wife, Mr. Roberts?" I asked. "Or have you been a bitter man all of your life? I saw a bumper sticker the other day and I thought of you. It read: 'Life's a bitch and then you die.' Is that your view of life, Mr. Roberts? And is that what you want to instill in Shannon—no hope, no illusions, and no faith? If that's the way you feel, then I'm sorry for you. Very sorry."

"I don't need your pity, Miss Weeks," he said, clenching and unclenching his fists at his sides. I looked at his white knuckles and wondered if he wanted to strangle me with those hands. The anger left his face, though, and then I saw the anguish in his eyes. "Shannon's mother was alive that morning, happy and carefree. She was planning a trip to the mall to finish her Christmas shopping. By nightfall, she was dead. Her car slid on an ice-covered road into a tree. Is it any wonder that I'm disillusioned and bitter?"

"No," I told him gently, feeling a wave of compassion for him that startled me with its intensity. "I can understand. Two years ago I was engaged. The wedding was just two weeks away when my fiancé decided that he wasn't through playing the field. When I found him with a friend of mine—one of my bridesmaids, by the way—he dumped me. It wasn't as traumatic and final as losing someone in an auto accident, but it was unpleasant and painful and disillusioning. I've managed to survive, though. For a little while there, I wasn't sure that I would—or that I even wanted to. But I still believe in the hope and faith and happy endings that Santa Claus and the Easter Bunny and the Tooth Fairy bring to all of us."

I grabbed my coat from the back of a chair in the hall and shrugged into it, fumbling blindly for my car keys.

"Just give it up, Miss Weeks," he said wearily.

"No!" I shouted at him. Tears started to flow down my cheeks. "I won't give it up! I love that child and I will not give up on her!" Or on you, I wanted to add. I suddenly knew that I wanted him to have faith and hope. I wanted a happily-ever-after ending for him. "I'll change your mind if it kills me." I tugged at the doorknob, but it refused to open. "Open this door."

He took a step toward me. "No, wait. You're upset and you can't drive in this weather. It's practically a blizzard out there."

"And what do you propose I do about it? Walk home?" I asked, taking refuge in sarcasm.

He looked around uneasily and pushed a hand through his dark hair. It stood up in unruly spikes, making him look younger and more worried. "You could stay here, I guess," he said hesitantly.

"Stay here? Stay here, cooped up w-with—" I sputtered with rage, searching for words. Finally, I finished triumphantly with, "I'd just as soon stay here with Scrooge or the Grinch!"

His mouth twitched and then he laughed. "You are preoccupied with Christmas, aren't you?"

"Why not? It's Christmastime," I muttered, disconcerted by that laugh. The darned man looked almost human there for a moment—human and much too attractive for my peace of mind.

I tugged on the door again. It opened suddenly and, caught off guard, I stumbled backward against Max. For the briefest of moments, his hands touched my waist, steadying me. He released me immediately and I moved away, feeling like I'd been burned where the feel of his touch lingered.

I stifled a dismayed gasp as I looked out at the huge amounts of snow shrouding the shrubs and covering the cars in the driveway. I looked up at the sky and groaned inwardly at the amount of snow that was still coming down.

He caught my arm as I put my hood up and moved out onto the porch. My car was in the driveway, unrecognizable under all of the snow. My heart was in my mouth.

I can't drive in this weather, I thought. I'd be a fool to even try.

"Miss Weeks. Kristin, please don't try to drive in this. It's dangerous."

He sounded genuinely worried and my anger evaporated. But I wasn't about to give in. I could be as stubborn as he could be. "Don't worry, Mr. Roberts, I'll be fine. I have four-wheel drive and I don't have far to go."

"I won't let you! It's too dangerous, I tell you. You're upset and the roads are treacherous. You have to stay here."

"No, Mr. Roberts, I don't," I told him gently. "You can't be afraid that every time someone drives on icy roads they'll have a wreck and die. You can't live the rest of your life with that hanging over you. And besides, I'm not your wife."

His mouth thinned in anger and he put his hands on my shoulders, giving me a little shake. "No, you aren't!" he groaned from between clenched teeth. "You're not one thing like her. You're little and dark and she was tall and fair. She was soft-spoken and agreeable; you're pushy and bossy and always sticking your nose into matters that don't concern you. She was . . ." He trailed off and looked down at me, an expression of dismay on his face. "I'm sorry. I don't know why I'm . . ."

"It's all right, Mr. Roberts. I understand," I said, not understanding at all really. Why is he comparing me to his dead wife? Something fluttered frantically in my chest; it was like a wild animal trying to escape. Is it hope? Fear? Excitement? I wondered why it should matter—why anything about that cynical man should matter to me.

Get out of here, I told myself. Forget Shannon's problems and forget Max Roberts. You've been hurt once. Don't tempt the fates again. I hurried out the door and down the driveway as though the devil were at my heels. The whole way, I was conscious of Max's eyes on my back.

Somehow I made it home in that awful snowstorm. My heart was in my mouth every inch of the way.

A couple of hours later, Lila called me. "Where in the heck have you been?" she asked. "Max Roberts called here. He was worried sick that you'd had an accident. He asked me to call you and make sure that you got home all right. What's going on with you two, anyway?"

"Not a blessed thing," I snapped. My heart did a little tap dance when Lila said that he was worried about me. But then, considering how his wife died, he probably worries about anyone dumb enough to drive in a blizzard. "Call him back and tell him that I'm fine."

"Okay, girl, but you've got some serious explaining to do. I want to hear everything."

"There's nothing to hear, Lila. I drove Shannon home because he was running late and I stayed with her until he got home. We had a fight. That's all."

"I don't believe a word of it," she declared. "Something's going on here. I'm just not sure what it is yet."

Five days later, on Christmas Eve, Lila sat on my couch dressed in a black-sequin dress and watched me stuff brightly wrapped Christmas gifts into a super-sized, black garbage bag. "He's going to kill you—you know that, don't you?" she asked, her expression fluctuating between amusement and exasperation. At the moment, exasperation had the upper hand. "He's going to catch you red-handed and wring your silly neck."

"He's not going to catch me," I muttered, stuffing an unwrapped Lullaby Baby doll into the bag. I did my best not to muss the doll's nightgown. "I'm just going to leave these gifts for Shannon on her front porch, get back in my car, and drive off. He'll never know who left them. Maybe the wretched man will think that Santa left them."

Lila rolled her eyes. "If you don't expect to be seen, may I ask why you're wearing a Santa suit? And a very ill-fitting suit, at that."

"Well," I explained, "this is just in case Shannon sees me. I want her to think that Santa brought the gifts."

Lila stood up and put an affectionate hand on my arm. "Kristin, honey, give it up. You're just going to get hurt because the bottom line is she's Max Roberts's kid—not yours. Go put on your best outfit. Wear that black miniskirt and go to this party with me. You've had Shannon on your mind to the exclusion of everything else and you need a break."

"I can't," I said. "I'm determined to do this for Shannon. I want her to have a happy Christmas." My lips tightened. "Can you believe that man? He wouldn't even let her participate in the Christmas program!"

Lila sighed. "He said that she had a sore throat." She held up her hand when I started to disagree. "All right; do it your way. You will, anyway." She grinned and gave me a fierce hug. "But you're positively the worst-looking Santa I've ever seen. That suit's a mile too big, your pillow tummy is slipping, and your beard's been eaten by moths. Let's hope that any children in the vicinity only see you from a distance. Up close, you'd be a bitter disappointment to a starry-eyed youngster." She adjusted the pillow I'd stuffed in the waistband of the red Santa trousers. "Where did you get this thing, anyway?"

"I rented it." I twitched my nose where the scraggly beard tickled it.

"Well, they sure saw you coming, honey."

"Run along to your party, Lila, and have a good time," I told her, closing the neck of the bulging garbage bag.

"Well, call me tomorrow if he doesn't ring your silly neck."

After Lila shut the door behind her, I flopped down onto the couch and stared morosely at my feet in the rubber boots that were so big that they threatened to fall off with every step. "She's right," I mumbled, my stomach churning. "He'll kill me." I remembered his anger at our last meeting and shivered.

As I drove out to the house, I wanted to turn back at every intersection. Lila's right, I realized. I'm getting ready to do something totally stupid.

The man has his own ideas about his daughter and how to rear her. He has his own ideas about Santa and Christmas and a thousand other things concerning Shannon and he has a right to his opinions. And Shannon is his daughter—not mine. I really have no business interfering. If the situation were reversed and Max was going against what I thought my child should believe, wouldn't I be angry? I sure would. Maybe it's time to be sensible about the whole thing. But then I looked at the bulging bag in the backseat and the toys I'd picked out so carefully and I knew that I wasn't going to be sensible.

The houses in the neighborhood all looked like the houses on Christmas cards. They sat snugly on their snow-covered lawns, wreaths hanging on the beautiful doors and Christmas tree lights blinking in the windows. Shannon's house looked cold and somber with only one light burning in the living room.

I parked on the street and climbed awkwardly out of my car. I hoisted the garbage bag onto my shoulder and prayed that no one would see me. I shuffled toward the house, trying to stay behind the hemlock trees that lined the driveway.

I put the bag on the porch and was turning away when I had a dismaying thought. What if they don't come out of the house tonight or tomorrow morning? What if it rains or snows? Shannon's Christmas gifts could get ruined or sit for days before someone finds them. There was only one thing to do: I'd have to ring the doorbell and hide until the bag was taken inside.

I pressed the bell with shaking fingers. What if Max catches me . . .

When I heard the melodic chimes ring through the house, I ran across the lawn and around to the side of the house where I hid behind a bed of rhododendrons.

A minute or so later the porch light came on, the door opened, and Max stepped out. He bent to look at the plastic bag. Shannon appeared at his side, squealing when she saw the bag. "It's Santa! Santa came! Oh, Daddy, Santa came! You told me that he wouldn't come, but he did! He did! Look at his little footprints. He's an elf, you know. That's why his feet are so little."

She tugged at the bag, trying to drag it inside.

Max was looking at my footprints with narrowed eyes. He lifted the bag, hefting it in his hands. He probably wants to toss it out onto the lawn, I thought, knowing I'd attack him physically if he dared.

He put the bag in the foyer and, leaving the door open, stepped out onto the porch. He jumped down onto the lawn and before I could gather my scattered wits he was looming over me. "Come out of there!" he ordered.

Taking a deep breath, I looked at his face. It was dark with anger and his mouth was clamped tightly in impatience and irritation and exasperation. "Are you going to wring my neck?" I asked with an almighty effort. "Lila said that if you caught me, you'd wring my neck."

He gave a short bark of laughter. "Lila sounds like a woman with some sense." He shook his head ruefully. He pulled me up the steps, frowning at me when I had to stop and put one of the boots back on. "You—you're a different kettle of fish. I've never met such a bullheaded, dreamy-eyed, idealistic woman in my life."

We made it into the foyer and he shut the door behind us. Shannon wrapped her arms in a death grip around my leg. "I always knew you were real, Santa! Miss Weeks told me you were real and I just knew that you'd come!"

I put my hand on her shiny, little head and looked defiantly into Max's face, daring him to disillusion her.

"Wipe that look off of your face," he muttered ruefully. "Much as I'd like to and much as I probably should, I'm not going to wring your neck. Not in front of a four-year-old witness, anyway. And, contrary to your opinion that I'm a combination of Jack the Ripper, Scrooge, and the Grinch, I'm not going to be the one to destroy happiness like that," he said, nodding toward Shannon's radiant little face.

"Thank you," I whispered.

"You're welcome," he said, his face relaxing.

I saw something that might've been amusement pulling at the corners of his mouth. My eyes drank him in. He looked wonderful in a yellow sweater and tight-fitting jeans. I swallowed and looked away as Shannon tore into the bag, leaving a mass of ribbon and brightly colored wrapping paper on the living room floor. I was nearly as excited as she was. Max's eyes never left Shannon. His expression was thoughtful.

Shannon hugged the Lullaby Baby to her chest and rocked it gently. "How did you know that I wanted a Lullaby Baby, Santa?" she asked, her big, bright eyes shining. "I only told Miss Weeks. Did she tell you?"

I nodded and Shannon, satisfied, sat down in the middle of the presents to examine the doll. I looked at Max and found him studying me, his face impassive. "I know I should apologize," I told him, "but somehow I just can't."

He shook his head. "What am I going to do with you?" he asked softly, and I wondered if I was only imagining that his eyes were shining as brightly as his daughter's.

I shrugged. "I don't know. Put up with me, I guess, because I'm not going away. You might as well get accustomed to me. I'm going to see to it that Shannon is happy. I'm going to see that she gains some weight, that she gets a haircut when she needs it, and I'm going to tell her about Snow White and Rapunzel and Cinderella." I was way out of bounds there and I knew it. I took a deep breath, bracing myself to get thrown out the front door. "And I'm going to make her believe in happily-ever-after endings!"

"And what about me?" he asked. Now there was no mistaking the glow in his dark eyes. "Don't you think I deserve a happily-ever-after ending?"

"Yes, of course," I said shakily. My knees started to wobble.

"Well, then, come here," he murmured, opening his arms wide and holding them out to me.

I was totally bewildered at the speed with which things were happening, but I went into his arms without hesitating and without questioning. It was only the third time I'd actually talked with him and so he was pretty much a stranger. But as his arms closed warmly and securely around me, nothing about our embrace seemed strange. It was as if we'd embraced many times before; it felt like we'd been away from each other for a long time—too long—and now we were back together.

He pulled down the ragged beard and bent toward me. His kiss took my breath away even though it was a light, tentative kiss. Anything else would've been too much, too soon. But the promise was there.

"I can't fight you, so I might as well join you," he whispered. "Anyone who gives this much happiness can't be all bad. I'm willing to give it a try because I'm tired of being bitter and disillusioned and tired of coming home to a house where there's no warmth or love. If you can put up with me while I'm working on it, I'm ready to give happily-ever-after endings a try." He shook his head and I could feel him shake with laughter. "I can't believe it took a ragtag Santa with a beard that looks like a rat's nest who delivers gifts in a garbage bag to make me understand what living is all about." He sobered and looked down at me with his daughter's serious, deep eyes. "Will you help me, Kristin? Will you help me start to live again?"

"I'd be delighted," I whispered. "Lila says that all children need lots of love and hugs and kisses," I told him. "I think that might work with adults, too, don't you?"

"I told you Lila's a woman with sense," he murmured.

I felt the muscles flex in his arms as they tightened around me and thought hazily, Just wait until I tell Lila.

Shannon tugged impatiently on her father's pant leg. "The song says Mommy kissed Santa Claus—not Daddy." Her smooth, little brow furrowed with puzzlement.

"It's all right, honey," he told Shannon. "Daddies can kiss Santa if it's a special time like this."

Shannon's face cleared and she transferred her grip to my leg. "I just love you, Santa Claus!"

"Know something, honey?" Max smiled at me, his dark eyes warm and indulgent on my flushed face. Then he said something I'll remember for the rest of my life: "I'm sure, in time, I'll come to love Santa, too."

THE END

A Chance Encounter Put Me—
IN THE MOOD FOR MISTLETOE
It's great for the holiday spirit!

After the way Christmas turned out the year before, I decided to boycott the holiday that year. Oh, I still decorated the tiny tree I purchased for my apartment, but other than that I intended to turn my back on all of the parties and frivolity.

When I was at home, it was easier to avoid than when I ventured out. Tucking my head deeper inside of my down-filled jacket, I tried to ignore the brightly decorated holiday windows, happy couples, and laughing children. The red, suede toes of my new boots kicked up tiny puffs of snow as I hurried along.

"Hey, watch out!"

The warning came at the same exact time as the impact with the completely immoveable object—a broad, denim-clad chest. Dazed, I looked up into the warmest pair of chocolate-brown eyes I'd ever encountered.

"Are you okay?" the man asked. As he spoke, he didn't make any move to take his hands off of my arms where he'd reached out to steady me.

"I'm so sorry," I finally said. I shook my head to clear it and noticed a torn grocery bag and scattered items on the snowy ground at our feet. Dropping to my knees, I started picking up the man's groceries.

He knelt down and pulled me up to my feet. "I can get those," he said.

"I guess I wasn't paying attention."

"Nope, but if you had been, we would never have met," he said, holding out his gloved hand. "Jerome Tillotson, at your service."

I shook it. "Susanna Meadows."

"Well, Susanna Meadows, if you don't mind staying here for a second while I run back in and grab another bag for my groceries, I'd love to take you out for a cup of coffee."

"N-no thanks," I stammered. "I really should get home."

A flash of what looked like disappointment flickered across his face before he asked, "Someone waiting there for you?"

"Just the goldfish, but I don't think they can tell time."

"Great!" he said. "Then say you'll agree to have coffee with a stranger to celebrate the holiday season."

I was sorely tempted, but then I remembered my vow to boycott the holidays. Celebrating wasn't really on the agenda for me—not when Christmas Day marked the one-year anniversary of my divorce.

Jerome mistook my hesitation for agreement and strode back into the store to grab a bag. A nagging voice in the back of my mind told me that it might not be a bad idea to just have coffee with a handsome stranger—especially since I'd been alone for the better part of a year. Well-meaning friends had set me up on a couple of disastrous blind dates, but other than that it was me, the TV, and my goldfish spending nights together.

"You're still here, so you must've decided to take me up on the offer."

"I did change my mind." I flashed him a hesitant smile and handed him the cans of tomato paste I'd recovered from the sidewalk.

As soon as the groceries were tossed into the plastic sack, Jerome grabbed my hand and led me toward a little café that bordered Main Street. Soft red and green lights danced on the tiny Christmas tree that sat in the front window. It was nestled amidst a coating of fake snow and a bunch of beautifully wrapped gifts.

"Jerome, Merry Christmas!" The barista came out from behind the counter. She was drying her hands on a towel that was draped over the waistband of her black jeans.

"Right back at you," Jerome said with a laugh after planting a light kiss on the blonde's cheek. "Betty, I want you to meet Susanna. We just . . . um . . . bumped into each other and I begged her to have coffee with me."

"Hi, Susanna." She ignored my outstretched hand, grabbed me, and pulled me into a light, quick hug before turning back to the counter.

I wondered who Betty was and how she knew Jerome. I knew I had no right to think any thoughts about that, though, and couldn't even figure out why that question popped into my head. Still, I wondered if Betty was a sibling, a family friend, or an old girlfriend.

Jerome's touch on my sleeve brought me back to the present and I realized that Betty was talking to me. "I assume it'll be the usual for you, Jerome. So, what will you have, Susanna?"

I was almost embarrassed to say what I wanted since it was getting so cold and blustery outside, but I did, anyway. "I'll have a frozen mocha shake, if you make them."

A quick smile sliced across Jerome's face before he turned to me. "Ah, a girl after my own heart!"

He put his hand on the small of my back and guided me toward a table tucked into the corner of the coffee house and offered to take my oversized jacket. I was so glad that I'd paid attention to my outfit when I got dressed for work that morning. I always feel good when I wear my dark-green sweater with its deep V-neck. I reached up and untangled my thin, gold chain from one of my curls. Once it was untangled, the tiny unicorn charm dangled between my breasts.

I looked over at Jerome. He was hanging the coats and I caught a glimpse of my reflection in the window. My eyes appeared to be twinkling in the lights of the Christmas tree. My cheeks looked a bit flushed; it was probably from the chilly night air. I admitted to myself that I liked the way my soft curls framed my face—they weren't too flattened or too full of static from being inside the hood of my jacket all that time.

"Here's your drink," Jerome said, startling me out of my reverie. He handed me my glass, but continued to stand, looking down at me for a minute. His perusal gave me a warm feeling in my belly. I glanced at him and flashed a quick smile. He shook his head, laughed, and sat down. "You have the most beautiful eyes I've ever seen," he finally said.

"Cat eyes, my mom always says." I felt a warm blush color my face at his comment. It had been so long since anyone had commented on my appearance.

As we enjoyed our whipped cream, chocolate, and espresso-filled drinks, Jerome told me that he works in the city as an architect and that he'd lived in the same town for his whole life.

"I work at the newspaper downtown. The weekly paper," I told him before taking a sip of my drink. "I've been here for about five years. I moved here from California."

"What brought you this far across the country?" he asked before leaning across the table to wipe a bit of whipped cream off of my lower lip.

The warmth of his thumb as it grazed my lip sent a thrill through me. My tongue flicked out toward where his finger had been.

"My . . ." I hesitated. "My husband's job transferred him here."

I saw his eyes dart toward my ring finger—my bare ring finger.

"I'm divorced." It didn't hurt too much to say the words, but I did still feel a bit like a failure for not having been able to make my marriage work. It seemed like Paul and I should've been able to make it. We grew up together, dated all through high school, drifted along together during college, and finally got married once we'd graduated. By the time the two of us stood up in front of the justice of the peace, we'd been together for close to fifteen years.

"I'm sorry. Was it recent, the divorce?" he asked.

Try as I might, I couldn't bite back the sarcastic bit of laughter. "Christmas day will be one year."

His hand shot out to cover mine, its warmth penetrating my chilled fingertips. I felt the calluses on his work-roughened hands. For some reason, I liked knowing that he took part in the actual work involved in building a house or an office building. Maybe that was because Paul had been such a hands-off manager. And a hands-off husband, as far as that went, I admitted to myself.

"That truly sucks," Jerome said, shrugging. He was at a loss for words.

"That was just Paul being 'practical,' " I explained. "He handed me divorce papers along with two Christmas gifts—a key to a new apartment and a paid, one-year lease. He said that it would be easier to begin a new life on the first of the month and he didn't want to ruin New Year's Eve with discussions of the end of our marriage."

I was surprised that I could talk about it without crying. But, like my mom and sister had said, I knew the marriage was over long before the papers were signed. They were merely a formality.

"So, that means that your lease is up in a couple of weeks. Are you going to stay in town?" he asked.

"I love my job, so I'm staying put," I said. "I really miss my family, but I'm hoping to get home in the spring."

We put the awkward conversation about my marriage behind us and continued to talk until it was closing time at the coffee shop. We found out that we had so much in common—from our love of old, black-and-white movies to the books we read, the vacation spots we dreamed of, and the funny dysfunction of our respective families. We decided that his brother and my sister would make a perfect couple because their quirks would mesh.

"Do you need a ride home?" he asked as I shrugged my way into my coat. He laughed and said, "You just look so tiny inside that big bunch of material!"

"I still haven't acclimated to the cold, so I bought the biggest, puffiest jacket I could find." I tugged at the zipper. It was stuck on my sweater.

"Here, let me." Jerome brushed my hands away and leaned forward to work the sweater yarn out of the zipper's teeth.

The smell of his spicy aftershave drifted toward my nose. One of his sandy-brown curls fell across his forehead as he worked, and completely on their own my fingers reached out and brushed it back in place. He looked up at me with a smoldering heat in his eyes so warm that it melted the icy core I'd built around my heart over the past year.

"Hey, you two!" Betty called out. We looked over and saw her pointing above our heads. "Mistletoe."

A smile tugged at the corner of Jerome's mouth as he slanted a glance toward the ceiling. "May I?"

I flashed him a tentative smile and nodded. It was my last thought before his mouth claimed mine in a warm, persuasive kiss. I thought then that maybe I wouldn't boycott the holidays, after all. Once Jerome's fingers wove themselves into my hair, pulling me closer as his tongue danced with mine, all further thoughts were lost beneath the magic of the mistletoe.

THE END

I FOUND LOVE FOR CHRISTMAS
This was the best gift ever!

It was Thursday—the day before Christmas Eve. The entire office was abuzz with excitement. As I sat in my cubicle, I listened intently to the various topics of office chatter.

Some people were talking about spending the Christmas holiday with friends, while most talked of spending quality time with their family. I decided to ignore the incessant chatter and get back to the piles of work in front of me. The void in my heart was big enough to hold half a country.

My fingers tapped busily against the keyboard in front of me until Marcus, my cheery coworker, peeked his head over my small cubicle, temporarily erasing my train of thought.

"Hi, Roslyn. I know you're not working! It's four thirty. The market's closed now. You don't have to worry about any more stock sales until tomorrow."

I smugly looked up at him. "I know that, but it's best that I keep working. I have a lot on my mind," I said.

Marcus pressed forward in his questioning, leaning dangerously close to me. "Come on, Roslyn. Get into the Christmas spirit," he sang, before reaching behind his back and retrieving a large Mexican hat. "Here," he playfully demanded. "Pick a name out of this hat. The least you can do is participate in the office grab bag this year."

I really wasn't in the mood. But Marcus had the persistence of a pit bull. I knew that the only way to get rid of him was to pick a name at random. The office participated in this every year, but I usually declined. The look on the friendly man's face, however, signaled I wouldn't be able to give any excuses this year.

Other than his pushiness, Marcus truly meant well. He wasn't the blame for my "Scroogelike" behavior.

"Whatever," I said. "If I pick a name already, will that make you leave me alone?" I questioned.

"Yes, it sure will," he replied, easily.

Quickly, I dunked my hand into the large hat he held steady in front of me. I pulled out a small strip of paper that read: Pedro—eight years old.

My heart sank to my knees. That age struck a chord with me—it was the age my son would've been had he survived the tragic car accident that took him from me two years ago.

I stuffed the paper into my purse before darting out without more than a nod at Marcus. I was at a sudden loss for words amongst the joyous chatter in the room.

"Wait, Roslyn! What's wrong? Did I say something wrong?" Marcus asked, as I rushed from him. I didn't respond to his question. It was nothing he personally did, but I didn't have time to explain that. The pain in my heart was increasing by the moment, and if I hadn't left at that moment, I swore I'd faint from emotional distress.

Once I was outside the building, I took a big gulp of air deeply into my lungs. Yet, I could feel my heart beating faster as I flew into my car.

All of a sudden, the painful memories from the past resurfaced. My son would've been eight years old this year, too! I knew then there was no way for me to readily forget the life I once had.

I turned on the car, and practically burned the rubber on my tires bolting out of the parking lot. I flew through the streets like a bat out of hell. Depression had taken such a complete hold over me, all at once, that I was beginning to feel as if I didn't have much energy to completely steer the car.

When I finally made it home, all I could do was collapse on my living room couch in tears. I clutched the pillow close to me as if it were my late son, nestled in my arms.

All the memories of that Christmas Eve past had hit me each year around the holidays. The memories always seemed like yesterday— the day I lost both my son and my husband.

I had worked late that particular night in order to organize some badly constructed files. Jacob called me while I was deep into working overtime. His voice was amazingly peppy and upbeat. I hadn't heard him sound so well in some time.

"Hey Roslyn, honey. Working late?" he asked.

"Yeah, Jacob. But I'm gonna get out of here in just a few minutes. I'll pick up Jarrett from the after school program as soon as I leave. I'm going to call the teacher, now."

"No, don't worry about that," he said.

"Well, I don't want to be late picking him up."

Jacob sighed. "You don't have to worry because I've already picked Jarrett up. He's with me, now."

My heart raced suddenly. "Is he all right?" I asked.

"Of course," Jacob scoffed. "Why wouldn't he be all right? He's with his father. They let us out early today so I thought I'd scoop him up today and give you more time to work. "

I quickly asked to be put on the phone with our son. Jacob handed him his cell phone. My six-year-old's voice was like sweet music in my ears after such long, hard days. "How are you, today?"

"Fine, Mommy. Daddy's taking me to go pick up the Christmas tree!" he said, his voice full of excitement.

"Oh really," I said. "You make sure you pick out the best tree. Mommy will help you decorate it," I announced, proudly.

"Thank you, Mommy," he said. "I love you."

"I love you too, Jarrett. See you later," I said. Little did I know that would be the last time I spoke to my precious son. "Put Daddy back on the phone, okay."

He did as I said, and in seconds, I was speaking to my husband. The topic of the conversation soon changed to making Jacob the focus of conversation.

"Are you all right? I mean, you haven't been drinking tonight?" I asked.

For a moment, he was quiet; but then, he freely discussed his prior drinking habits that led him to rehab for the past month.

"Of course, I'm fine," he said. The confidence in his voice was unlike I'd heard it in a while. He and I had been trying to mend our broken marriage, due to the problems his drinking addiction had created in the past.

"Jacob," I began.

"Roslyn give me a chance, please. I've been clean and sober for a month, now. You know that. Give me a chance to bond with my son and to prove your doubts wrong, at least."

The sincerity in his voice allowed me to drop my guard. I figured, people were allowed second chances. "Okay, Jacob. But call me as soon as you guys get there. I'm leaving out of here in about a half hour, then."

I had allowed my husband to take our son to pick out that tree, primarily because of the excitement in my son's voice. I believe he was pleased at how much of an interest his father was taking in him. Just a few months past, his father was more interested in tipping the bottle than spending time with him.

My son had always cried out for his father's attention, but when Jacob was consumed by alcohol, the last person he could focus on was his own son. Nights of putting up with his drunken ranting and raving was too much. The final straw was when my husband's drinking started to consume every inch of his life. He even drank at work during his lunch break and would come home reeking of liquor from head to toe.

I was at my wit's end during the final week of his out of control drinking sprees. Quite regularly, Jacob would go to the bar with his coworkers at the day's end. They'd all drink themselves stupid, and managed to drive home every time.

Jacob was the worst of them, sometimes, not remembering how he made it home the next morning.

It was that risky behavior that never allowed me to trust Jacob behind the wheel with our son. And I hadn't allowed Jacob to escort our child anywhere since then.

But all of this was before my family and I intervened, forcing

Jacob into Alcoholics Anonymous. He had been clean for a month and was showing tremendous progress. So despite my reserve, I allowed myself to calm down and relax my nerves under the circumstances.

Soon, I hurried to finish up the last bit of work left on my desk.

Once my work was finished for the night, I shut off my computer, ready to head home. I darted out the front entrance, and to my car in the parking lot. The pale evening sky was illuminated by the full moon.

I hopped in the car, started the ignition, and peeled out of the parking lot onto the main road. My cell phone sat in the passenger seat next to me. I glanced down at it, realizing no one had called me on it. I thought I might've missed Jacob's call.

It was seven o'clock by the time I got inside the house.

"Jacob. Jarrett," I called. There was no answer. I looked in the kitchen for a note on the refrigerator like Jacob would usually leave if he were running late. There was no note left for me.

The phone nearby displayed no messages left on the answering machine. There was also no Christmas tree in the living room, so I know they hadn't been back.

I picked up the phone to call Jacob on his cell. It rang until his answering machine picked up. I hung up and immediately dialed again, but I was met by the same greeting. This time, I left a message at the sound of the tone.

"Jacob. What happened to you? Call me. I'm home. Let me know that you're on your way, all right. I'm starting to get worried," I said, before hanging up.

Minutes had passed, but Jacob never called me back. It was unlike him. I tried to calm my nerves by imagining his cell phone had died on him. He had a habit of forgetting to charge his phone the night before.

As another hour soon passed, I began to get really worried. Pretty soon, I was becoming a mess. At anytime, I expected my family to come home. Jacob would criticize me for overreacting.

Maybe they stopped for a bite to eat, I thought. Although I remembered telling Jacob earlier, I had planned on making dinner.

I was about to pace the floor before the doorbell rang. I rushed to it, swinging the door open with force.

"You guys had me really worried," I began, before the words in my throat ceased. Instead of meeting my husband and son, I was face-to-face with two solemn looking officers before me.

"Mrs. Rodriquez?"

"Yes, that's me," I slowly responded. My body had frozen into place, suddenly. There had never been any reason for the cops to ever visit my place. I looked at them with a look full of skepticism and fear.

The taller, deep-voiced officer stepped forward. I focused on the movement of his lips as each painful word left his mouth. "May we come inside for a minute? I think you may need to sit down."

"Why? What? What's happened?" I asked. I couldn't feel the feet beneath my legs. As if driven by instinct, the other officer gently grabbed me by the arm, and led me to my couch.

Something had to be terribly wrong, but I had hoped they were here to tell me Jacob's car had gotten stalled somewhere, and they were being brought home by a tow truck or something.

The deep-voice officer looked down at me, the corners of his eyes turned slightly downward. "We're sorry to inform you that there's been a terrible accident. Your husband and son collided on I-95 with another car, and they were killed."

I sat still for what seemed like minutes. My face and body froze. How could this be? They have to be lying to me, I thought. There is no way the information is true. At first, I refused to believe the tragic news.

"How can this be? Are you sure there's no mistake here," I pleaded.

"Miss, we've identified the bodies through personal articles in the car. We believe alcohol may have played a big part in the accident. I'm sorry. The coroner is going to run some tests to see if your husband was legally drunk at the time of the accident."

My face and body froze. The cops continued speaking to me, saying words I no longer dared listen to. My life had been stolen from me in a matter of seconds.

I hopped up from the couch, paced the floor for a moment, and let out the loudest scream I could muster before collapsing to the floor. Honestly, I didn't remember much once the officers left my house.

The coroner's results shortly thereafter, did conclude my worst fears: Jacob had lied to me. He had been drinking that night. The investigator on the scene of the accident suspected Jacob was speeding, and he was killed instantly when he jumped the divider and collided head-on with the truck driving in the opposite direction.

I was numb for days after that, and I couldn't even bear to handle any of the funeral arrangements. My mother and sister had to handle all of the funeral and wake planning. They helped me with everything, although the tasks were no easier for them than it would've been for me.

After the funeral when I laid my family to rest, I sunk into the deepest depression in my life. I took a leave of absence from my job and cocooned myself inside my house.

I couldn't bring myself out because life seemed too painful. How am I supposed to live my life, now? I thought. If I even heard a family's laughter, I broke down in a fit of tears. Working became almost impossible because I couldn't focus on any one thing for long.

My weight had dropped significantly. I was practically skin and bones within a few short months. Suicidal thoughts entered my mind on a daily basis, but even that would've required more strength than I had.

Yet, I decided to write out a will, which would designate my personal possessions to members of my family. I knew I couldn't go on living much longer without any food in my body.

On one lonely Sunday afternoon, I set aside some time to write my will. An abrupt ring at my door alerted me to move from the desk near my living room door. I slowly crept to the front door, opening it slightly.

My mother was standing before me, her Bible clutched tightly under her arm. "Roslyn, honey," she sang.

"Hi, Ma," I said, welcoming her inside with the easy gesture of my hand. "Come in."

My mother walked inside, and clutched my hand in hers. Tears slowly crept from her eyes as she sat next to me on the couch. "Roslyn."

"You don't even have to say it, Ma. I know you're hurting over their deaths, too," I said.

"Yes," she answered. "But I'm more hurt over you. You've been inside this house for months. You have to go back to work and move on with your life."

"But . . ." I argued, staring my mother directly in her eyes. How could I have been expected to carry on with my life, alone?

As if reading my mind, my mother began speaking again, but this time, with much determination. "Roslyn, this isn't healthy. You can't live your life waiting to die. I know you're hurting inside, but it's time you moved on. I lost my son-in-law and my grandson. I don't want to lose my daughter, too," she said.

The pain in her voice shook my insides. I'd never known my mother to be so serious about anything. She was always the one who joked around and made everyone laugh. But here she was aching for me; her heart was just breaking. Naturally, I couldn't have possibly lived much longer with denying myself food and any human contact.

Even though it was one of the most difficult decisions in my life, I believed my mother was right. So after two weeks of counseling and prayer, I returned to work.

That was over two years ago, and the painful memories from that time still existed in my head. It seemed as if the Christmas holiday placed me back in time every year. I relived the tragic memory of my family's death over and over again like a broken record.

After a night of crying myself to sleep, I woke up the next morning puffy-eyed and exhausted. Nevertheless, I had to go to work. It was Christmas Eve, and the last place I felt like being was at work. But there were bills to pay, and every year, we received our Christmas bonuses on Christmas Eve.

No sooner had I come through the door did I notice Marcus approaching me. He had a large smile on his face and a big gift in his hand. The present's bright red wrapping seemed almost blinding to my weary eyes.

"Good morning, Roslyn. Here's your present. I picked your name from the office grab bag," he sang.

I grasped my mouth. I remembered picking the eight-year-old boy's name out of the hat he handed me yesterday. I hadn't even begun to think about buying Pedro's gift. My mind suddenly went blank.

I took the gift with a halfhearted grin on my face. "Thanks Marcus. You didn't have to get me a gift, though."

"But I picked your name. Some of us picked coworkers, and others picked from the names of kids at the local group home," he said, matter-of-factly.

My eyebrow raised curiously. Each year, I had never cared to ask where the names of the children came from since I hadn't participated since my family's death. "Did you say these kids are from a group home?"

"Yeah," he said. "I heard something about that kid you picked— Pedro. His mother is in rehab, and she is a crack addict. Saura, over in accounting, and I, always visit the group home every year. Some of those kids would never see any gifts if we didn't come around."

A desperate pain hit my heart. Suddenly, I thought about the boy. Ironically, the boy whom I'd never met shared more in common with me than he may have known. We were both without a family.

I thought of how lonely and desperate he must've felt by not having any one to turn to except the workers at his group home. It was on my mind, so I had to ask Marcus a little more about him.

"Where's Pedro's father?" I asked, matter-of-factly.

Marcus's nose frowned slightly as he spoke. "Dead, I think. He died from gunshot wounds in a fight he had with a drug dealer over money—or at least, that's the story his social worker gave me."

Marcus's eyes briefly misted over as if he were going to break down in a fit of tears right in front of me. I had the urge to grab him in my arms and tell him everything was going to be fine. But I was barely the spokeswoman for happiness myself, so I maintained my distance.

Yet, I felt even more drawn to this boy from his story. "So what group home is he in?" I asked.

Marcus cleared his throat, and spoke with the usual calm reserve that was his nature. "Halloran House. It's about twenty miles from here in Gary," he said. "Pedro is a smart boy. He has a really big heart. He's going to love that bike you bought him!" Marcus exclaimed.

Oh my God, I thought to myself. I haven't gotten Pedro's gift, and Christmas is tomorrow!

"Marcus," I began. "I was supposed to bring Pedro's gift in with me to work this morning like everyone else, but I don't have it with me. I didn't buy Pedro's gift."

Marcus looked at me concerned. "What happened?"

I allowed tears to trail down my pale skin. "I just didn't get around to buying it. I usually don't participate, but now . . . is it too late for me to get the bike to him?"

Marcus smiled. "Of course not. If you want, you can leave on your lunch break and get him the bike."

I shook my head from side to side. "No way. I have that big project for Jacob to finish today remember . . . transferring over all those old accounts for Mr. Sotomeyer. If I take a lunch, I'll never get it to him."

Marcus pondered his next decision so much he had developed a cute little dimple above his right eyebrow. I studied it intensely until his eyes locked with mine in a momentarily powerful glance. "Well, Roslyn. Saura and a few others in the office are taking over the gifts at the end of their lunch hour. You'll miss them. What if I go out and get the bike Pedro wanted, and you just reimburse me next week?"

That wasn't an option for me. I was always backing out of life and letting others make decisions for me ever since Jacob and Jarrett died. It was time for me to finally face the music, and do something for myself.

"No, Marcus. I'd like to see to it that he gets his bike personally . . . from me."

Marcus's eyes lit up. "Well, there is one way we can resolve this. Pedro is on the group home's baseball team. They practice throughout the year, and they're having their last practice for this year, tonight at Lowell's Field. It's a little field down the street. Practice starts tonight at six thirty. Do you think you can make it?"

I nodded at him, fighting back tears at the same time. "Of course, I'll make it. E-mail me the directions and I'll be there. I'll go to the toy store after work to pick out Pedro's gift, and I will meet you at the field, later."

Without warning, Marcus stretched his long arms out, and he pulled me in for a tender embrace. For a matter of moments, I could hear his heart beating steadily next to mine. The intense heat of his body warmed me, instantly. I patted him on his back, signaling he should release his penetrating hold on me.

"Thank you, Roslyn. He's going to be so happy."

Marcus had a newfound glow that had warmed him all over. As he walked away, I shook with emotion.

Jacob, my late husband, had always seemed so much more interested in alcohol than in how our son was feeling and what he was doing. Yet, Marcus, an unmarried, handsome man, was devoted to making any needy child happy—and he didn't have to.

I tried to focus on work for the remainder of the day, but all I could do was think about Pedro. I couldn't focus on much else. My heart just went out to him, an eight-year-old facing a crisis he probably wasn't even that aware of. It wasn't his fault his mother was addicted to crack, but he found himself facing adversity all on his own.

Immediately, once work was done, I was on a mission to find the best bike I could for Pedro. Since I didn't have much time, I made my way over to the local toy store at the mall, with quickness.

I walked from aisle to aisle, aimlessly searching for which bike many of the boys were riding. The sad truth was I wasn't up on toy trends at all. After my own son died, I pretty much stopped watching toy commercials and distanced myself from any nearby children—that included my neighbor's kids, and any of my nieces and nephews. So I was at a loss. My mind drew a blank. I did not know anything about this boy's personal taste or dislikes. I didn't have a clue.

Luckily, a nearby sales clerk noticed the confusion on my face and sauntered over in my direction to assist me. It only took a matter of minutes before I decided to buy Pedro the "hottest bike" in the toy store, as the sales clerk put it. It was a stunning mixture of black and metallic silver.

The rugged dirt bike looked perfect for a boy his age. I also picked out the matching knee and elbow pads, along with a sporty little helmet. Hopefully, this boy would take an interest in this bike. I wanted to make him happy in the way I physically couldn't make my son.

A helpful clerk helped me carry my items to the checkout line. After having him lug them into my car outside, I stuffed them into the trunk and drove right to the field where the kids would be practicing.

I wandered around the field after parking my car discreetly nearest the exit gate. I didn't have to stumble for long before Marcus came running toward me. "Roslyn, you made it."

He was dressed in a baseball uniform. The snug fit of his outfit allowed me to see the strong muscles protruding from his arms. His eyes sparkled as he stared at me in a way I had only remembered my late husband staring at me on our wedding day years earlier.

Bashfully, I turned away from his gaze, and I stared down at my feet for a moment. "I'm here. Hey, I didn't know you volunteer with the kids. You're really decked out."

"Well," he said. "I do this on the evenings I can. I love children, but since I don't have any of my own, this is the closest I can get to kids."

I blocked away the shock of seeing so many children near my late son's age. It was difficult for me at first, but somewhere in my heart, I imagined one of those kids being my Jarrett reincarnated in a sense, allowed to live out his carefree childhood.

Marcus gripped my hand in his as he led me down to the dugout where the young kids were. Briefly, he whispered in my ear before we walked any further. "I know how much it took for you to come out here and be with these kids. And I know that you've had a rough couple of years. I truly do appreciate you being here, Roslyn. I know that things are going to get better for you. Pain doesn't last for always."

Those sweet words softened up the inside of my heart. "Oh," I said, glancing back at my car in the distance. "I left Pedro's bike in the car. I should go get it."

Marcus stopped me with a gentle tug at my left arm. "Leave it there—for now. How about you just sit through the practice and relax? These kids are full of comedy, too. They'll give you a good laugh."

"Okay, Marcus. I'll follow you."

Marcus led me to the crew of happy kids, for some reason they weren't like I imagined them. Though they must've faced their challenges like anyone else, these kids' faces were full of joy, energy, and anticipation. They rooted for one another when they stole bases, and patted each other on the back when they didn't. It was as if they were their own little family. Suddenly, my problems didn't seem so large.

Some of the children were without any family at all. Some would never know who their real families were, and some would live out their childhood in the group home unless they were adopted—which accounted for half of the kids there.

But despite their fears, no child showed happiness more than the feisty Pedro, who seemed to be such a natural at baseball, he could've passed for the next Babe Ruth. I stood up and cheered for him as he stole all the bases and landed a home run.

Marcus was right there by my side as if we had known each other much longer than the four years we spent working together.

The practice was over, seemingly just as soon as it had begun. However, I knew that time hadn't flown by that fast. I was just having too much fun to notice the passing of time. And that had been something deeply unusual for me.

When someone you loved more than anything in the world died, the thing you find yourself doing most, is watching time pass on a regular basis. Every moment of every hour is spent usually thinking of that other person and how different life would've been had they still been alive. I wasn't thinking about that tonight—for the first time in the past two years.

As practice ended, Marcus turned to me. His face drenched with sweat and said, "There's someone I'd like you to meet, Roslyn."

Within seconds, the team's star player, Pedro Ramos, ran over to me.

Marcus introduced us, immediately. "Pedro, this is Roslyn. She picked your name in the grab bag, and she wants to give you a little something."

"My gift?" he asked me innocently.

"Yes," I said.

Marcus gripped the boy's hand. "You'll have to walk with us to get it. You don't mind getting your gift a few hours before Christmas morning."

"No way. I'll beat you to the car," he sang.

"Last one there's a rotten egg," Marcus teased, before letting Pedro get a head start in the race.

The little boy shot out in front of Marcus.

I watched the two of them as I walked behind. It was as if I were looking at my vision of what Jacob and Jarrett should've been. I shook the thought out of my head. This time, I was making it a point to be happy in my life.

By the time I made it to the car, the both of them were out of breath and gasping for air. I interjected, "Okay guys. It's time to take a break. And Pedro . . . it's time for you to look at your brand-new bike."

I lifted the trunk of my car and walked the wide-eyed boy around to the back. Marcus diligently pulled the bike out of the trunk and placed it in front of Pedro. All he could do was place his small hand over his mouth.

But soon, like a bolt of lightening, Pedro shot over to me and embraced me. It was the tightest, warmest hug I had felt since Marcus's enormous hug before. My body was practically frozen. I could feel the boy's tears of joy on my shirt.

"Thank you, Roslyn! Thank you. This is the best Christmas ever!" he shouted, excitement shining in his eyes.

Marcus eyed me, throwing an infectious smile my way. All I could do was smile back at him, thanking him for saving my life. It was as if life had ended so long ago, and this was the most pleasure I'd felt.

Pedro turned to me, and asked: "Are you sure I can take this with me? This isn't some kind of a joke? I mean, this is a pretty nice bike. You sure you don't want it back?"

I bent down to his height and placed my arm on his shoulder while reassuring him. "It's all yours. You deserve it. Enjoy your bike, my friend."

"Thank you," he said, planting a quick kiss on my cheek. "Can I ride it now?"

Marcus spoke to him like the father figure he was. "You can ride it back to the van, but then I'll have to put it in my car, and I'll drive it over to Halloran House for you."

"Thanks, Marcus. Thanks again, Roslyn!" he howled, before darting away on the bike at a breakneck speed.

Marcus and I watched him drift away just as quickly as he had approached us. It was so heartwarming to see this little boy so happy.

Suddenly, he gripped my hand in his. "Roslyn, you don't know how much that meant to him . . . and me. I don't know how to thank you."

"You can take me out to dinner," I said, noting that it was the first idea that came to my mind.

"Dinner, it is," he said. "And do you have a preference of restaurant, or favorite food?"

"I really like seafood," I offered.

"I like seafood, too. I know of a great little restaurant down by the shore. It's a bit of a drive, but if you really like seafood, this place is the best, Roslyn."

"Say no more. But tomorrow is Christmas," I said. "Who in their right mind is going to be open on Christmas?"

He simply shrugged his shoulders softly. "There's always some place that's open. Trust me," he said.

Not knowing what to make of that comment, I just left his words without further interpretation. We parted ways, but as soon as we did, I quickly wished that I could've run after him. His words, the way he stared at me and took such time with me, was overwhelming my psyche.

I wanted to be in his comforting embrace. I didn't want him to let me go for any length of time. I had been closer with Marcus than I even had with my late husband. Slowly, I got inside my car to begin driving home with Marcus and Pedro on my mind.

My thoughts hadn't been on much else but having dinner with Marcus. I spent the day cleaning out more of Jacob's belongings I had held. Since it was too much for me to view my son's empty room, I had cleaned it out years ago.

Yet, I did manage to find a picture of the last time I saw Jarrett. We had gone to his favorite amusement park. Our expressions were full of laughter and joy. I suddenly wanted to remember Jarrett that way always. I hadn't wanted to remember anything else about the accident.

I was also determined that other mothers wouldn't have to be sitting in my place. I called and left a message with the local chapter of Mothers Against Drunk Drivers. M.A.D.D. would be the organization that would help me feel as if my son's death wasn't in vain. I couldn't allow it to be. There had to be a way to finally transform the pain into happiness.

That night, I was determined to keep a positive outlook. Sometimes, I noticed I'd slip into depression for seemingly no reason. It was as if I was holding myself from being happy because I believed that I was betraying my family.

Yet it took all these months for me to realize I wasn't betraying Jacob and Jarrett by allowing myself to be happy. Beside, there was no way I could try to support laws against drunk drivers if I was a miserable mess. I had to be dynamic. I had to move on.

I met Marcus at his house hours later as he'd requested. We were supposed to go to the restaurant from there. But to my surprise, Marcus greeted me at the door with a tuxedo on, and a bright red rose in his hand.

I eyed him suspiciously before he hurriedly placed the rose in the palm of my right hand. "Here you are, Roslyn."

"Oh Marcus, you didn't have to do that," I said.

His eyes gleamed against the pale moon in the sky above us. "A beautiful woman like yourself deserves some roses."

His gesture and comment made me blush for the first time in years. I could feel a sudden warmth surround my body. It was as if I were floating on a cloud, and the whole world had disappeared.

I reached over and gave him a quick embrace. He returned it with a soft kiss on my cheek. As soon as he welcomed me inside, I noticed the table set up with a lavish assortment of cheeses, wine, and breads. To the left of that assortment, was a lobster big enough to feed a family of four, and at the right, rested two plates fit for the main course.

My mouth dropped open. I couldn't believe Marcus went through all of that for me. "Marcus, why did you go through all this trouble?" I asked.

"Because you're a special woman. And you have the biggest heart of anyone I've ever known. I remember how distraught you were years ago, and I just want you to know that I think you're an incredible woman who's survived serious life events that would've broken most people. You're much stronger than anyone I know."

I don't know what made me do it, but I pulled him to me and kissed him hard on his lips. All of me melted under the strength of his muscular arms as he welcomed my kiss, exploring the contents of my mouth with his own. There was no place else I'd rather have been than there.

Another strange feeling that opened up inside me was peace. I had a purpose in life, and a sense of peace. I had only been hiding from happiness because I believed I wouldn't be respecting the dead with my joy. But now, I realized God didn't want me to live the rest of my life contemplating my own suicide. He wanted me to move on, and I believe he sent this man to allow me to move on.

That night changed the rest of my life. After an evening of laughter, food and romance, I was hooked. There was no turning back to my past. Besides, I don't think my son would've wanted to see his mother living in continual grief.

One year later, Marcus and I got married in a small ceremony in the field down the street from Halloran House. Pedro and my coworkers were there. It was one of the best days of my life. Unlike my marriage to my late husband, we didn't have any preexisting condition stopping us. He didn't drink or even smoke at all, for that matter.

It didn't seem unusual that we got married on Christmas Day. That day just had such a special significance to us that we couldn't resist. Besides, now every year I didn't have only painful memories to dwell on. I had an anniversary to celebrate.

As a matter of fact, when our first anniversary rolled around, Pedro and his now clean and sober mother spent the day with us. That was another blessing in disguise for Marcus and me. Although I wasn't able to save my late husband from alcohol destroying his life, Pedro didn't have to see his mother suffer the same fate. She had stayed off crack for an entire year—no doubt a feat that would've literally killed someone with a weaker sense of self.

As Marcus and I looked over across the table to see Pedro and his mother sharing small talk in between conversations with us, I couldn't help but remark. "Marcus, this is beautiful."

"What? The fact that we're here with each other?"

"The fact that my dreams came true after all. I was allowed a second chance. I never thought this day would come. God bless you for loving me."

Marcus smiled, shyly. "Who would've known that my future wife had been working with me for four years and I never even realized it? I really love you, Roslyn."

"I love you too, Marcus," I said, leaning in to plant a sweet kiss on his gentle lips.

"Ugh," Pedro pointed out. "You two are not going to start kissing again! I mean, no offense, but I've seen enough."

His mother laughed, tapping him on the shoulder. "Baby, stop that. They can kiss if they want to," she teased.

"All right," I agreed. "No more kissing for a while—at least until we're alone so we don't gross you out, Pedro."

That evening, we laughed, talked, and played video games well into the night. God had truly blessed me in a way I'd never imagined. Love had given me a second chance, and in three short months, Marcus and I were expecting our first child!

Whoever said "happily ever after" didn't exist, must've gotten their wires crossed. The truth was love was never ending, and my life was living proof of that.

THE END

A Super-Romantic Holiday Story—
SELLING CHRISTMAS TREES . . . WITH ATTITUDE!
The job I dreaded made me feel spunky
and sexy—and ready for love!

Maybe it was the dull, defeated look in Vida's eyes when she told me that somehow she'd "make it" this Christmas. Maybe that's how I wound up selling trees on the corner of Belmont and Forest in below-freezing temperatures. I just had to help Vida out.

Vida and her husband, Pascal, had been supporting their two grandchildren, Skylar and Owen, ever since their daughter, Vicki, had taken off with a man who was going to "show her the world." This was about the sixteenth guy, and Vicki wasn't getting any closer to her dream. We all knew she'd end up in a one-room dive over an all-night convenience store until her folks bailed her out. But Vida and Pascal couldn't bail Vicki out of her drug habit.

And it was killing them.

In fact, Vicki probably figured strongly in Pascal's heart attack—not that Vida would ever blame her. Now, though, Vida was going it alone. Skylar was only four, and Owen was five. They were little bundles of energy with big Christmas dreams.

But this Christmas was going to be tough. Pascal had used to work that tree stand like it was a McDonald's. Customers drove in with big hopes and drove out with reasonably priced trees. Everybody was satisfied. Oh, Pascal's trees weren't perfect, but they were affordable. He sold trees "with attitude." Oh, they might have a bare branch here or there. But ornaments, lights, and a lot of love worked wonders—that's what Pascal always said. And the money from the tree sales filled in a lot of holes for Vida and Pascal during the year.

Now Vida was just left with the holes.

The rent was cheap in our building; I'll vouch for that. In fact, the rent had been one selling point when I'd been looking for respectable apartment that would fit into my budget. Clerks at Kirsten's Kloset didn't make much. Sometimes, I worked a six-day week, including Tuesday and Thursday nights, just trying to make ends meet.

But this was a tough year. As the holidays got closer, Kirsten gave me the bad news: Women just weren't looking for expensive crepe blouses or cashmere slacks these days. This was going to be a year of wearing last year's holiday fashions.

I tucked my extra pair of comfortable shoes into a Kirsten's Kloset shopping bag, along with a black cardigan that I'd pull on for those cold winter mornings when the shop was chilly, and headed home.

As I dragged myself up my apartment stairs that day, my shopping bag banging against my leg, Skylar hurtled down the stairs, chasing after her brother, Owen.

"You take that back!"

"Will not! Will not!" Owen turned to taunt her. Then he saw me and straightened up. "Hi, Inga!" He threw me a deceptively innocent smile.

What a pair they were!

Vida appeared at the top of the stairs, wearing one of her polka-dot aprons, her arms folded over her ample stomach. "Both of you. Upstairs."

Now, when Vida used that drill sergeant tone, those kids minded, let me tell you. Heads down, they scampered up the stairs, and I followed. Skylar turned at the top, and when Vida wasn't looking, she stuck her tongue out at Owen. "There is too a Santa Claus!" she hissed.

Owen passed Vida, head down, and then picked up speed, chasing Skylar into the apartment.

"Well, now, what are you doing home in the middle of the afternoon?" Vida pushed some gray tendrils off her damp forehead. Her kitchen was sweetly scented with fresh-baked cookies.

Dropping my bag, I plopped onto a stool in her kitchen with a sigh. "Looks like I'm gonna be home a lot of mornings." Short and sweet, I gave Vida the dismal details.

Without a word, Vida scooped two chocolate chip cookies onto a napkin and poured me a glass of cold milk. "My, oh, my," she said as I started munching. "Looks like everybody's in trouble this Christmas."

I stopped in midcrunch. "Hey, I'm really sorry, Vida. Here I am, bending your ear about my problems, and this is the first Christmas without Pascal. I'm sorry."

But Vida shook her head and held up one hand as if she just didn't want to hear it. Everybody missed that man. "Without the money from the Christmas trees this year, well, I just don't know what we're going to do." She shot a worried glance into the living room, where Skylar and Owen sat in front of the TV, hypnotized by Big Bird.

Her words soaked in. "The trees." Pascal always sold trees during Christmastime. Why, the whole neighborhood depended on Pascal. He even took time to balance the tree for you if you brought your stand with you. And he always shaved a couple of dollars off the price for widows and single moms.

"Pascal always made sure that everybody had a tree. And his trees were never expensive." Even as I said it, I couldn't help thinking of all the disappointed families this Christmas.

"Worse than that." Vida slid the empty cookie sheets into a sink full of sudsy, hot water. "Those trees, why they kept us going all year." Her shoulders sagged as she began to wash the pans.

"No trees this year?" I was still trying to grasp it. I guess I'd been too busy with my own life to put two and two together. "No more trees with attitude that people can afford? You mean, we'll all have to buy our trees from Greene's Greenery?"

My milk soured in my mouth.

My brother, Mike, and I had gone to high school with Chris Greene. He was the guy who scored all the touchdowns, and dated Missy Burnes, head cheerleader. Stuck up—that's what Chris Greene was. BMOC—Big Man On Campus. And we'd have to buy our trees from him?

Now, that was disgusting.

Vida nodded as I groaned. "Won't be the worse thing, Inga. Somehow, we'll get by."

"No way." I'd rather opt for no tree at all than give Greene my hard-earned cash. Then it hit me that I wasn't really earning any cash at the moment.

Vida finished washing the dishes. She took off her apron and hung it on the hook next to the phone. "That's right, darlin'. No dirt-cheap trees for this neighborhood. No precious trees for folks to love up."

Greene's Greenery charged an arm and a leg for their trees.

Vida snatched a piece of paper tucked under the phone. "Supplier called me, but I told him, 'Mister, Pascal's Pines is out of business.' And that's the end of that."

I snatched that paper right out of her hand. "Oh, no, Vida. We're calling him right back. They can deliver those trees. We, meaning me, are in the tree business!"

Vida looked at me like I'd just told her I was going to be a stripper. "You sure about this, Inga? That tree lot was a lot of work."

But I was already headed for the door, phone number in hand. "Don't worry about a thing."

Taking the stairs two at a time, I sprinted up to my third-floor apartment, jammed my key in the lock, and within minutes, was on the phone with some guy in northern Michigan, telling him to put me on the schedule.

Pascal's Pines was resurrected, just like that.

Then I called the owner of the corner lot, which had been a gas station at one time, but so long ago that no one even remembered what kind of gas they'd sold. I negotiated for "Pascal's rates" and explained why I was doing this.

"Pascal was a good man," Mr. Thomas said. "Sure, use the property. It's not doing anybody any good, anyway, right now."

The trees would arrive in only four days, so I had to hustle. In fact, things happened so fast that I didn't even have time to feel bad about losing my job at Kirsten's Kloset. Sometimes, life is just like that—the faster it moves, the happier I am.

Of course, not everybody saw it the way I did.

"You're going to sell Christmas trees this year? On Pascal's corner?"

My older brother, Mike, looked really confused, as if I'd just told him that I was going to morph into Santa Claus and he was waiting to see how that would happen. I'd stopped off at the fire station where he'd been a firefighter for the past seven years. He was polishing one of the trucks with a bunch of the guys.

"Right." I spoke with what I hoped was calm certainty. "You know, on the corner of Belmont and Forest?"

When Mike was confused, his nose still crinkled up, just like when he was a little boy and couldn't understand long division. "Right across from Greene's Greenery?"

"You bet. Right across from the guy you hated in high school."

Mike's face turned a little red. "That was a long time ago, Inga. Things change. Chris's an okay guy. Anyway, who's gonna help you?"

Now, I'm just over five feet tall. Although I think I'm a pretty feisty lady, there are moments in my life when I can act really helpless.

This was one of those moments.

I stubbed the toe of my boot against the heel of the other and tilted my head to one side, letting my blue eyes grow wide with wonder. "Gee, I don't know. Do you think I'll need help?"

Mike twisted around and called out, "Hey, guys, want to help out Vida and sell trees at Pascal's this year? Maybe a couple hours a week?"

"You bet."

"Count me in."

"No problem."

They all chimed in, giving me reassuring smiles and waving their waxing rags. Well, tears prickled in the corners of my eyes. I wanted to hug them all. "Thanks, guys." I twirled around and threw them kisses, giddy with excitement. This was really going to happen. I was in business!

"You really think I'm gonna need this much help?" I asked Mike.

He grinned. "You have no idea, my little chickadee." He ruffled my hair and I swatted at his hand. "You're in for some loooong hours out in the cold. Remember: Pascal didn't have a fancy trailer or anything. He did it the hard way."

I flipped my hair back over my shoulders. "No problem."

But what did I know? You wouldn't believe what goes into selling Christmas trees. I mean, it sounds easy enough, but it can get pretty complicated.

We started in Pascal's storage shed. Skylar and Owen came along.

85

Together, we went down into the basement, past the entryway with all the mailboxes, through the door that led to the chilly, dark, dank basement. That's when Skylar and Owen pulled back and let me take the lead. When I got to the row of doors in a plywood wall, I found the right lock and opened it. The door creaked as I shoved it open.

It smelled damp and dusty in there, but when I pulled the light string, there it all was—the signs, the wooden slats for displaying the trees, and all the colored lights wound into neat loops. The sign read: Pascal's Pines! Good Prices! Pascal had never changed it in all the time he'd sold those trees, even though some of us had urged him to charge more, telling him that times had changed. Now, I looked at the sign, and then grabbed a marker. I stuck an arrow above the word Pines! and scrawled: With Attitude! Owen ran his hand over the wooden slats with reverence while Skylar took a string of lights and looped it around her head.

"I'm the Christmas queen!" She twirled, promptly got tangled, and fell down.

"You're the Christmas klutz," Owen shot back. He picked up the sign. "You gonna put this up this year? Or is it gonna be Inga's Pines now?"

I shook my head. "Naw, I don't have time to make a new sign." But the truth was, I felt I just had to use that sign. It was like I needed Pascal's blessing.

With a little help from Mike and some of the guys from the station, before long, we had the stand all set up and ready for business. The planks were tented in neat rows, red lights strung from the high points of the display. The Pascal's Pines! sign hung proudly at the front. We were ready for business.

Well, almost.

"Where is that truck?" I strained my eyes down Belmont Avenue, looking for the semi that would bring the trees wrapped tightly in twine.

"Hold onto your horses, Inga," Mike chided me as he climbed back into his van. "Guy said he'd be here, didn't he?"

"Yeah, sure. But when?" I shifted my gaze to Greene's Greenery, kitty-corner from our lot. Of course, their trees had already arrived. Sparkling Italian lights were generously strung above a dazzling array of trees, and a huge sign blinked invitingly at the curb. I sighed.

Mike drove away and I opened up my card table chair in the middle of the empty lot. My excitement had spiraled down into a tight, nervous knot in the middle of my stomach. I felt like a little girl Santa had forgotten.

Just then, a car door slammed, and I jumped up, hoping to see the truck, brimming with my trees. Instead, Chris Greene was striding toward me.

He hadn't changed a bit. I started seeing red immediately—and not the Christmas kind. He moved with confidence, like he was walking down the hall at Wilbur High after having beaten the Kenmore Blue Devils. And just who did he think he was, anyway? Santa, with his red parka and green, knit cap?

I wanted to slap the smile right off his face.

"Going to try your hand at selling trees this year, Inga?" His eyes swept over our setup, and I knew what he was thinking: Pretty pathetic.

"You bet." I pointed to the sign. "Just like always."

Chris took in Pascal's hand-lettered sign, and my changes to it. Then he looked across at his own lights, blinking confidently across the street. I could even hear Christmas carols coming from a sound system across the way. Give me a break!

He turned to me and quirked one brow. "With attitude, huh?"

I straightened my shoulders and put my hands on my hips, pulling myself up to my full height. "You got that right."

Chris nodded as he looked around and circled back to me. "This is nice, Inga. Pascal would've liked this."

My jaw dropped.

Chris must've seen the surprise in my eyes. "Pascal was a friend of mine. He was a very good man; we used to play gin rummy on slow afternoons. Helped pass the time."

Silence fell between us like a heavy blanket of new-fallen snow. But just then, a huge semi pulled up, braking at the entrance to the lot, and then pulling right in. Trees were mounded in the back of the trailer.

Thank goodness!

I breathed a sigh of relief. It was like Santa had just squeezed himself down the chimney and landed, splat, right in my living room with a bag full of presents.

Chris's eyes narrowed as he read the name on the side of the driver's cab. "Inga, watch it with these guys," he said quietly.

Spoilsport. He wasn't going to scare me. Ignoring him, I hustled over to the semi, waving my arms. "Over here! Glad to see you! Pull right in!" It was going to take a lot more than this for Chris Greene to discourage me, that's for sure.

Chris walked back across the street.

By the time the trees were unloaded, I sure wished that Mike had stuck around. I had areas marked off in the lot; Douglas firs would go there, and long needle pines over there. After I dragged a tree to the right section, I cut the twine and stood the tree up against the slats of wood.

At first, I buried my face in the sweet-smelling branches of each tree. Oh, this was what it was all about! This was the smell of

Christmastime! The trees weren't perfect, but they had character, just waiting to be released in appreciative homes.

But as the afternoon wore on, my arms and back started to ache. My gloves were sticky with sap, and I'd gotten some on my face by pushing back my knit cap. I needed a hot bath and a cup of strong, hot coffee.

I needed some help.

Just then, a Ford Escort pulled into the lot and a young couple holding a sleeping baby piled out of it.

"So, you're selling Pascal's trees this year?" the husband asked while his wife checked the sign, just to make sure she'd seen right.

"You bet." All of a sudden, I had new energy. My first customers!

Within ten minutes, they'd decided on an eight-foot pine. Like all of the trees, it had a bare branch here and there, but they thought it was just beautiful. That was the important thing. The mother kissed her baby on the forehead and the baby gave her a sleepy smile, curling up one tiny fist.

"This will be your very first Christmas," the mother whispered tenderly. "We'll take a picture so you'll always remember this beautiful tree."

Boy, that did my heart good! This was going to be great.

Meanwhile, the husband was counting out the money. He hesitated, and then handed me another five. "Put this in the pot for Vida. Merry Christmas."

"Hey, thanks." I tucked the bills into the money belt under my hooded sweatshirt and parka and waved good-bye as they pulled back out onto Belmont.

After that, I didn't have a minute to think about my sore shoulders or my aching back. After that, cars kept pulling in, and I really had to hustle. I tried to remember if any of the guys from the station were coming down that night to help; a pile of trees still stood at the edge of the lot, waiting to be sorted. Of course, Mike thought we didn't have the trees yet.

By about ten o'clock, traffic slowed and it got quiet. I collapsed onto the card table chair, tensing when I felt the cold metal beneath me. Exhausted, I let my head fall back and looked up at the stars. They seemed to shine so brightly that night.

Pascal, wherever you are, things are going to be just fine. Vida and the kids are going to be all right.

And I felt really good about that. The rest of the trees could wait until morning.

When I got to the lot the next day, all the trees were sorted and standing tall. I made a mental note to thank Mike and the guys later; what would I do without them? Then I settled into a routine of long days that made my hours at Kirsten's Kloset seem like a part-time job.

Usually, I opened the lot by ten in the morning and stayed open until ten at night. If business was good, well, I kept warm by just hustling around, bending, shaking, and holding trees so people could measure them, and then standing back to see if this was the tree that would make their Christmas complete.

Some wanted their trees to be fat and full. Others wanted tall, narrow trees for small rooms. A lot of the older people wanted tiny trees to set on tabletops. We didn't have many of those. But somehow, we found a tree for just about everyone. I never sent anyone away empty-handed.

And how good it felt to see all my trees going to happy homes! Kinda like they were my children, and I was sending them out into the world well prepared.

Yeah, I felt great when it was busy. But when things slowed down, well—I just about froze to death.

Thank goodness, the lot was just down the street from my apartment. Vida would stop by with a Thermos full of coffee or hot chocolate, and every afternoon at about four or so, she'd arrive with supper, packed neatly in a basket. I could usually smell the chili or meat loaf, and sometimes my mouth would be watering before I even saw her coming, with the kids tagging along behind.

"You are a lifesaver, Vida," I'd say, giving her a hug before I dug into the basket.

"You need to be good and strong to sell these trees!" she'd laugh. "Pascal always said with supper under his belt, well, he could sell trees all night long."

Well, Pascal had done a lot more than sell trees. I remembered how he would take time with each customer—check up on their family, listen to their problems. He never offered advice, just nodded his head as if he could feel the pain, the worry, right there in his heart. I wasn't Pascal, but I knew these people; they were from my neighborhood, and it was exciting to be a part of their Christmases.

And Mike and the crew from the fire station didn't let me down. They all came to help, as promised. "Hey, thanks for finishing up with the trees," I told Mike the next time he came to the lot.

"What are you talking about? I told you we'd help you sell the trees."

"No, big brother, that's not what I'm talking about. I'm saying thanks for sorting out that first shipment. I was dead on my feet that night."

No look of comprehension. He shrugged. Then a customer drove in and we forgot about it.

Sometimes Skylar and Owen would hang around in the afternoons. Vida would go home and stop by an hour later to pick them up. They were no trouble; Skylar liked "dusting off the trees," as she called it, and Owen would build a snowman or go to the curb and wave his arms at cars, trying to get them to turn into the lot. Customers seemed to get a kick out of talking to the kids.

"What do you want for Christmas?" one young mother asked Skylar.

"Let's see." Skylar rolled her eyes heavenward and started to tick things off on her fingers. "I want a doll that cries and a stove that really cooks like Grandma Vida's and a computer game and . . ." The list went on and on.

As I listened to Owen launch in to his list, I pitied Vida. How would she ever handle their Christmas lists? She always wanted to do so much for them, but could she this year? I patted the belt at my waist for reassurance.

Mike and the guys from the station began to take regular shifts, working two hours or so on their time off. Since a lot of them had kids, I thought it was really nice and generous of them.

When it was busy, the time flew and it was great. But when it slowed down, the minute hand on my watch seemed to crawl. I'd stamp my feet, cradle a cup of coffee in my hands, and wish I had one of those fancy trailers like the ones I saw over at Greene's Greenery.

Oh, yeah. Across the road, the cheery, white lights blinked, and carols played—"Frosty the Snowman" or "Silent Night." The music positively boomed across Belmont on the cold air. Sometimes, I'd hum along—until I caught myself. I would not hum to Chris Greene's music! After that, I brought my Walkman to the lot; I'd pop in my own CDs. I began to carry two or three of them in my jacket. Crazy, but if I kind of danced around behind the trees, it kept me warm.

But Greene had that big, red trailer. It made me mad, just looking at it. Guys would go in and out of that trailer, laughing and cracking jokes, mugs of steaming coffee in their hands. On the coldest nights, I'd imagine the warmth of that trailer, maybe a comfortable sofa, and, most importantly—a bathroom.

One slow night when I was jiving behind a line of the trees, snapping my fingers and swaying my hips to Eminem, I looked up, and there stood Chris Greene, with a big smile on his face. My hands fell, and I immediately stripped off my headphones.

"You here to buy, or just snooping?"

The smile slid right off his face. "I just wondered how things were going. Wondered if you needed any help."

"Everything is just fine, thank you."

I've never been known for my tact. I started picking up loose branches that had fallen or been cut off the trees and tossed them into a pile. Some people took them home with them just to make their houses smell good.

Chris was being really quiet.

"I guess I was a little rude," I finally offered, not looking up at him.

He gave a quiet chuckle. "Yes, you always were known for telling it like it is."

I jerked up and stared at him. He was smiling at me. Had he always had that dimple in his left cheek? His cheeks were ruddy from the cold and he looked like he'd stepped out of an ad for some ski lodge, with his unruly hair escaping from beneath his green cap. And those eyes . . . hot chocolate, that's what they were. Warm and . . . hey! What was happening to me?

A crooked smile cracked Chris's face. "Yep, you always were a little spitfire."

"What do you mean?" Like he'd ever noticed.

His smile broadened. "Oh, you weren't hard to find. Always in the front row at the games. Tiny, little Inga with the great, big voice."

I guess my face was pretty red by then. And was I ever steaming! Chris ran his hand over one of the small trees and looked up Belmont Avenue like he was counting the cars.

"Listen, Inga, if you ever want to use our trailer—you or Mike and the guys—you're certainly welcome."

The wind whipped a strand of hair across my cheek. Chris brought up one gloved hand, and for a crazy minute, I actually thought he was going to tuck it back under my stocking cap. I jerked back.

"Thanks. But I'm okay. We're doing fine." I wiggled my toes in my boots. My feet felt like two blocks of ice.

Chris nodded, and the redness in his cheeks seemed to deepen. "Okay, well, the offer still stands." He looked at me and caught his bottom lip between his teeth like he was going to say something else, but the words didn't come. Instead, his eyes shifted to the trees lined up against the slats of wood. I had a lot of holes; my stock was selling out.

"Your supplier coming through for you okay?"

"Yeah, sure," I lied. Fact was, my shipment was late, and I was getting a little nervous about it. All of my six- and seven-foot trees were gone, and they were the most popular sizes.

But I wasn't about to admit to Chris Greene that I was having any trouble.

"Well, good." He pulled his hat down tighter on his head. "You know, I think what you're doing is just great, Inga."

I glanced away from his searching brown eyes. It sure was cold out, but all of a sudden, I was warm. "It's nothing."

Right then, Vida arrived with her basket of goodies, Skylar and Owen trailing behind her. "Why, hello, Chris. Good to see you!"

I took the basket from her arms.

"You here to buy a tree?" Then she broke into one of her belly laughs that started deep in her belly and just kind of worked their way up and out.

91

Chris touched his hat politely. "No, ma'am. I was just offering Inga a little help . . . which she doesn't seem to need, after all."

"Uh-huh." Vida's eyes flitted between the two of us. Then she busied herself with her basket, pulling out Tupperware and a Thermos. "Want to stay for some hot soup, Chris? You always loved my beef-and-barley."

Chris looked tempted. But he began to back away. "Actually, I guess I better be getting back, but thanks for the offer." Then his eyes locked with mine. "The offer still stands, Inga."

"Yeah, thanks." I bent my head and studied my boots.

As Chris Greene swung across Belmont Avenue, back to his colorful tree lot and warm trailer, Vida started right in on me. "There a reason you're being the ice queen tonight?" She took one of the spoons and shook it in my face.

Casual. I tried to be casual, and not act as confused as I was feeling right then. "Not really." I took the Thermos of soup from her. The fragrant steam teased and tantalized my nostrils. "But, after all, he is the competition, Vida."

Vida put her hands on her hips. "Girl, Chris Greene and his fancy, high-priced trees are no competition for us! Never in a million years! Why, the folks who buy from Chris are the same folks who have him take care of their homes up in Bower Ridge, with all their fancy bushes and shrubs! His crews cut their lawns during the summertime, and when Christmas comes, they send someone down to pick up two or three trees, or he delivers them. Our trees, well, they're different. These are for our folks who just love these trees."

Her eyes ran lovingly over the trees, as if they were her children. "The folks who bought from Pascal, why, they live in apartments, and those little row houses right down the street. For three or four weeks at Christmastime, these trees fill their homes with magic. That's what Pascal used to say." Her voice drifted off then, and her eyes filled. I gave her a quick hug.

Skylar and Owen were chasing each other around the trees. Skylar shrieked when Owen picked up a huge handful of snow and threw it at her. "Grandma! Grandma! Owen's being mean and nasty to me! He's not being a gentleman!"

"Owen, are you being a gentleman?"

I smiled as Vida, in her usual quiet voice, began to pull Owen into line. As I sipped the soup, I thought about what Vida had told me. What really surprised me was that Pascal and Chris Greene had been friends. But I didn't have long to think about it. Nope, worries about my late shipment of trees crowded everything else out.

The next morning, I got on the phone and was assured that the trees were on the way.

"You're way ahead of Pascal's schedule," the supplier snapped at me, like it was my fault or something.

I explained to him that this year, the trees were serving as sort of a fundraiser for Pascal's family. "Because of this, it seems like more folks are coming out."

"Yeah, whatever. Everybody's got some emergency."

He hung up.

Well, it was two days before the guy pulled up with my trees. By then, the lot was getting pretty bare. Chris Greene had stopped by twice and had had the nerve to offer to help. I'd told him in no uncertain terms that I could call the supplier myself.

He'd held up his hands and backed right off. "All right. Just trying to help." He'd had this crooked smile on his face, like my getting mad really tickled him.

When the driver finally pulled up, I raced to the truck. "You're late!" I cast my eyes back on the trees. "I've been waiting for you!"

The driver shrugged. "Whatever, lady. I'm here now. You want these or not?"

I bit back my anger. "Yeah, sure. Of course. Pull right in." He was three feet away from me, and I could swear I smelled alcohol on the guy's breath.

Well, he dumped the trees while I scurried to arrange them. The trees were just stacked in haphazard piles; thank goodness Mike was coming later with Steve Swanson and Rick McBride, because I didn't know if I had the energy to drag all those trees around. And the driver had already climbed back up into the cab of his truck.

"Hey, are you still bringing the next shipment in four days?"

He pushed his hat back on his head. "Maybe. Don't rightly know."

"But our contract calls for another shipment in four days, even though this one is late."

My words hung on the cold air as he pulled away. I had to keep myself from running after that truck.

Boy, I was really boiling as I dragged those trees around, standing them up and cutting the twine. "Yeah, great. Be back next week. Probably more like next year." I was muttering to no one but myself, but it felt good.

Then suddenly, Chris was behind me, a tall tree in hand. "Need some help?"

My shoulders ached. My head was spinning, and it was so darn cold out. "Not really. I think I'm okay."

But my voice kind of wobbled on that last word, and I guess that gave me away. Chris just gave me a look, then thumped that tree on the ground, and it plumped right up. He leaned it carefully against the slats, turning it to find its best angle. And then he headed back for more. I opened my mouth to stop him, but thought better of it. Instead, I quietly tramped along behind him, with my head held high.

Looking over at Greene's Greenery, I saw two men in the standard Greene red uniform jackets bustling around, helping customers. I guessed they didn't really need Chris. Must be nice; as Christmas got closer, Mike and the guys at the station didn't seem to have as much time to help me.

Chris and I worked in silence for a little while. Chris stacked two trees for every one that I managed. By then, my whole body ached, and it had turned gray and miserably cold. A cold wind blew in from the north; I could feel my nose turning red as I turned up the collar of my jacket.

Meanwhile, Chris was whistling under his breath, giving me a quiet smile every now and then. "I never get tired of the smell and feel of a real pine tree. No, siree," he said at one point.

"Me neither," I reluctantly agreed. "Reminds me of the Christmas mornings when I'd come downstairs and my dad would have made some footprints in the fireplace soot, right next to the plate of cookies. He'd nibble on a few, just to make it look real."

"Hey, that's pretty creative." Chris folded his arms across his broad chest and his eyes got kind of dreamy. "Well, Dad never did the footprint deal, but he or my mom would always nibble on the cookies—and the carrots, too."

I wrinkled my nose. "Carrots? Did you think that Santa liked carrots?"

Chris looked at me like I'd just asked him if the sky was blue. "The carrots were for the reindeer!"

Well, I couldn't help but chuckle with him. Then I jerked myself up straight. What was happening here? Suddenly, it almost felt like we were friends or something!

While we were standing there, reminiscing, Vida dropped in with a sack under her arm. "I thought you might want some hot chocolate, Inga."

Her eyes flitted to Chris, and then back to me. She gave me a knowing smile and I frowned at her. I wanted to say, "This isn't what you think."

"Good thing I brought some extra cups," she said with that mysterious note in her voice, filling one cup and handing it to me, and then another for Chris.

"This is great, Vida," Chris said, taking a deep gulp.

I could tell by the familiar way they had with each other that they knew each other pretty well. That still surprised me; stuck-up Chris Greene—friends with the likes of Vida and Pascal? It just didn't fit, in my mind. Still, it began to dawn on me that maybe Mike was right, after all: People change. Only, I didn't want to admit it.

"How's Vicki doing?" Chris asked Vida.

Vida's smile faded instantly. "I don't rightly know, Chris, to tell you

94

the truth. But I pray for her every night."

"She was always so handy around the greenhouse. She had a real knack for plants—a regular green thumb."

Vida nodded. "She used to tell us stories every time she came back from your place, Chris. How she loved working there!"

It got real quiet then. You could almost hear the snow falling. I stood there and wondered what the heck they were talking about. When had Vicki worked in Chris's greenhouse? I was beginning to think I'd been living in a time warp or something!

"Well, I've got to get back," Chris said, crushing his Styrofoam cup and throwing it into the trash bag I had next to my chair. The tree lot was a very simple operation: a small box of tools, a chair, and I kept the money in my money belt. "See ya." He nodded to both of us.

"'Bye, and thanks, Chris." Okay, so it was hard for me to squeak out the thanks, but he didn't seem to notice.

Vida had gone home by then, and Mike pulled up. Then customers started arriving, and I was sure glad we had those extra trees. While we worked that night, hoisting trees onto cars, helping people secure them to their roofs with twine, or balancing them in the trunks, all I could think of was a pair of brown eyes. Sometimes, they were like M&Ms, all shiny and tempting. Other times, they were like hot chocolate, or melted chocolate that you drizzled over Christmas cookies.

What was happening to me?

The next day when I woke up, snow had blanketed the city. I could hear the plows shushing through the streets outside as I flipped open my blinds and peered outside. Belmont had been transformed into a winter wonderland. Any cars parked on the street were now mysterious, white humps lined along the curb. Their owners would sure have a heck of a time digging out. But it was beautiful!

Pulling on my jeans and a sweatshirt, I quickly brushed my teeth, threw on some makeup, brushed my hair, and pulled on a cap. I realized I'd have to tromp on down to the lot and shake off the trees. But would I have to have someone shovel out the driveway? Up until now, cars had been able to drive into the lot very easily. But this was heavy snow.

On my way down, I knocked on Vida's door. I thought that maybe the kids would enjoy coming with me to play in the snow. But when Vida answered the door, her face was drawn. She could hardly meet my eyes. She held a crumpled handkerchief in one hand, and she kept dabbing at her eyes with it.

"Vida, what is it?" But inside, I knew. Whenever Vida looked like this, there was usually only one cause. "It's Vicki, isn't it? What's happened?"

Her voice breaking, Vida told me that she'd gotten a call from a hospital in another city, two states over. "Drug overdose." Vida twisted the handkerchief in her hands. "My baby almost died." Then she began to cry openly. Thank God, Skylar and Owen were still asleep. "I've just got to get to her, Inga! My baby needs me!"

Instinctively, my hand went to the money belt around my waist. I'd been taking money to the bank regularly. And, after paying for the trees, the money was to help Vida. I was only taking enough out to pay for my groceries. Even though I had reservations about Vicki's latest "emergency," I figured spending some on an airplane ticket made sense.

After a few phone calls, I found a flight for that afternoon.

"But what about the kids?" Vida cast a worried glance down the hall toward the bedroom door that stood ajar in the early-morning light.

"I'll take care of Skylar and Owen," I said. Now, I didn't exactly know how I was going to do that, but somehow, I knew I would. "Now, you go and get ready, Vida. In the meantime, I'm going to make a few calls."

But Mike couldn't help. "We're all out on calls, Inga. Sorry."

Head down, I trudged through the snow to the lot, my boots making fresh prints in the snow. There was one person I knew who had a Jeep—a tough, all-purpose Jeep that might take Vida to the airport for me.

Passing my lot where the trees stood like silent, shrouded figures in the newly fallen snow, I hiked across the now-quiet intersection of Belmont and Forest to Greene's Greenery. Some guys were out on the lot already, shaking the heavy snow from the tree limbs. A plow was clearing a section so people could park on the lot.

When I knocked on the door of the trailer, Chris answered. He smiled—and then he saw my expression.

"What's wrong?"

He threw the door open. Inside, the trailer smelled like coffee and cinnamon buns. In fact, it was more like a mobile home than a trailer, with a kitchen, bathroom, and another room in the back.

"Vida needs a ride to the airport," I began. Then I filled him in on the problem. "I don't know how much you really know about Vicki . . ." I said uneasily.

Chris just nodded slowly. "Enough. It's a damn shame. Of course I'll take Vida." Then his face clouded. "Of course, we'll have to make sure that the airport is open this afternoon, but it sounds as if the plows are out."

I hiked back to the apartment to give Vida the news, and then went to the tree lot. For the next hour or so, I shook snow off the trees, trying to get my mind to stop jumping around. It was just so strange to me that Chris Greene was helping us through this crisis.

Early in the afternoon, I hightailed it back to the apartment building. "All set?" I called out when Owen answered the door. Vida's battered suitcase stood just inside the door.

Vida bustled out of her bedroom, patting her hair, clearly nervous about her upcoming trip. Skylar rocketed toward Vida and clasped her around the knees.

"Don't go, Grandma! Why do you have to go?"

Vida didn't want the kids to know that she was going to see their mother, didn't want them to get their hopes up. I squatted in front of Vida and gently pried Skylar's fingers from Vida's legs and held them in my own. "You know, Skylar, you and Owen and me, why, we're going to have just the bestest time while Grandma's gone. You can work with me at the tree lot, and make tunnels under the trees in the snow. Would you like that, precious?"

"Yippee!" Owen howled, running to get his jacket.

"Get your things on, Skylar," I coaxed. "I'll help you with your boots."

Vida threw me a grateful smile.

"Hey, everything's going to be okay," I assured her. "You just see how Vicki's doing. Call me when you get there, after you've talked to her."

Vida nodded. Then a horn honked outside, and I went to the window, drawing back the lace curtain.

"Chris's here."

As I opened the door, suitcase in hand, Chris bounded up the front steps.

"I'll take that."

He took the suitcase in one hand, and Vida's elbow in the other, clearly the man in charge. That time, I didn't mind Chris's take-charge manner. Hey, I needed help!

"Let's hit the road," he said. "I don't know what the traffic will be like, although the state police report that everything's clear."

They disappeared down the stairwell, and my prayers went with them. How I hoped that Vida wouldn't be disappointed. But Vicki might not want to be rescued. She never had before. Still, I knew that Vida just had to see Vicki with her own eyes and make sure that she was all right—make sure that she'd cheated death one more time. And maybe this time, things really would be different.

While I was making hot chocolate and filling a Thermos, Skylar tromped into the room wearing a hot-pink summer jacket and winter boots.

"Hey! You're going to need something a whole lot warmer than that, Skylar!" I said, laughing.

"But I want to wear my pink jacket!" She wrapped the jacket tightly around her. "My winter jacket's brown. It's yucky."

"But it's warm," I insisted. "And today, warm is what we're looking for."

Owen appeared dressed in a quilted, navy jacket and a hat pulled down over his ears. Before too long, we were on our way. As we walked toward the lot, we held hands against the wind that smacked veils of snow across our faces. I wondered briefly if they could really handle the cold; I didn't want them to get sick or anything. I searched my mind for someone who could take care of them, but I wasn't coming up with anyone. Most of the people in our building were two days older than water. I knew that they would never be able to keep up with Owen and Skylar.

When we got to the lot, the snow had stopped. "Brush the snow off the trees," I told them. "Just use your hands and shake the branches you can reach until the snow falls off. Each of you, take a row."

"I can do it faster!" Skylar challenged her brother.

"No way!" Owen set off in a flurry, shaking each branch vigorously.

By three in the afternoon or so, the people did start coming in for trees. The snow seemed to have jolted everyone into the Christmas spirit. But by that time, Skylar and Owen had had it with the cold. The Thermos of hot chocolate was empty, though, and Mike wouldn't be stopping in for another hour. In the meantime, the kids were bored, and they were cold.

Worry gnawed at me. What if Vida came home from one hospital, only to find her grandchildren in another hospital, suffering from frostbite? Maybe I'd bitten off more than I could chew. After all, what did I really know about taking care of kids?

These were my cheery thoughts when Chris Greene pulled up in his Jeep.

"Vida get off okay?" I asked him.

"Like clockwork. Everything's open again." He cast a glance over at his lot, which was full of people. "Looks like the weather has gotten everyone in a tree-buying mood."

"Looks like it."

"Hey, Inga? I'm cold." Owen sidled up to me. His cheeks and nose were like red cherries. "I wanna go home and watch TV."

"Me, too! Me, too!" Skylar chimed in. "And I'm hungry!"

Bad situation. "Well, you can't go home just yet, because I have to stay here. And it looks like it's going to be a very busy day. Tomorrow, though, I'll look for a sitter for you two." Another expense, I thought to myself. This pot for Pascal that was supposed to get Vida through the year was disappearing fast.

"Hey, why don't they come to the trailer with me?" Chris suggested, squatting until he was at eye level with the kids. "We have hot dogs and chips—nothing fancy. But you guys can watch TV and stay warm."

"Yeah!" Skylar and Owen perked up in a hurry.

"Are you sure it won't be any trouble?" I looked over at his lot; that trailer was beginning to look mighty good.

Chris was already taking the kids' hands. "Naw. The guys'll love it."

"Hooray! We get to watch TV!" Skylar jumped up and down in excitement. Chris didn't even seem to mind the fact that she was yanking his arm along with each leap. He opened the Jeep door and Skylar and Owen piled in. With a wave, Chris turned the Jeep and headed back across the street.

Well, will wonders never cease? I thought as I watched him go. Picture Chris Greene—babysitting.

As the day wore on, I was more and more grateful to Chris. And I was relieved to have Skylar and Owen in a safe, warm place. The snow seemed to have brought people out in droves. They were laughing and full of the Christmas spirit—parents with children, young couples buying their first trees. They were all grateful for our reasonable prices.

Mike eventually showed up with some chili dogs, and then he helped me that night. I was feeling pretty good by the end of the day, but one look at the lot as night fell told me the sorry truth: I had about fifteen trees left. My shipment was way overdue.

I pulled out my cell phone and got on the phone and reached my supplier, who just about took my head off. Told me he'd have a truck down as soon as he could and to hold my horses.

"Does that mean tomorrow?" I asked.

"Lady, that means when we got time." He hung up.

I trudged back out to the lot and unplugged the lights. Head down and hands jammed in my pockets, I headed across the street to Greene's Greenery.

"How did it go?" I asked when Chris opened the door to the trailer and let me in.

"We played computer games!" Owen was beaming.

"I washed the dishes." Skylar straightened up with pride. They both looked warm and well fed. I collapsed onto the sofa; I was still steaming, and Chris seemed to pick up on that real fast.

"Why don't you two go back and watch a little more TV while I talk to Inga?"

They were only too happy to oblige. This guy had them under a spell, but I was too tired to care.

"You look exhausted." Chris handed me a mug of coffee and sat down on the sofa next to me. "Want some soup or something?"

I took the coffee. "No, Mike brought me some supper." But my voice was kind of thick. I gulped and tried again. "Whew! I'm beat." I didn't want Chris to see my tears.

"Why don't you sleep in tomorrow?" Chris angled his body and faced me. He had this way of giving me his complete attention.

"Yeah, right." I thought about Skylar and Owen, and their early-morning hours. I sipped my coffee and felt its warmth melt away the cold core inside my chest.

"Any word from Vida?"

I shook my head. "But she might be on my answering machine at home." Then I sighed and Chris didn't miss a trick.

"Hey, Inga, she'll be all right."

Then suddenly, Chris had his arms around me, and I was just about crying on his shoulder. Now, how did this happen? How did I turn into a wimp instead of the strong, fearless woman who makes her own way in the world?

But his broad shoulder felt good. He smelled of pine needles, and some kind of musky cologne. He smelled like a man who worked hard.

I liked it.

"My lot's almost empty," I murmured into the front of his flannel shirt.

"When's the next load due?" Suddenly, Chris was all business again, but one arm stayed curved protectively around my shoulder.

"Today, tomorrow—anytime, I guess." My voice cracked, and then the whole, frustrating story came pouring out of me.

A muscle twitched in Chris's jaw. He used to wear that same determined look when he addressed the student body at pep rallies. The gym would positively rock after he gave his little speech about team spirit and school pride. At the time, I'd thought it was all pretty corny.

"Do you mind if I give them a call after you leave?" Chris studied me, gauging my response.

But I was too tired to care. "Have at it." My eyes were starting to flag. I stood up, shook myself, and set the mug on the counter. "I'd better get them home and into bed."

Minutes later, he had Skylar and Owen all bundled into their snowsuits. They could hardly keep their eyes open. Chris insisted on taking us back to the apartment in his Jeep, even though it was only a block. I was relieved. He even warmed up the Jeep so that it was toasty warm when we got out there.

When we reached the apartment building, he carried Skylar up the stairs in his arms while Owen tagged along behind with me, clutching my hand. After I opened the door, they both disappeared inside.

"I can never thank you enough." I focused on some area just over his right shoulder, just not real comfortable meeting his eyes.

But those darn tears started again. I was just so tired! So he put his arms around me again. It was getting to be a habit—me crying on Chris Greene's shoulder.

And I kind of liked it.

100

Then he drew away a little and looked deep into my eyes. He was so very tall that I had to crane my neck to look up at him. His eyes were like two big pools of melted chocolate.

"Don't worry about a thing, Inga. And bring the kids back to me in the morning. Let me handle your supplier. After all, this is the first year you've done this. I've been at it a long time."

For a minute then, I thought he might kiss me. For a minute, I wished he would.

But instead, he gave my shoulders a squeeze and disappeared down the steps. He'd taken off his cap and now, he pulled it down over his glossy curls. I peered over the banister that wound down to the first floor and at the bottom, he looked up and caught my eyes following him. He threw me a wicked smile.

"Good night, Inga."

I gave a little wave. "Thanks again." Then I floated back into Vida's apartment.

Skylar and Owen had fallen asleep on top of the covers. They'd managed to get their jackets off, though. Carefully, I maneuvered them under the covers.

Then I went into Vida's bedroom, where the message light was blinking on her answering machine. I pressed the button and sat down on the bed.

"Hi, it's me." She sounded drained. "Got here okay. Doctors say Vicki will be fine. But this was a real close call, they say." Her voice got thick and I could hear her take a deep breath. "Anyway, I might stay a few days—if that's all right. I found a room with one of Pascal's second cousins; they're being real good to me. I want to talk to Vicki's doctor again, and to her social worker. Oh, Inga—Vicki is just as sorry as she can be!"

I'll just bet, I thought as I fell asleep that night. Vicki was always sorry—always just sorry enough that her parents would shell out more cash to help her. And then she'd be gone again.

Well, this time, I was the keeper of the funds, and Vicki would have to watch her step.

The next day, the kids woke me up at the crack of dawn.

"I want breakfast, Inga!"

Skylar shook me. I turned over and squinted up at her. The clock said seven. Slowly, I dragged myself out of bed, stretched, and padded off to the bathroom. Owen already had the TV on; I made a mental note to put out cereal bowls that night and a pitcher of milk in the fridge. This babysitting stuff was going to teach me a lot.

"Do we get to play games with Chris again today?" Owen asked as we ate breakfast.

"Yep, if you eat all your cereal."

Owen and Skylar both dug into their cereal as if they were digging

101

their way to China. Clearly, Chris had made an impression.

Davey O'Connor was already at the lot when I got there. "I was beginning to wonder," he said with a smile.

"Oh, you fellows have been so good to me."

As if he'd been watching for us, Chris pulled up in the Jeep right then, leaned over, and opened the door. "Anybody ready for doughnuts?" he asked.

"Me! Me!" Skylar shrieked, running for the Jeep. Owen hopped in, too. But then Chris got out and came around to talk to me.

"Your supplier said he'd be here tomorrow," he said, his voice level and very businesslike. "Let me know when he arrives, would you?"

I perked up. "Why? Is there a problem?"

Chris didn't meet my eyes. "Not really. I just want to know."

Well, the day was busy. Mike had the guys come and go. That night, I picked up the kids, and they tumbled into bed. Whatever they were doing in that trailer, Chris was tiring them out. Sometimes, I'd look over and see them helping the guys with the trees. Traitors, I thought. But in my heart, it was fine. I knew they were safe with Chris.

The next day, sure enough, about eleven in the morning, the truck rumbled up Belmont. I was so relieved; at that point, I had about ten trees left. I mean, I was getting desperate.

As if he'd been watching, Chris walked over, his eyes on the load of trees. When the driver hopped out of the cab, Chris just gave him a nod and went straight to the back of the semi.

"I'm Inga," I said, wondering where they ever got these scruffy mountain men who drove these trucks.

In a second, Chris was back. "We're not accepting these trees."

His tone was final. I looked from him to the driver, whose mouth dropped open. The toothpick he'd held clamped between his teeth fell into the snow.

"Looky here, mister. Them trees come all the way from Michigan, just like you wanted."

"Right. And they were cut when? Maybe two months ago? They're dry as tinder," he said to me. "We're not taking them."

I yanked Chris aside, my blood boiling. "Now you look, Chris Greene. I need these trees. Vida needs these trees. We're about out, and there're still two weeks till Christmas!"

I could see the wheels turning in his head. "I've got an idea," he said slowly. "I'm expecting a load myself today. You can have half of it."

I gasped. "But I can't pay the price you pay! People come here for bargain prices—for trees with attitude that they can afford!"

"So they'll have an extra-nice tree this year. Just call it my donation to Pascal's fund. Take the trees, Inga. Please?"

Well, what can you do when a man says please like that, and looks at you with puppy dog eyes?

"Okay."

Chris turned back to handle the driver, who was furious. Luckily, I was far enough along the process with this distributor that I was supposed to give him full payment on arrival, so I didn't lose any deposit. His check stayed tucked in my money belt. As the truck backed out, it knocked over some of the slats, and two trees fell to the ground. The semi rumbled away down the street, and when it hit a bump, needles fell from the trees at the back of the load. Chris had been right.

I turned to Chris. "How can I ever thank you?"

He grinned and got this mischievous look in his eyes. "Oh, I'll think of something."

I watched him walk back across the street. Pretty soon, there'd be a regular path between our two lots.

That night, Vida called. "We're coming home!" she said.

"We?"

"Vicki's coming with me!" Vida was so excited. "Just think, Inga: Vicki will be with the children for Christmas—the first time in three years!"

"Terrific." Although I wanted to share Vida's excitement, I had my doubts about Vicki's intentions. Was she coming home—or coming home to see what she could get?

"She's going into treatment, Inga."

Now this was news. Previously, Vicki had always resisted treatment, saying she'd do it on her own, or that she didn't need it.

"That's great, Vida. I mean it. The kids will be so happy. But I think I'll wait to tell them, okay?" I didn't want them to be disappointed. Vicki was known for changing her mind.

"Sure. And tell Chris that Vicki said thank you, and she'd be glad to try his plan."

"Okay," I said, not understanding what she was talking about. What plan?

Vida and Vicki flew home the following day. Mike took me to the airport to meet them; I still hadn't told Skylar and Owen about their mother's arrival, although they did know that their grandmother was coming home that day. They were with Chris, and I thought I'd just bring them over to the apartment after Vida and Vicki had settled in.

"It's so good to see you back!" I gave Vida a big hug when I met them at the airport. She was positively beaming. Then I turned to Vicki. "Skylar and Owen will be so happy to see you, Vicki."

Vicki had lost a lot of weight and her eyes were dark pools in her face, but she gave me a weak smile. "I can't wait to see my babies."

That night, when Skylar and Owen tumbled through the door, they

103

had expectant smiles on their faces. "Grandma! Grandma!" But they stopped dead in their tracks when they saw Vicki.

But when Vicki opened her arms to them, Skylar and Owen bounced right into those outstretched arms with screams of joy. She was their mother, after all, no matter what she'd done.

I turned away. Chris stood behind me, watching the whole thing. "It's great, isn't it?"

My curiosity got the best of me. "And just what role did you play in all of this?"

He shrugged. "I just told Vida that Vicki could work in the greenhouse. She needs a job, and then she'll meet with her social worker regularly. It's sort of a probationary thing."

Would I ever stop being surprised by Chris Greene?

I was still stunned when he tugged me out of the apartment and closed the door behind me. He leaned toward me then, resting a hand on either side of my head.

"Inga, I think you're a super lady," he whispered as he bent closer.

I gulped. "People change."

He drew back, and I inhaled the coffee in his laugh. "Well, you sure have!"

I opened my mouth to protest—but was silenced by his kiss, a kiss that made me glad I had the door behind me to hold me up. Then I forgot all about Christmas trees and Vida and Vicki, because I knew that kiss, well—

It was going to take us way past Christmastime.

THE END

A CHILD IS BORN
Will he bring Christmas joy?

It's Christmastime, the season of miracles. And I'm praying for a miracle now. I'm praying for the miracle of forgiveness, hope, and love. To some people, those three words may not seem like a miracle. I know if my prayers were answered, a miracle would have occurred.

As I sit to write about Michael, tears start to form in my eyes. He was born in a small town in Arkansas nearly twenty-two years ago. The memory is joyous and painful, but I need to write this. Words on paper can say things that I've never been able to utter. . . .

Nearly twenty-two years ago, I talked to Michael, even though he was still inside my body. That day, December 15, I had had back pains all day. I stretched to try to relieve the pain with my hands, bracing the spot of constant ache in the small of my back.

"What would you like to eat tonight, Michael?" I asked. I knew, somehow, the child would be a boy. Talking helped push away the loneliness.

"Don't say it. I know. You'd like prime rib." I laughed out loud. I rarely could afford even the cheapest cuts of meat. While reaching for the bottle of vitamins, I stopped midway, stilled by another sharp pain in my lower back. Sweat popped out on my upper lip without warning.

I started toward my only chair, but the pain subsided, going away as suddenly as it had come, leaving the usual dull ache.

"That sewing machine will be the death of us yet," I said to Mike, after swallowing one of the vitamins. In spite of my words to the contrary and a cramped back, I was thankful for that sewing machine.

When I came to this town seven months ago, I lied about my age to get a job. I lied about my name, too. I was sixteen and the job required a person to be at least eighteen. Thank goodness, twenty years ago, people didn't ask to see social security cards or other identification and paid in cash. The only job I could find was sitting behind that ancient sewing machine, eight hours a day, pushing through material. It was not the most desirable job in the world, but the Lord knew what he was doing by seating me behind Buzzer, my name for the oversized machine. I could hold the job until time to go to the hospital, then only three weeks away.

I might have been forced to quit any other job earlier, but nobody cared what I looked like at the factory. I was just another girl behind one in the rows of machines. Dusty signs overhead had spouted the company's philosophy, "KEEP 'EM HUMMING!"

I hated the job at first, while I fought to control that machine. I had tried to overcome my timidity to make friends with the girls on the machines next to me. But the foreman frowned on the employees talking much, and the girls didn't usually stay long enough for me to get up enough nerve to get acquainted. After a month or so, I just stopped trying to make friends. After all, I could always talk to Mike.

I sat down in my ragged rocker.

"Here, Michael. You hold the bowl," I said, placing the dish of instant soup on my enormous protrusion, my very pregnant no-lap. "Don't kick now. Be still while we eat." With the spoon poised for a bite, I froze as a pain seared my lower back. I lowered the spoon to catch my breath.

"I hope you're not too hungry, Mike. I don't think I can manage this, tonight." I set the bowl next to the cup of tea on the apple crate beside the chair. I boosted with my elbows to push my unwieldy body out of the chair and waddled to the single bed. Lately, my legs felt like a wishbone pulled apart after a Sunday chicken dinner.

The springs of the bed squeaked with my weight. Each time I lay down, loneliness attacked, making me wish I were back in Tennessee with my friends and family. Even fussing with Mother would be nice. I won't lie here long, I reasoned. I'll get up and take a walk.

Half asleep, my mind slipped back to an image of Skip, his auburn hair, his dancing brown eyes, his laugh, and his last words still echoing in my head.

"Get married? You crazy? Here," he had said, digging his billfold out of his back pocket of his jeans. "Here's some money. Get an abortion." I took the money in shock, surprised and hurt.

The next day, I took a bus. I meant to go to Oklahoma, but I got tired of riding on the bus and got off in Arkansas.

I squeezed my eyes tightly, trying to shut out Skip. I remember rolling to my side, searching for a comfortable position. My daddy always told his congregation that the Lord would provide. Well, the Lord had found me this job and this place to live and enough to eat. It took nearly everything I made, but I'd paid the doctor and the hospital in advance for delivery.

Probably anywhere else, my meager salary wouldn't have been enough. Things were less expensive in this rural part of Arkansas. I had told the doctor a lie when I said my husband had died in a car accident.

I flipped the switch on the transistor radio on the floor. The only station it would pick up was the local one.

"Now, we present the calendar of events, a public service of this station," whined the local announcer. "If you have announcements from your church or club, send them to this station and we'll air them. Get your pen. You may want to write down these upcoming events.

"On the calendar, today, is the annual caroling to be held on the lawn of the courthouse, tonight at 6:30. Choirs of all the churches will sing your favorite carols. Don't miss this, folks. This town is mighty proud of her great choirs." The announcer paused. "Next Saturday is flea market time again and—" I turned off the radio.

"That's what we'll do, Michael," I said to him, quickly forgetting the pain. "We'll go see Baby Jesus." The night was nice, warm for the season. The acute back pain hit once, and I debated going back. But the pain subsided, and I walked on. I really wanted to hear the music and see the scene.

A crowd was already gathering there. I liked watching the people until time for the program. Many sat on blankets, others stood in bunches, visiting. Children raced around, playing chase. A preacher said a few words and the caroling began. With the first notes of "The First Noel," I thought, Christmas is such a precious time. I hummed the tune.

A sudden pain took the starch out of my knees and my body moved downward. I caught myself before I reached the ground. When normality returned, I looked around, embarrassed, to see if anyone had noticed. But everyone was listening to the music.

The narrator quoted the Christmas story from the Bible. His voice sounded much like my father's booming with kind resonance and practiced patience. Hearing my dad's voice from the pulpit always had a tranquilizing effect on me, making up for his absences. Seems as if he had always been gone: gone to prayer meetings, gone to revivals, gone to the hospital, gone to the funeral home, always gone to help his flock.

Now, I was gone, a runaway, but I still missed my often-absent dad. A rush of loneliness and desolation swept over me like one of my mother's hot flashes. At that moment, it would even be nice to hear my mother complain about a hot flash.

The sweet music became background for the holiday spectacle. One by one, the nativity figures became animated, ending with Joseph and Mary in the stable. All I could see of the Baby Jesus were two little arms waving over the edge of the manger. Soon, Michael, will be waving his little arms like that, I thought.

The pain struck again, more fiercely this time. Tears came with a gasp. I was embarrassed, especially when a lady near me moved closer and touched my shoulder.

"Are you all right, honey?" the woman asked me, concern etched in her weathered face.

"My back keeps hurting," I managed to mumble.

"How? Like all the time, achy, or sharp and every once in a while?"

The woman's questions were interrupted by another sharp pain, curling me up.

"Oh, I see, honey. I think it's time we ought to be getting you to the hospital."

"But it's just my back not my stomach, not labor pains," I protested.

"Must be your first one." The woman helped me to my feet. "I never did have one pain in the front with my first one. The pains were all in the back."

Three days later, I took my sweet beautiful boy, Michael, home to my very tiny apartment, at least they called it an apartment. In reality, it was just one room above a single garage. I lay the quiet Michael in a garage sale bassinet and moved quickly to light the small open heater.

"To be so warm three days ago, it sure is so cold today," I said to my baby. No gas came through the pipe. The match almost burned my fingers before I could blow it out. Trying two more matches, I felt panic crawl up in my throat.

If I'd been alone, I could have done without heat. I was timid and shy, but my baby needed to be in a heated room. So I gathered Michael into his one blanket and trudged down the street to the real estate office where I paid my rent. When the secretary looked up at me with that "can-I-help-you" look, I hesitated as usual, fighting for each words.

I pushed out the words in a big rush of air. "I tried to light the heater in my apartment. I can't get it to work."

"Oh, yes. I've been trying to get in touch with you. There has been a break in the lines and the gas has been cut off. The serviceman says that they won't be able to get it back on until next Monday or maybe even Tuesday. I'm sorry." She turned back to her work.

"Oh," was all I could say.

"But you can pick up a small electric area heater at the local discount store and be nice and toasty and verywarm," the secretary added, shifting her papers to find her place.

"Oh."

"Is something wrong?"

"You don't have one I can use?"

"What?"

"A heater."

"No. I'm afraid not."

That scared me worse than ever. "How—how much is a heater?"

"Only about thirty dollars," the secretary said over her shoulder, never missing a click at her typing.

I stood there a moment longer, calculating my meager finances in my sixteen-year-old head. I walked out of the office and down the street to the town's only discount store. The tiny bundle in my arms whimpered. I held him closer. Inside the store, I stopped to catch my breath. How could six pounds be so heavy? My arm was going numb. Why was I so tired?

I looked at the array of electric heaters. Any one of them would take all my resources, leaving none for food or diapers. I went to the baby section and picked up a box of disposable diapers. My eye was drawn to a fluffy blue outfit with a hood. It was expensive, but it looked very warm.

Adding the items in my head, the total shocked me. My body drooped with fatigue, but I put the outfit, along with a can of formula on the checkout counter. I carefully counted out the total from my shabby purse.

I walked home just at dusk by the beautiful nativity scene. If I hadn't been so cold and tired and Mike hadn't needed a bottle, I would have watched it awhile. When I passed, a kindly looking man went to each figure individually and checked its animation before he turned it on to perform for the evening. I was touched when the man knelt at the manger to check the Christ child figure. It looked like he was praying.

My thoughts went to Mary, the mother of Jesus. I felt I understood how Mary must have felt, bearing the weight of outraged opinions of her community. They believed she was having an illegitimate child. Tears ran down my face.

Michael seemed to sense my anguish and put sound to my tears. The two of us cried the rest of the way to the cold room.

After feeding my beautiful son, I realized how much my early delivery affected my plans. I had been so elated that my last paycheck had paid the last of the hospital and doctor's fees. It hadn't bothered me that I had so little left. The doctor said I had two to three more weeks before my baby's arrival. So I thought that I'd have two or three more checks to sock away until I'd return to work.

I didn't need to look at my dingy spiral memo pad to know that the little I had left would not be enough. My tears dripped onto the new fleecy bunting that was much too big for a newborn. It swallowed him.

Much later that night, I put him in the manger of the Nativity scene with all of his meager possessions and a note saying, My name is Michael. I sat on the bus stop bench at the drugstore across the street and waited. Soon, a man whose name I learned later was Henry O'Malley, came to turn off the machinery in the display. I watched him place his hand on the off switch.

My baby couldn't stay out all night in the cold. I was struck with panic and fear. Then before I could utter a prayer, he noticed the Baby Jesus figure on the ground next to the manger.

Henry was angry. He picked up the figure and examined it for damage. Seeing none, he started to return it to its place. I watched him drop the figure and kneel beside the manger. With two big fingers, he moved a bit of fluff from Mike's face, my infant who was dressed in a blue, fleece-like bag, zippered to keep away the cold.

"Well, I'll be," I heard Henry say as he picked up my baby and nestled him into his arms.

The big blue and silver bus with a lighted sign saying CHATTANOOGA stopped in front of me. I boarded the bus and sat on the side where I could see my baby. I waved as tears ran down my face; then the bus drove away.

Michael made the national news. While I was watching the report, Mother called me away.

"I guess we'd better go, honey," my mother said. "The Christmas cantata is going to be excellent. I'd hate to be late."

"All right, Mother. I just want to see this on TV," I answered, straining to hear the newsman's words.

"The Arkansas town has responded with open hearts to the foundling," the reporter said.

"That sounds like a nice town, taking to that baby," my mother said.

"Yes, they call him Michael Christmas. People from all over the United States want to adopt him."

"Oh, look. Isn't he sweet?" Mother commented, as the commentator continued.

"Doctors examining the child say that he is in good health. The baby was about three or four days old when found by Henry O'Malley, builder of the display. Nothing is known so far, of the mother."

"I wonder what would make a mother leave such an adorable child?" Mother asked, but not expecting an answer. "We'd better go, now." She touched my shoulder, lovingly. "Everyone will be so glad to see you home."

I remember lingering to get one more peek at my baby. Then I followed mother from the parsonage across the lawn to the church. I dreaded prying questions. I hadn't told my parents where I'd been or why I left—and they hadn't asked. They just welcomed me home like a prodigal daughter. I remember thinking then if the hens at church only knew, they would have a lot to cluck about, the pastor's daughter, no less.

Then my thoughts returned to the present. I had to give up my beloved child. I was too young, too scared, and too broke to take care of him. I barely had enough money to return home.

I wasn't being selfish. I just knew that I couldn't give my child the life that he needed or deserved. And I didn't want him to die from living in a freezing cold apartment. And I felt guilty about being an unwed mother. Some people might think that's silly, but that's how I was raised. My parents probably would have accepted my pregnancy, but I let my pride take over. And I didn't want to hear a personal sermon about premarital sex. And I didn't want to destroy my father's reputation and all he stood for.

I've thought about Mike every day of my life and regretted the decision I made twenty-two years ago. I pray that he found a safe, loving home and that he knows I love him dearly. I pray for his forgiveness. And I pray that this story finds a way into his hands.

THE END

110

HOME FOR THE HOLIDAY
A toast to family, love, and
the man of my dreams.

I was excited about returning home for Christmas. New York was covered with one foot of snow after the previous night's blizzard, and I was looking forward to the warmer Southern temperature where I could walk around with just a sweater on, and having the sun against my skin. Yes, I was ready to escape.

My mouth was ready for some good home cooking such as okra stew with big jumbo shrimps and large, tender flakes of crabmeat over a bed of rice. My Nana Bell could put a hurting on her okra stew, and she'd toss in some butter beans and baby corn in a tomato-based sauce. She'd also make homemade biscuits topped with butter, and Lord, her coconut crème pie would melt in your mouth. Yeah, nothing's like going home for the holiday!

I had already missed the annual visit to Memorial Hospital where we spent Christmas Eve entertaining sick children. Some had minor illnesses, and others had cancer, or were terminally ill kids who were in the hospital during the holiday season. We brought them laughter and gifts to make their stay much more pleasant. Nana Bell started that tradition forty years ago; and each year, she and our family made their annual visit.

I just checked in at the airlines, because there were flight delays at airports along the eastern seaboard because of the previous night's blizzard. I figured that's what I got for not leaving with the rest of my family.

Sitting at my desk on Friday afternoon, I watched as storm clouds passed over my office building. I had a feeling as I looked out of the window, and then listening to the forecast on the radio, the impending snowstorm would affect my leaving on Saturday morning as I had planned.

There I was at eight a.m. on Christmas morning, waiting for my flight to arrive. Pulling out my cell phone, I pressed the digits to connect me with my Nana Bell. I knew she'd be placing her turkey into the oven just about then.

"Merry Christmas, Nana Bell."

"Well, Merry Christmas to you, Angel. Are you on your way? Everyone else has arrived, and you're the last one to come home," Nana Bell added.

"No, Nana Bell, because of the snowstorm, the plane hasn't arrived in New York. I hoped to be there before dinner is on the table. We're sitting down for dinner at four o'clock, right?"

"Yes, four o'clock and I just put my turkey into the oven, the okra stew is done, and your sisters and Aunt Celie have prepared the other dishes."

"Nana Bell, did you make my favorite: coconut crème pies?" I asked.

"Now, Betty Lou Griffin, you know I made that yesterday. I need a whole day to prepare and bake my pies. I've made two sweet potato, two apple, and three nine-inch coconut crème pies."

"I know I'm being selfish, but would you please hide one coconut pie for me? If my brother-in-law, Gregory, cuts into the pie by the time I reached home, there will be none left for me."

"Angel, I didn't teach you to be selfish, but to share everything. Besides, I made one small coconut pie just for you. Now, get off this phone and let me get myself dolled up. My new man will be joining us for dinner, this year. I'm not as young as I used to be, and it will take me longer to dress these old bones."

"Nana Bell, you're one beautiful woman, and he will be blessed to have you in his life. I'll see you soon. Love you."

"Love you too, Angel. Take care, and fly safe."

When I disconnected the call, I walked over to the observation window to take a look at the weather outside. Even though the snow had stopped falling, the city was slow in getting the plow trucks and the salt on the road. The airport had just cleared the runway for the airplanes to arrive and take off; and then, I was just waiting for the darn plane to arrive from Charleston.

I prayed I wouldn't be stuck in New York for the holiday. I could almost taste Nana Bell's okra stew, and that coconut crème pie was calling my name. I tried, but no one could burn like my Nana Bell!

Turning away from the window, I viewed a fine, tall brother talking to the same agent who processed my check-in. My eyes traveled the length of his body—his well-toned, muscular body—zeroing in on his round behind. My hands were itching to stroke and caress him. That was so like me to be attracted to a man's backside without even seeing his face.

He must have felt my eyes on him, because he turned around slowly, and his intense hazel eyes scoped me out.

Astounded, I smiled as I recognized Lance Edwards, from my hometown of Monck's Corner, South Carolina. I hadn't seen him in three years; and Lord, did he look scrumptious!

It appeared that he had been lifting weights. His body was well-defined, his shoulders broad, abs tight, and he had muscular arms and legs. And the way his clothes fitted the body—especially his pants—just made me want to scream. I wanted to examine for myself all of the new changes to his sculptured body. After all, he was my first way back in the day. He was a gentle and giving lover, who saw to my needs first, before taking his own pleasure.

"Hey, Betty Lou; imagine finding you here. Going home for Christmas?" He asked, while pulling me into his arms.

"Lance!" I exclaimed, slipping into his arms, and getting a good whiff of his cologne—my favorite, Dolce & Gabanna.

He still wore that cologne.

"What a wonderful surprise," I said. "It's good to see you, too."

I wanted him. My . . . my, the body remembers how he would send me into twilight zone when we made love. He was that good, and my hormones went into overdrive. I had to push away from him or else I would've embarrassed myself.

"Girl, you're looking good. Have you joined a gym?" he asked.

"No time for the gym, just working hard. I barely have enough time for a lunch break. I lost twenty pounds since I saw you last," I proudly declared.

"It looks good on you. Hmm, and you smell good, too. Come here and give me some sugar."

"We're in an airport, Lance. I don't think we should," I said, suddenly becoming shy.

"Who's watching, and if they do look, who cares? This is New York, and I haven't kissed those lips in years. I want to see if they taste as good as I remember."

In his arms again, I couldn't deny that I didn't want to kiss those lips and why not? We were both adults, and it was only a kiss. As I gazed into his eyes, I didn't see when his lips touched mine, but I sure felt the effect. It was a gentle peck on the lips, but his tongue started to outline my lips, and I immediately opened my mouth, and he slipped it in. He thoroughly familiarized himself with my mouth, and he tasted like butterscotch candy. I knew he loved to eat butterscotch, and he must have just finished a piece. I don't know how long we were at it, but I felt shaken and wet all over. I had to stop that, or else we would be making out inside of a crowded airport!

Pulling out of his arms, I saw an older woman who could've been my grandma, giving me the evil eye, and another woman covering her little five-year-old daughter's eyes.

"You should be ashamed of yourselves. Didn't the two of you get enough of each other at home?" she asked, dragging her daughter to another chair. She wanted to get as far away from us as possible.

"Oh, don't mind them. Come, there are two seats over in the corner. Come sit with me," Lance suggested.

On weak legs, he led me to a seat away from prying eyes. Sitting down in the chair next to Lance and bumping next to his strong body had my heart racing. The kiss was bad enough, but the combination of everything was hurting me. Lance watching me, his manly scent drawing me closer, and his soft caress against my arm, was too close for my peace of mind. It reminded me what it felt like to have a man in my life. There wasn't one right then, and I hadn't been on a date in months.

"Girl, what's new besides your losing some weight?" he asked, smiling into my eyes.

"Nothing much has been happening to me. How about yourself? How's the family?" I asked him, not wanting to reveal how boring and lonely my life had become.

"My baby sister, Rena, got married last year, and she just gave birth to my first niece. That's another reason I decided to travel home for the holiday. Since Mom died, the house doesn't feel the same. I still miss her," Lance whispered, turning his head away—not wanting me to see his tears.

I raised my hands to touch his chin, forcing him to turn back toward me. The sadness on his face and a lone tear slid down his cheeks. Stroking his face, the tears continued to flow onto my hand.

"Lance, it's okay to still miss your mother, it's been ten years since the Lord called my mother home, and I still miss her every minute, every hour of the day."

We just sat there gazing into each other's eyes. Words were no longer necessary. Each of us was into our own personal thoughts.

The announcement from the airline stating the cancellation of flight 105 to Charleston brought us out of our quiet moment. Many angry passengers crowded the terminal desk, complaining and trying to make alternate travel plans. I was disappointed that I wouldn't be home for Christmas, but if the weather conditions, and the airplane weren't in tip-top shape, I didn't want to fly. I valued my life, and if this was God's will, why would I mess with it?

"We could go back to my place, pick up my car, and drive to Monck's Corner," Lance suggested.

"That's a fourteen-hour drive, and besides, we wouldn't be home in time for dinner, Lance. It's now ten a.m., and I don't want to be on the road on Christmas Day."

"Okay, how about I take you out for Christmas dinner?" Lance offered.

"No, why don't I make us dinner, instead?" I asked.

In my freezer were several containers of frozen snap beans and collard greens, but I would have to make a stop to the grocery store. I hoped that one would be open to pick up the other things I would need.

"You're sure you want to do this? A restaurant would be less work, and you could rest until I picked you up," Lance added.

"No, I don't want to eat in a restaurant; and, besides, I can make us our own Christmas celebration. You know the address, see you at five p.m."

I quickly dragged my one piece of luggage out of the airport revolving door, and headed toward the cab line.

Ten minutes later, I was in a cab heading toward my apartment in Rosedale, Queens. I was lucky to find a two-bedroom apartment in a quiet residential area, in a private house. The cab driver pulled in front of my place at eleven o'clock, and I had only six hours to get my dinner ready, and my place together for Lance.

By 4:45 p.m., I had taken a quick shower to refresh myself, and slipped into a red velvet warm-up suit and matching red slippers, spraying myself with my favorite cologne.

Because I planned to be home in Monck's Corner for the holiday, I didn't bother doing a lot of decorating, but I'd always set up my small, three-foot Christmas tree in the living room next to the glassed mirrored wall. On my coffee table, I displayed my Christmas villages. Every year, I added another piece to the collection. I had been a collector for the last fifteen years, when my mother bought my first piece.

The apartment felt warm, and cozy, and I set out a pine candle, burning it to give the apartment a fresh pine scent. Even though it was an artificial tree, you couldn't tell unless you touched it.

The dining room table was comfortably set for two. A red velvet Christmas cloth was laid out with matching napkins, and a large round red candle sat as the centerpiece. I wrapped pine garland around the candle, used my best china, and silverware. A bottle of sparkling apple cider was on ice, chilling for our meal. Both of us didn't drink alcohol, and the cider was one of my favorite sparkling drinks.

The Cornish hens were almost done, and the macaroni and cheese was browning nicely with a buttery brown color, and the cream was oozing on top. I didn't want it to dry up, so I told myself to remove it from the oven in another ten minutes. There wasn't time for me to bake a turkey, so I had improvised and baked two Cornish game hens, instead. Corn bread stuffing, dirty rice, and corn muffins along with collard greens, completed my meal. I was able to pick up an apple pie for dessert, and in the freezer was a gallon of French vanilla ice cream. I was happy to have pulled that all together in just under four hours.

I was still a little in love with Lance, and should have stayed in touch with him. Nana Bell was disappointed I wouldn't be home for Christmas, but when I told her I would be spending Christmas with Lance, she gave me the thumb's up. She said, if I wanted him, I'd better make a move, because the man was getting finer every time she saw him, and he wouldn't be alone much longer! She eyed the ladies checking him out at church the last time he came home. My Nana Bell was right, and I had every intention of starting something that night.

Nat King Cole's Christmas CD was playing on my Bose system, and I dimmed the lights in the dining room. Everything was ready and in place. The house smelled of pine trees and baked corn bread. My mouth watered because I hadn't eaten anything that day, except tasting my meal for seasoning as I cooked.

I hurried to the door after hearing the chiming of the doorbell, checking my appearance against the mirrored wall.

Lance was wearing a black leather trench coat, and in his hands, was a large shopping bag filled to the brim with goodies. Kissing me on my cheek, he stepped into my home.

"Hmm, hmm, something smells good in here. Girl, what's for dinner?"

Lance removed his coat and handed me his shopping bag while heading toward the kitchen, following the aroma of dinner.

"I see you remember the direction to the kitchen, Lance."

"Yes, my nose can always find the kitchen!"

Walking through the dining room, he stepped into my kitchen, opening the oven door, and put his nose inside to take a quick peek.

"The Cornish hens smell good, and macaroni and cheese—my favorite. Girl, you've outdone yourself. When can we sit down and eat? My stomach has been rumbling ever since I walked through your door."

"Lance, I see the way to your heart is still through your stomach. No 'you look beautiful,' or the place looks lovely,'" I teased.

"Girl, you know you look good; I told you so in the airport, and I like the outfit you're wearing. Red is your color," he added, taking me into his arms. "Hey girl, are you feeling neglected?" He asked, kissing my chin and working his way toward my lips. "We can have dessert now, if you like. I'm not that hungry," Lance murmured in my ear as his hand stroked my back, easing inside of my sweatsuit.

Wrapping my arms around Lance's neck, I drew him closer, while I returned his kisses. Feeling the heat from the oven's door against my legs forced me to remember dinner.

"Lance, I need to check on our dinner."

"Okay, we can continue this later, girl," he said, winking at me.

Lance ate every drop, and he even went back for seconds. Afterward, he stretched out on my sofa and picked up the remote control for the wide screen TV. I heard him as he flipped through the channels, searching for something to watch, while I cleared the dining room table of our dirty plates.

Warming a slice of apple pie, I dropped a double scoop of the French vanilla ice cream on his plate and brought it over to Lance. We watched the ending of Miracle on 34th Street, while eating the apple pie a la mode. After eating dessert, we both were stuffed and comfortably wrapped in each other's arms on the sofa. I couldn't move, nor did I want to, so I snuggled closer to Lance who'd fallen into a deep sleep. He started to snore in my ears, but I didn't mind.

Being in his arms again felt wonderful. Hustling to get dinner just right, and eating a hearty plate myself, made me sleepy. I drifted to sleep alongside Lance, and I felt content.

I was awakened from a deep sleep by Lance's warm hands stroking my breasts, causing my nipples to peak and harden to his touch. I elevated my body off the sofa, bringing him closer to them. I stroked his face and kissed his lips, hungry for more. His hands caressed, teased, and explored my body pushing me to a breaking point. Lance's hand teased me and found my readiness.

I led him into my bedroom where we could stretch out on my king-sized bed. I lay in bed and watched Lance undress eagerly, slipping into bed beside me. I was still dressed, and he took pleasure in removing my clothing piece by piece—kissing me in between each article of clothing removed.

The sheets were cold to the touch, but soon, Lance had me so hot I had to hold my tongue between my teeth to stop myself from screaming my delight. His hard body pressed against mine, and his lips traced a sensuous path.

When we became one, my body remembered the feel of his skin, his heady, masculine scent. Old memories resurfaced about the first time we made love, the last time we made love, but nothing could compare to this time. Slowly and with perfect ease, his body took over mine—knowing he'd come back home.

"Damn, it's been too long," I groaned, afterward when Lance's body curved into my backside. With his arms wrapped around me, I drifted off to sleep.

Two days of being snuggled up in my apartment, making love, eating, and watching TV with Lance; we had the place to ourselves. My landlord and her family went to Florida for the holidays and weren't expected home until after New Year's. With free reign to express ourselves, our lovemaking became very vocal—and I didn't hesitate to shout my joy!

Lance ran out of condoms, and he also needed a change of clothing. He was tired of walking around my place in only his underwear. I decided to take the ride with him after being confined in my apartment for two days. I was stir-crazy, and had overdosed on lovemaking. It felt good to get outside when I finally got some fresh air. Besides, I hadn't been to his place in years, and I was curious to see how he decorated his home.

We pulled up in front of a brownstone in the Park Slope section of Brooklyn, and his apartment was on the second floor. He had a duplex. His living room, kitchen, and den were on the first level, and his bedrooms were on the second level. As I strolled around being nosey, looking into every nook and corner, I couldn't believe how well his place was decorated. I was about to ask him who did his décor, when a tall, tanned woman walked down the stairs, coming from the second level in only a tank top and matching panties. She appeared as if she belonged there, and she looked at me as if I were an intruder.

"Honey, you're finally home. Where have you been?"

"What are you doing here?" Lance demanded.

"Melinda, our relationship ended two months ago, and I thought you returned my key. Why are you dressed like that? This is my place, and I want you out!"

Lance was angry, and I saw it on his face; but Melinda smiled—not afraid—and she sashayed right up to him, sliding her sensuous body right up against his. I could see she was doing it intentionally, and I waited patiently for Lance to get rid of her.

"I have a surprise, and I couldn't wait for you to come home. I was afraid you went home for the holiday. But then I found your suitcase in the living room, and realized you wouldn't be gone long; so I waited."

Melinda's voice dripped with sweetness as she rolled her eyes toward me.

"Lance, you didn't introduce me to your friend."

"There's no need for me to introduce the two of you. You're not staying, I want you to march up those steps, change back into your street clothes, and leave my home," Lance stated firmly, trying to keep his temper in check.

"Don't you want to hear my surprise?" Melinda asked.

"We ended our relationship, and as far as I'm concerned there's nothing left to say. I'm seeing someone else now as you can see, so be an adult, and get out."

After spending the last two days with Lance, I knew how she felt, and I was starting to feel sorry for the girl. Some sisters just don't know when to leave, I thought.

"Just give me five minutes, alone; please, Lance. I'll make it quick," Melinda whimpered.

Fresh tears welled up into her eyes, and started to roll down her cheeks.

"Lance, I need to use your bathroom," I said, giving him some privacy with her.

"It's up the stairs and the third door on the right," he directed.

I climbed the steps and walked swiftly to the bathroom. Admiring the décor, I didn't really have to use the bathroom, but I couldn't stand by and watch her humble herself before any man.

Heated words carried on up the stairs and toward the bathroom. I couldn't hear what was being said, but their voices got louder, and someone came storming up the steps, and then, a door was slammed. The vibration from the door slamming could be felt in the bathroom, and rattled the wall sconces.

I eased the door open, and peeked out to see if the coast was clear before walking back down the stairs looking for Lance. He stood quietly by the bay window looking out, and he didn't hear me as I eased up close to him. I wrapped my arms around his waist, and he jerked out of my arms—looking down at me with a hurt and sad face.

"Lance, is everything all right?" I asked.

I watched him open his mouth to speak to me, but nothing came out. Melinda came running down the stairs, and entered the living room with a bang.

"My baby and I will be okay without you in our lives," she shouted and stormed out of the apartment.

"Lance, she's going to have your baby?" I whispered. Shocked, I turned away from him as hot, burning tears slid down my cheeks. "I wanted to have your baby. It's too late for us. You need to go after her, Lance. It's your baby she's carrying, right?" I questioned, wishing he would tell me it wasn't possible. His reaction and the sadness on his face spoke for him.

"Yes, it's my baby, and I don't love her. It's always been you, Betty Lou. We can work this out. I'll support Melinda and our child, but I want to be with you."

"No, Lance. Melinda needs you. Take care."

I pushed past him and ran out of the door just like Melinda. Hurting badly, I ran down the street toward the R train.

I took the train to Pacific Street, and caught the Long Island Rail Road into Queens. Holding back on my tears, two hours later, I walked into my apartment, feeling lonely and miserable.

Lance's scent was still in the apartment. A burst of energy came from somewhere deep inside of me, and I proceeded to cleanse and wash his presence from my life. My answering machine light was flashing, and without playing my messages, I deleted them all. I couldn't bear to hear his voice, and I needed to make a clean break from him.

I couldn't stand the quiet house, and since I didn't go home for Christmas, I returned to work before my scheduled time, immersing myself in my job. Working long hours each day helped me to forget about Lance in the daytime hours, but my nights were the hardest. My dreams were all on Lance and how he made me feel.

Three weeks later, I found Lance outside of my front door with a dozen red roses in his hands. He had a big grin on his face when I walked up to my door.

"Hi," he said, his eyes smoldering with desire. "Can I come in? We have something to discuss."

After I opened my front door and led him into the living room, he handed me the flowers and kissed my cheek. We stood there, staring into each other's eyes, just smiling at each other.

"Don't you think you should put those flowers in water?"

119

When I walked into the kitchen, he followed me to the sink where I dropped my flowers and turned to him.

"What do you want, Lance?" I asked.

"I want you, girl."

"What about Melinda and your baby?" I whispered.

I couldn't help it; tears welled up in my eyes and rolled down my cheek. I tried to turn away from him, but he pulled me into his arms.

"Betty Lou, there's no baby. Melinda was just trying to hold on to me. And you know, I believed her, but I prayed and asked God to help me to make the right choice for my child. I was ready to commit, and I insisted we go as a couple to see her doctor. And that's when she confessed to the lie. I'm free to love the girl of my dreams, and that's always been you."

"Really, Lance?"

"Yes, I've always loved you," he whispered, stroking my face and lips. "I don't know why I waited so long to tell you. When we met at the airport, I believed God answered my prayers. And this situation with Melinda made me realize all the wasted moments we've let pass. I'm declaring my love right here and now."

"I love you, too, Lance."

A year later, Lance and I are living in his brownstone, and we opted to elope instead of the big wedding and the mass of confusion over who would be the best man, maid of honor, and the number of people we should invite to the wedding. Instead, we went to City Hall with just two witnesses, and we had a big celebration with our family and friends a month later. Nana Bell was disappointed we didn't have a big, flashy wedding; but more important, she was happy I finally had the man of my dreams!

THE END

CHRISTMAS HEARTACHE, NEW YEAR'S JOY
I was wishing to be home for the holiday.

I glanced around my tiny apartment with its shimmering Christmas tree and gorgeous red flowers that Amy's Flower Shop had delivered. The flowers were from Hal, and just thinking about my boss, the man I loved, made me long for his warm body; the heat turning into my eager passion. Fingering the gold heart-shaped locket Hal had given me, my heart beat with joy.

Hal and I met when I moved to Milwaukee after high school graduation. Meeting Hal had been like a scene from a romance novel—we'd fallen for each other like a ton of bricks. Soon, I'd be his wife, and hopefully my dream for two children—a boy and a girl—would finally become a reality. Loving Hal seemed too good to be true.

There was only one bad aspect about my relationship with Hal—he insisted that it was important that we keep our romance a secret.

"I'm not bragging, Connie, but I was friendly to one of the women in this office and she took me too seriously. If she guessed that we were involved, she'd start stalking me again. It gave me the creeps. I told her to lay off or I'd have to find a way to legally stop her."

"How'd she stalk you, Hal?"

"She'd take her break when I took mine and then hang around outside the café where I got coffee. Then, when I left work, I had to get her off my trail by circling around before driving home. Sometimes, I'd pull into an alley and wait a while."

"How awful, Hal. Of course I'll keep our love a secret, honey."

He hugged me hard. "Someday, we can forget the secrecy, Connie."

"I know. I understand." Someday we'd send wedding invitations to everyone in the office and then no one could complain.

In the meantime, I had the jewelry, flowers, and cell phone Hal had given me. With my starting salary I couldn't afford to buy a cell phone, but Hal's thoughtful gift had kept us in touch, and I even had enough free minutes to call home. I felt like a princess.

A knock on the door broke my thoughts, and I hurried to see if Hal had arrived earlier than promised.

Instead of Hal, I stared into the blazing blue eyes of a willowy blonde who resembled a Miss America contestant.

"I'm Melissa, Hal's wife," she said. "I know this is strange. I checked out a jewelry store receipt that came in the mail. I see you're wearing the locket described on it. I checked at the store for the delivery address and that is how I found you. I've done some good detective work."

I stared at the woman in disbelief.

"I'm warning you, Connie Weaver, you're just the latest 'other woman' in my husband's life. You should know that before you make any future plans. Since my father owns the company at which you both work, you will receive your termination notice the next time you try to return to your job. Your paycheck will be mailed to you."

Before I could speak, she whirled and marched down the hallway.

"Wait!" I called to her. "I didn't know!"

"The other women never know," she snapped, before pressing the down button at the elevator.

Sick at heart and shocked right into my bones, I managed to sit down by the window and watch Melissa drive away in a sleek white luxury car. My fingers shook as I stared at the falling snow and wondered what lay in my future. I couldn't even phone Hal's wife at home—he'd already told me the number was unlisted. He always said that he'd write it down for me someday, but he always seemed to forget. He'd never told me his address either, or I'd drive there and give him a fiery piece of my mind.

Then I remembered that I had the cell phone. I called Hal's cell phone and had to leave a message. I wanted to shout, "You cheating jerk!" into the phone.

Instead, I forced calm into my voice. "You need to explain why you kept your marriage a secret from me, Hal. You owe it to me."

How dare he deceive me! I guess I'd asked for it. I'd been too eager for a new life in the big city. I'd been too anxious to get away from my small hometown. So many nights, I'd gone to sleep longing for the day when I'd drive away on the old blacktop highway that curved through town. Sure, I'd return to visit my parents and little brother, but eventually, I'd visit with my successful husband in a streamlined van and announce my first pregnancy.

My thoughts faded as I gazed out the window at the thickening curtains of snow. I saw people streaming into the nearby Cornerstone Community Church for the Christmas Eve service. My family would be going to church right about now. Instead of glorying in my Christmas Eve romantic interlude with Hal, I would be alone. I felt a shiver run through me as Melissa's words repeated themselves in my mind. I was disgusted with Hal; I felt as if he'd stabbed me with poison arrows.

My memories fled back to the summer I'd left Martin Valley, after my high school graduation. I'd majored in Business and graduated fifth in a class of fifty. It had been quite easy to find a job as an executive secretary to Hal Hanford.

The first time I sat by his desk and felt his gaze on me, the office filled with electricity. Currents of desire hit my body and made me shiver all over. I'd never believed in love at first sight, but it happened to me at that moment. I gazed into his dark eyes that were drawing me to him like a magnet. I trembled with a sudden longing for him to hold me. I knew he was a dozen years older than me—I was only eighteen—but I didn't care. Love doesn't have boundaries.

During my job interview with Hal, he kept looking up from his question list and smiling. I was wearing a revealing pink sweater and a matching snug skirt. I'd never felt beautiful like some of my cute classmates, but my former boyfriend, Rusty, had said I was pretty. Basking in Hal Hanford's admiring glances, I finally felt sexy.

For a moment, my thoughts dwelled on Rusty. Although he'd been very nice to me, I realized he had been part of my young wild years. Rusty had settled for working in his dad's local hardware store in Martin Valley. He also was an EMT on the local ambulance crew. His thick auburn hair and admiring green eyes came to mind. Kid stuff. I was ready for a new life with a sophisticated man like Hal. It amazed me that I'd felt so drawn to someone I'd just met, but my feelings were very real.

Now that I'd met the man of my dreams, I felt finished with Rusty. I'd grown so tired of our town during my senior year, and all I'd wanted to do was to flee. I longed for the kind of life that Cindy Matthews had—Cindy had gone to Chicago and returned on the arm of a gorgeous hunk of a husband and bulging with her pregnancy. I wanted to be like her.

I didn't tell anyone about my romantic dream. My parents had respected my decision to move, and they had taken me to Milwaukee to find a furnished apartment with a well-lit parking lot.

Mom said, "Be careful."

Dad added, "Living alone means you need to wait before trusting strangers, honey."

When I left home a week later, I kissed my parents and my brother good-bye and promised to visit soon.

The first day at my new address, I felt as though I was walking into a brand new chapter of my life; one entitled "Adventure and Romance." Most of my friends had decided to stay in our hometown and work as supermarket checkout girls and nurse's aides. They told me that romance could happen in our town as well as in the city.

My best friend, Kitty, said, "Our parents found romance here, right? How else did we get here?"

I didn't think it was as easy as she said. We'd all known each other for years—there was no gorgeous stranger waiting for me in my hometown.

It took me two months of wandering around Milwaukee to get a job and to meet my new boss, Hal.

As time passed, I began to feel so lucky I'd met Hal. We later told each other about the desire we'd felt during my job interview. He was cautious and never let on to others that he was interested in me—and I kept our relationship businesslike.

The few times my coworkers saw me with Hal in the coffee shop during breaks, they had scowled at me.

Tracy, who had worked in that office for two years and was engaged to a navy man, shook her head and said, "Watch out for Hal, Connie, he's a lady's man—and too old for you."

Remembering that our love was a secret at work, I countered with a sweet smile. "Oh, Tracy, he's my boss—it is my job to be near him. Thanks for the warning."

I knew from Tracy's scowl that she was jealous. Hal and I got along as though we'd been friends for years—we always talked and laughed in his office. I never mentioned that I suspected Tracy's interest. If it wasn't true, I didn't want to cast a shadow over her character. She was a kind person and I respected her.

However, I felt confident that if Hal had asked Tracy to go out, she'd go in a second. She flirted with him a lot. Sometimes, she would stare intensely at him when she thought no one was looking. Her actions made me think she might even break her engagement if Hal paid attention to her. I couldn't blame her, though.

One day, Tracy got so close to Hal in the break room I knew she was hitting on him. I later teased him to get his reaction.

He shrugged. "I knew Tracy had a crush on me after I bought her coffee a few times. Her fiancé, Tim, had to leave on short notice for duty. She was crushed and seemed so darn lonely. I was being cordial."

"That was nice," I said, relieved.

I was so glad he didn't want Tracy.

When we were alone, Hal and I joked about Tracy's warning to me. As he laughed, his soulful brown eyes shimmered like our favorite pond in the moonlight. We both laughed, then we talked about our plans for the weekend. We could hardly wait to meet at the Riverside Motel, located a dozen miles outside the city. It was on an obscure, private place where we could really be together.

I felt more secure about our love with each passing day. I could hardly wait to drive into my hometown with him.

As I drove home from work, I'd picture my cozy dream home edged with flowers. A sandbox and swing set would grace the backyard, and our boy and girl would play as I cooked dinner.

I'd pictured Hal helping me tuck in the kids. Then we'd go to our room and kiss, feeling the ache of throbbing passion which would lead to hours of sweet lovemaking.

Then, suddenly and cruelly, my dreams had been shattered like broken glass. After Melissa knocked on my door and slammed her words at me, I felt torn apart. My romantic future splintered to bits, and the glorious new chapter of my life ended with brute force.

As the snowfall outside my building thickened, creating a beautiful white Christmas, I felt even worse. I had already told my parents I would not be home for Christmas. They had wanted me to share the holidays with them. They had also hoped that I would bring Hal home to meet everyone.

When I had spoken to my mother, she had said, "I have to ask. Do you know Hal's life history, honey? You were careful to find out, right?"

"I know he's wonderful and that he loves me with all his heart and soul, Mom."

"I'm so glad. Daddy said you'd be sure to fall in love with a good man. We liked Rusty and I'm sure we are going to like Hal as well. In fact, I was buying tree lights at the hardware store and Rusty told me to tell you that he hoped all was going well for you. I hope he finds another girl, Connie, like how you found Hal. If you love Hal, he must be wonderful."

Mom nearly cried when I'd phoned to say I couldn't be home for Christmas. She said Daddy would feel sad. "But it's your life and we'll try to understand."

Now I was alone on Christmas Eve, feeling stabbed with the sordid truth—I'd fallen in love with a jerk!

It was at that moment that I knew I had to go home for Christmas.

Packing a bag, I grabbed the cell phone for the trip. It would be handy now that I was risking a trip alone in the steady snowfall.

Once I got behind the wheel and started down the street, I saw how fast the wet snow collected on the windshield. The wipers labored as they swished the snow away. I thought about going back to my apartment, but my urgency to get home for Christmas to enjoy my parents' love kept me heading down the highway.

When my tires slipped and the car fishtailed, I gasped loudly, but then I remembered that I had new tires with good gripping power—they could get me through the storm. I decided to take the secondary road with graveled shoulders to the highway, figuring it would be plowed. I could drive with my two right wheels gripping the stones and not slide on the icy spots.

I sighed with relief as I turned onto Route Eighteen, which headed north to Martin Valley.

The snow got heavier, but I felt secure with my cell phone. When I tried to call my parents, however, I couldn't get a signal.

"I'll keep trying," I thought. "There has to be a hill ahead where I can get a signal."

As I drove on, I thought about calling Rusty. He would be in town and maybe we could go out for a pizza and talk about old times. Then

I recalled how I'd been rude during our last date. He might tell my mom he missed me, but that doesn't mean he wants to hang out.

Rusty had taken me out for dinner on my eighteenth birthday last April. I'd dressed up in his favorite red dress. I almost asked him if we were going to the Pine River Supper Club, a known place to celebrate events, but I decided that I'd let Rusty surprise me.

Surprise me he did—he parked by Ma's Diner on Main Street where the top menu items were burgers and hot dogs.

Other students were hanging out there, talking a mile a minute and eating.

"This is your surprise for me?" I gasped, then realized I'd meant to sound pleased.

Rusty stared at me. "We're students, Connie. All my money is going towards the hardware store right now; I want to be the owner someday."

I nodded. "You hinted that you had a surprise and I'm not surprised, that's all." I quickly added, "The food's great here."

I'd put a damper on our evening but consoled myself by thinking how I'd soon leave town and Rusty would be in my past. I'd send him a present for his next birthday to make up for my rude remark.

I checked my cell phone again and still no signal. I kept driving and the roads kept getting worse. Where were the plows?

The farther I drove, the thicker the snow got. The unplowed road was filling so fast with snow, and I worried my little car would stall in it. I kept going but my heart kept pounding with fear.

I sighed with relief when I saw a path on which a four by four must have been. I followed its twin tracks down the middle of the road as the wind whistled and slammed heavy, wet snow against the windshield.

A stop sign loomed ahead and I hoped I wouldn't slide into the intersection. As I neared the stop sign, I gently braked, then clicked my lights from bright to dim. The car slid sideways as I stopped, then lurched forward again as I pressed the gas.

"Turn back!" I told myself. But Melissa's angry face and hurtful words were back there. I needed to spend Christmas with people that loved me. Sure, I could handle being alone, but on this Christmas I needed my parents. I had to hug my Mom and tell her she'd been right to warn me about not trusting a stranger.

I kept driving. Somehow, my trembling leg managed to stay on the accelerator. My top speed, as the storm worsened, was thirty miles an hour. Gritting my teeth, I hoped my car would groan its way up the hill. When I reached the top, I prayed that I wouldn't get dragged into a ditch on the way down. Somehow, the wheels stayed on course.

At the next stop sign, I saw my cell phone had a signal! I called home but no one answered. My parents had mentioned being invited to our neighbor's place after the midnight church service, so I left a message on their answering machine.

"I'm driving home in a storm," I said. "If I don't get there by the time you hear this message, call for help. The snow is so heavy and the road unplowed. I'm at Marshall Corners and Highway Eighteen now."

As I was on the outskirts of Martin Valley, I began to wonder if my parents might have decided to visit Aunt Ruth. I felt desperate enough to risk being ignored by Rusty and called him. I left a message. "I'll call you from my parents' home, Rusty." I told him where I was on the highway. I wasn't sure if I'd ever hear back from him.

I tossed the phone on the car seat, checked the rearview, and gasped.

Flashing yellow lights were gaining on me. "A snow plow?" I wondered, my pulse racing. "Are my taillights covered with snow? Would the plow run into me?"

Stepping on the gas to escape being hit, the steering wheel refused to take me where I wanted to go. I slid far enough to the road edge to let the plow pass me.

The plow driver must have thought I'd planned to pull over, but I was stuck and my tires kept spinning and whining in the drift. I felt my car being pulled deeper into the snow with each effort to get free!

I tried to get free for such a long time that the motor finally died. The cold soaked into my body—I shivered and my teeth chattered as the minutes passed. I felt so scared. I would freeze to death on Christmas Eve—and all because of that jerk Hal! Melissa's news got me so riled up I didn't think straight and plunged into a blizzard. How stupid of me! How foolhardy!

I had to forget Hal and fight my exhaustion. I had to stay awake so I would not freeze. I wiggled my toes and fingers, shifted in my seat, and pulled my wool cap over my head. The car got colder by the minute. I hadn't even been wise enough to bring a blanket in case of trouble.

Time ticked away and the snow formed a thick white quilt over my windshield. I felt so tired but knew I had to stay awake. So, to stay alert, I sang "Jingle Bells" with as much zeal as I could muster. I thought of other peppy songs, too, but I could hardly keep my eyes open. My song fizzled, faded, and I felt sucked into another dimension.

"Connie, wake up!" I heard Rusty's voice. "Oh, baby, stay with me!"

I opened my eyes, knowing I'd only dozed for a minute or so. I gazed straight into Rusty's worried green eyes. "I'm here to take you home. I'm so glad you called, Connie."

It felt so good being put on the back seat of Rusty's warm SUV. He placed a cozy blanket over my body and cranked up the heat.

At home later, with Rusty and my parents watching over me in my bedroom, I burst into glad tears.

127

They all hugged me and said soothing words about being glad I was all right.

"I am, too. Oh, so glad!"

Rusty's caring smile and shimmering green gaze melted into my heart, and I knew that his kind of love had taken care of me, not exploited me.

Then another thought hit me. I'd given myself sexually to Hal, and Rusty was too good of a person for me to lead on. I'd have to confess what my life had been like lately. He may have lost romantic interest in me, anyway.

On the day after Christmas, after I'd had a good rest and a cheerful visit with my parents, Rusty asked me to go for a ride to look at the town's decorated homes.

I went for that ride, and Rusty asked if we could resume our relationship.

"Pull over and we'll talk for a few minutes, Rusty," I managed to say, with knots in my stomach.

I told the entire sordid story about my illicit affair with Hal, and I felt sick when Rusty frowned. Then, his shock turned to tears. "Oh, you poor girl, Connie!"

"I was foolish and that's why we can't resume our relationship. I ruined everything," I said, as unwanted tears filled my eyes. I blinked them back, knowing I had to grow up and face my mistake.

Rusty was silent for a while and there was tension in the air.

Then, Rusty spoke slowly. "I'm not perfect either, Connie. When we were going together, I flirted with Stacy Edwards a lot. She was the homecoming queen and so popular—I felt special being around her."

"Oh, you were so bad!" I said, needing to smile at his attempt to try to make me feel better.

We gazed at each other for a long moment before I reached out to hug him. He pulled me close.

"I've always thought of you as my girl, Connie—and I mean it. I can forget your relationship with that guy, Hal, if you can. You were just trusting and innocent. Let me help you get over it, okay?"

That was two years ago. After that difficult Christmas, Rusty and I drove to my apartment to move me back to Martin Valley. We got engaged, and married three months later in a beautiful spring wedding. Rusty is saving to buy the hardware store and I'm working as a secretary in a local attorney's office.

I'll be leaving my job in seven months to have our first baby. If we have a girl, we'll call her Merry. If we have a boy, we'll name him Noel. After all, it was the spirit of Christmas and the luck of the New Year that changed my life from terrible heartache to exquisite joy.

THE END

SANTA AND
THE SINGLE GIRL
I met him at the office party!

It's amazing how one little word and a few glasses of wine can change your whole life. At the time this happened to me, I was appalled and mortified by my uncharacteristic behavior. Now I realize that sometimes you've just gotta say the first thing that pops into your head—and then face the consequences.

My coworker, Libby, was the first person to tell me that a new employee would be starting in our office. I guess you could say that she started it all.

Late one Friday afternoon, Libby came over to my cubicle and perched on the edge of my desk, inadvertently knocking over the orderly piles of client files that I'd just alphabetized.

She sipped from a bottle of flavored water and handed me a memo. "Check this out. There's a new guy starting in Documentation on Monday. His name is Mark and he's transferring from Cleveland." She rolled her eyes. "I hope he's not a drag. Everyone in the group is getting along fine. Well, almost everyone." Libby nudged me with her elbow. "Are you going to Milo's?"

I shook my head. "Nope, not this week. I told my aunt that I'd come over for dinner." It was a small lie, but I just couldn't bear to spend another Friday night at Milo's.

"Okay, fine. Suit yourself." Libby took the hint and walked off toward Accounting. "You know where to find us," she called out over her shoulder.

I certainly did. Each Friday, everyone from the office congregates at a local bar called Milo's. It starts out with people having a few drinks and playing darts, but by the end of the night, my coworkers are hopelessly sloshed and/or on the prowl, looking to hook up with anyone who comes within reach. It's not my idea of a fun evening at all, yet Libby practically dragged me there every week as part of her "loosen up Erin" campaign. Despite my protests, she was determined that I shed my shell and come out of hiding. I was known as the "quiet girl" around the office, and I'd developed a reputation as a stick-in-the-mud.

The labels didn't bother me. I was content with the social life I had outside of work, with people I genuinely liked. I would've rather rented a movie and stayed home alone than go out with people from my job.

I have nothing against having a good time, but I work with these people for forty hours per week. I don't feel the need to "join the crowd" and waste my time getting drunk and rowdy at a bar every chance I get. The last thing I want is to make a fool out of myself and be reminded about it every day. I'd seen it happen all too often in their circle of friends. The members of that group share everything, and I'm not comfortable with that. After all, I'm here to work—not to socialize.

At the time, I wouldn't have dreamed of mixing business with pleasure. But that was before Mark came along.

Libby rushed over to my cubicle first thing on Monday morning. "You've got to see this new guy. Come on."

"But Mr. Bartlett wants me to run these reports," I protested. It was no use. Libby dragged me out of my department and down the hallway, grinning like a Cheshire cat.

I peeked into Documentation and immediately spotted the new guy. How could I not? He stood about six-feet-four and had a muscular build. His burly biceps stretched his white dress shirt tight when he reached up to brush a lock of sandy-brown hair out of his eyes. A small crowd of women from the office had gathered around him.

I swallowed hard. Mark was the most attractive man I'd ever seen. His nose was slightly large, but he had high cheekbones and a strong jaw. Things had certainly improved around the office.

"Go talk to him." Libby nudged me forward. "Introduce yourself, make friends."

"Are you crazy? Not on your life!" I turned away and cast Mark a glance over my shoulder. As gorgeous as he was, I knew I had to stay away from him. If I started giving in to a crazy crush, I'd only get my hopes up and my heart broken.

Libby followed me back to my desk and sat down. This time, she knocked my stapler to the floor. "Erin, you're not even going to say, 'Hi' to the new hunk? Why not?"

I arched my eyebrows at Libby. "Why? Do you even have to ask me why?" I opened a file and frowned. "Let me save him the trouble of telling me that I'm not his type."

I pursed my lips. "Not my type" was a phrase that had haunted me all through high school and most of college. It seemed like every guy I had a crush on told me that he was flattered, but that I wasn't his "type."

After too many rejections, I'd decided to give up on men altogether. I kept telling myself that someday, someone I liked would want me, too, and then my true nature would shine through. I knew that deep inside, I was an open-minded and adventurous person. I'd had boyfriends before, and I knew that I could be wild, but it had to be with the right guy. I had standards, but Libby didn't seem to realize that.

"Oh, fine!" Libby stood up. "Don't say that I didn't try. We're having the drawing for the holiday grab bag in the lunchroom at three. Don't forget."

I breathed a sigh of relief as Libby headed back toward

130

Documentation. Why couldn't she see that I wasn't extroverted like she was? I didn't understand why I had to date someone at work to be accepted by people I barely knew. Libby considered her "team" of coworkers family.

Just because I took my job seriously and didn't use it as a social club didn't mean that I wasn't fun to be with. My boss, Mr. Bartlett, seemed to appreciate my attitude. He could be a bit of a stickler for propriety, and I was one of the few reliable people who he could always count on to stay late and get the job done.

I treated everyone professionally. That is—until I ran into Mark.

I'd just left the tiny computer room and was walking down the hall with reports for Mr. Bartlett. My head was bent down and I was proofreading a sales chart when I crashed into something. I yelped and fell flat on my behind. My papers flew into the air and scattered all over the beige carpet.

"I'm so sorry!" a deep voice rumbled. I gazed up into the handsome, chiseled features of a very worried-looking Mark. I couldn't help but notice that his eyes were the color of tea, and that he had a tiny nick on his chin from shaving.

I stared at him for a minute, then swallowed hard. Just being this close to him took my breath away. I was at a loss for words.

Mark knelt down and touched my shoulder. A flash of heat seared through me and I felt my heart skip a beat. "Are you okay? I didn't hurt you, did I?" He sounded upset.

I shook my head and said. "No, I'm fine." I glanced at him out of the corner of my eye. "Just a little stunned. You sure are solid," I blurted out before I could stop myself. I closed my eyes and bowed my head. Of all the stupid things to say. I looked up and gave him a little smile.

He grinned and let out a laugh. "Well, that's not something I hear every day." Mark extended his wide hand and I placed my palm in his. My skin tingled as he hauled me to my feet effortlessly. I stumbled forward against him and ended up planting my hand in the center of his broad chest. I gazed into his eyes and knew that I was hooked. I took a deep breath and was pleasantly pleased to find that Mark smelled like sandalwood.

"Oh, I'm sorry." I pulled away in a hurry and looked around, praying that there weren't any of Libby's spies nearby. The last thing I wanted was for someone to catch us standing in the hallway together, practically in each other's arms.

"It's my fault. I'm really a clumsy ox." He grinned and shook his head. "Here it is my first day, and I go and trample my coworker." Mark bent down and started gathering up my reports. I knelt next to him and caught him looking at my legs. He glanced away. "I know we haven't met. I'm Mark."

"I know." I bit my bottom lip. "I mean, I heard that there was a new guy starting and . . ." I trailed off as I felt my face grow warm.

"Then why weren't you part of the harem?"

I was shocked. "The what?"

He chuckled. "I showed up at nine to start work and I was the social event of the season. I had about eight women sitting on my desk, asking me all kinds of personal questions and offering to show me around the office today. They were even so kind as to extend an invitation to dinner and a tour of the local hot spots."

He stacked the papers together as he stood. "The men aren't much better. They all want to buy me beers and sign me up for their dart teams." Mark handed me my reports and leaned closer to me. "I'm sure they're just trying to be friendly, but doesn't anyone have a personal life around here?"

I shook my head. "As a matter of fact, no. Everybody knows everybody else's business. They're all best friends and one big, happy family." I sighed. "And if you're not 'in' with them, they'll either torment you until you 'join the club' or they'll decide that there's something wrong with you for not being 'one of the gang.'"

I realized how bitter my words sounded, and I gave Mark an apologetic smile as I stood up. "It's not really that bad. I'm sure you'll make a lot of friends here." I licked my lips and glanced down at my reports. "I've gotta get these collated and in to Mr. Bartlett. It was nice meeting you," I said, and hurried down the hall.

Libby was sitting on my desk when I returned from Mr. Bartlett's office. "I heard you collided with Mark. He's solid, huh?" She grinned.

I rolled my eyes. How had word gotten around the office so fast? I was tempted to ask her which spy had been creeping around, but I thought better of it. "So? I thought you'd be happy that I talked to him. He's nice." Nice was an understatement. Mark was the hottest and sexiest man that I'd ever met. Even though I'd had a ridiculous conversation with him, I knew I was hooked. I'd replayed our entire encounter three times in my head while I was standing in Mr. Bartlett's office. How long will it be until I see Mark again? I wondered.

"Well, I've got bad news, Erin. He's taken. He's got a girlfriend back home in Cleveland. Karly told me." She shrugged. "I guess another one got away. I just came to tell ya before you got your hopes up. See you at three at the party."

I remained calm until Libby left, then I stomped my foot. Damn! Even though I knew I didn't stand a chance with Mark, part of me had wondered, What if? I sat down and tried to concentrate on my work for the rest of the day, but it was no use. Thoughts of Mark kept distracting me every five seconds. He was nice and sexy; of course he was taken. For a moment I'd gotten my hopes up, but now all Mark could ever be was an office fantasy.

Three o'clock came faster than I thought it would. The entire office was gathered in the kitchen to pull names for the "Secret Santa" grab bag. I closed my eyes and reached my hand into the cardboard box.

"Come on, pick a good one," Libby said.

The company was having its "official" party for employees, family members, and clients at a local hotel on Saturday the twenty-first. Our office was having an "unofficial" celebration in the office on Tuesday the twenty-fourth. We were only working a half-day, but everyone was bringing in food and we were going to exchange grab bag presents then. Mr. Bartlett always waited until the office party to hand out the Christmas bonuses—just to be sure that everybody would show up.

I pulled the folded piece of paper out of the box and opened it. I frowned and then glanced around the kitchen, hoping that nobody saw my reaction. I didn't have to worry. Everyone was busy laughing and joking with each other and virtually ignoring me. I sighed and shoved the paper with Dominic's name on it into my pocket. Dominic was another member of Libby's social club. At least he'd be easy to buy a present for; he drank like a fish. "Any bottle is a good bottle" was his motto. I looked around the crowded kitchen, hoping to catch a glimpse of Mark, but he was nowhere to be seen.

I turned in the direction of the door and was yanked back when Libby grabbed my arm. "Hey, look! I got Mark's name for the grab bag!" she exclaimed.

My stomach twisted and I bowed my head. Of all the luck. "Really? Wanna trade?" I asked hopefully.

"Not on your life." Libby scowled. "Where are you running off to? We're not done yet."

"I already picked my name out. Besides, I have to go to the bathroom," I lied. "I'll see ya later." I hurried out of the kitchen and headed back to my desk. Maybe it was for the best that I'd picked out Dominic's name and not Mark's. After all, what would I have bought him? I barely knew him and—

I stopped as I heard Mark's deep voice rumbling from the other side of the partition.

"No, no, it's going okay. Everyone's very friendly—very friendly." He emphasized the last two words. "Yeah, I had a full-blown welcome; you should've seen it." He laughed. "There are a few people who seem genuinely nice, but the rest of them, well, it reminds me of high school." Mark was silent for a second. "Yeah, okay, Val. I'd better go. See you on New Year's Eve."

I swallowed hard and closed my eyes. Val? Mark must have been talking to his girlfriend.

"Hey there."

I opened my eyes and looked up at Mark. He was leaning over the top of his cubicle.

"You okay, Erin?"

How does he know my name? I wondered. I cleared my throat. "Yes, I'm fine. I wasn't listening, really. I was just going back to my desk and—"

He shook his head. "Don't worry about it. I don't mind. I thought I'd be able to have a moment's privacy with everyone else gone." He shrugged. "Are they all still in the kitchen?"

I nodded. "Yeah. They're carrying on and drawing names for the grab bag. I snuck away while I could. Mr. Bartlett only puts up with so much from them. I think he's being extra lenient because of the holidays. I expect we'll get the usual memo on office behavior in January." I smiled.

Mark laughed. "I hope so." He licked his lips. "Are you going to the office party at the hotel?"

"Yeah. Everyone does. It's sort of required." I brushed a lock of hair away from my face. "It's not that bad. The food is usually good and the company reserves a block of rooms for people who want to stay over." I stared into his eyes. "You're going, right?"

He arched an eyebrow. "I guess I have to. I'm the new guy. I'll probably end up getting a room, though. My apartment is almost an hour away and if this thing goes too late, I won't feel like driving home." He snuck a glance at my legs. "What does everyone else do?"

"Oh, them? They leave after dinner and head over to Milo's. They're all locals, so they just go home or back to someone's apartment." I giggled and stepped a little closer to the partition. "You were right about this place being like high school. I never thought of that before. Now I know why they drive me so crazy."

Mark grinned. "I had my share of folks like them in high school, too. Don't worry, it always works out in the end. Just stick to your guns. You'll come out on top."

I was going to answer him when I heard Libby's throaty laugh from around the corner. I glanced at Mark. "I'd better get back to my desk before they see me here. 'Bye." I hurried away before he had a chance to say anything else.

I made my way to my desk and sat down. My heart was pounding out of control, and I felt like a giddy teenager. Mark sure was friendly. We'd not only had two semi-private conversations, but now we shared a little secret. I smiled. If he hadn't had a girlfriend, I would've been tempted to buy him lunch. But after a few seconds, my elation faded. As nice as it was living in that fantasy world, the truth was that Mark did have a girlfriend. And no matter what I dreamed, in reality, I didn't stand a chance.

My phone rang and I picked it up. "Hello?"

"And why don't you want them to see us together?" Mark asked.

My pulse skyrocketed. "Well, I, uh, it's just that—" I swallowed hard. "They like to talk and make up rumors. Libby's our town crier."

Mark laughed. "I understand. So, even if I come over there to ask you a work-related question, there would be . . . more to it?" he teased.

I crossed my legs under my desk. I wanted to answer, "I'd hope so," but I didn't have the courage. "Probably. Then the gossip would start about how you just moved here and you're already cheating on your girlfriend and—"

"My girlfriend? Damn! You know about her already?"

I closed my eyes. I'd blown it for sure. Why had I said that? "Yeah. Word gets around fast here."

"I can tell." He let out a long sigh. "Okay, then. That's good to know, at least. I'd better hang up. The clique is back. 'Bye."

I hung up and cradled my head in my hands. I could tell by the tone of Mark's voice that he was annoyed. Is he angry that I know about Val? I wondered. Is he bothered by the fact that he's only been here a day and everyone knows his personal business? Either way, I figured I'd let the whole thing rest.

The next two weeks went by in a blur. I was hurrying to finish up a big, end-of-the-year project for Mr. Bartlett. I kept myself busy at my desk all day and I tried to stay out of the rumor mill as much as I could. That was nearly impossible, though, with Libby perched on my desk every hour, giving me the latest Mark updates.

Within ten business days, everyone knew everything about Mark. A photo of him with his arm draped around a pretty blonde appeared on his desk; we all assumed that she was his girlfriend. Mark brought in a coffee mug with a Grand Canyon logo on it and casually mentioned that he used to work at the park when he was in college. He read Skydiving Monthly and had two cats. He had a tattoo of a dragon on his upper thigh and had spent a month in Italy backpacking around the countryside.

It really was more information than I wanted to know, but I, like everyone else, absorbed it all. Mark's life was interesting and exciting. I couldn't imagine why he was working here and what had possessed him to leave his girlfriend behind.

Mark and I bumped into each other at least three times a day. We always managed to meet up outside the computer room, and on more than one occasion, we were headed down to the coffee machine at the exact same time. As the days passed, I got more comfortable around Mark, and we shared pleasant, private conversations.

Even though he never mentioned any of his exploits to me, I was still wild about him. He starred in all of my daytime office fantasies and I had more than one erotic dream about him. All this wishing and hoping was nice, but it sent my hormones into overdrive. That's probably part of the reason why I did what I did at the Christmas party.

I arrived at the hotel at six and immediately looked for Mark. He was standing in the corner with Mr. Bartlett, surrounded by managers and clients. I smiled. He looked dashing in his navy-blue, three-piece suit and tie. He saw me from across the room and gave me a little wave. My heart fluttered. If it hadn't been for Val . . .

The night went on and I suffered through the office party dinner. Libby's group started drinking at the open bar and I indulged in two glasses of wine. At one point, I surveyed the room, looking for Mark. He was nowhere to be seen. We hadn't had a chance to talk all night and I was hoping to say hello. I wandered over to Libby.

"Where's Mark?" I asked.

She swallowed her scotch. "Oh, your lust man left. I saw him grab his coat and take off about ten minutes ago."

I was crushed. "Damn!" I muttered.

Libby laughed and patted the barstool next to her.

"Here, hop on up and have a drink." I was feeling pretty low. I'd been longing to talk to Mark all night and see what he thought of my new look. I'd decided to wear my long, wavy hair loose and I'd bought a short, low-cut dress for the party. Nobody even noticed the change. Against my better judgment, I sat down next to Libby and swilled down three more glasses of wine. What seemed like fifteen minutes later, Santa Claus came barreling into our party. The man in the costume marched into the room ringing a bell and carrying a sack full of presents. Everyone flocked around him and I got off the barstool and lurched in his direction. Something about his deep voice sent a shiver up my spine.

I waited for Santa to hand out the first round of gifts and I leaned in close. Santa smelled like sandalwood. "Mark?" I asked.

He winked and made a point of looking me up and down. "Well, Merry Christmas! Are you having fun here tonight, little girl?"

I giggled and nodded. "Yeah, the wine's really good."

Mark let out a hearty laugh. "And what would you like for Christmas?" he asked.

Maybe it was the wine, or maybe it was my overactive hormones, but I licked my lips and uttered the one word that changed my life: "You."

Mark's gaze met mine and he arched an eyebrow. I couldn't see if he was smiling, but I saw his white beard twitch. "And were you a good girl this year, or have you been naughty?" he whispered.

I swallowed hard and ran my finger along the white-fur trim on his red jacket. "That all depends. Is it naughty to fantasize about you while I'm at my desk?" Just at that moment, Mr. Bartlett appeared at Mark's side and tugged on his arm. "This way, Santa. We have more guests for you to greet."

My heart sank as I watched Mr. Bartlett pull Mark away before he could answer me. What had I done? The drunken part of me didn't care that I'd just offered myself to Mark, but the reliable, reasonable Erin was dying inside. What would happen when we went back to work on Monday? Would Mark think that I was just as bad as Libby and her friends?

I didn't have to wait too long to find out. Half an hour later, I was standing at the dessert table, pouring myself a cup of coffee, when Santa walked up behind me. He tapped me on my shoulder and I turned around.

"No," he said.

I looked down. "That's okay. I didn't—"

"That's not what I meant. The answer to your question is: No." Mark leaned close. "That's not naughty. That's what Santa considers nice." He chuckled.

I felt my pulse soar and I gazed into his eyes. "Does that mean?"

"Yup. Meet me by the elevator and I'll give you your present."

My heart skipped a beat and I managed to put my coffee down before I dropped it. I gazed around the room. Most of the party was breaking up and nobody would notice if I disappeared. Libby and her friends had left for Milo's about ten minutes earlier. I slipped out the door and hurried toward the elevators. I was nervous as all hell. Part of me didn't believe that Mark would go through with it. After all, he had a gorgeous girlfriend and an exciting life. I was just a mousy coworker from the office. My heart hammered out of control. I'd never done anything this wild and impulsive before.

I smiled when I saw Mark waiting for me by the elevators. He was still dressed in his Santa suit. "Are you going to wear that?" I asked.

He pulled me into an elevator. "I will until you take it off of me."

His mouth covered mine and I melted against him. We made out like a couple of teenagers all the way up to the tenth floor. I moaned as Mark slid his hands up the back of my short skirt and squeezed my buttocks. He yanked me forward and I yelped as I felt something hard press into my stomach.

"My, Santa, what a big candy cane you have," I teased.

He laughed. "God, Erin, you look so sexy. It's no wonder you don't dress like this at the office. Nobody would get any work done." He kissed me again and his tongue worked magic in my mouth. "You don't know how badly I've ached for you all night."

The elevator doors opened, and he led me down the hall to his room. I was ecstatic. Mark wanted me—really wanted me. I'd sobered up enough to know what I was doing, but there was still enough wine in me to loosen my inhibitions.

We made it into the room and Mark closed the door behind us. He scooped me up effortlessly and I wrapped my legs around his trim waist. I leaned closer and nuzzled his neck. He groaned and looked into my eyes. "Are you sure?"

I nibbled his earlobe. "Yes, Santa. I want my present. I want you to fill my stocking real good."

He laughed and kissed me down to my soul. "Don't let anyone know, but Santa likes naughty girls."

The next morning I woke up naked, lying facedown on the bed. I rolled over and blinked a few times. Mark was asleep on his back, snoring a little. The curtains were open a crack and I had just enough light to see around the room. Our clothes were scattered everywhere and it was almost eleven.

I bit my bottom lip. What had I done? I got out of bed as quietly as I could and picked my clothes up off the floor. I scrambled into my skirt and top and slipped my shoes on as flashes of the night before came back to me. I'd acted like a wild woman in bed. No wonder Mark was still asleep. He'd "delivered me presents" three times the night before, and we would've made it four, but we ran out of condoms.

I rummaged around for my bra and panties and found them on the other side of the room. I vaguely recalled throwing them there in a fit of passion. I tucked them into my purse and was halfway to the door when Mark rolled over and sat up.

"Erin? Where are you going?"

I panicked. I didn't know what to do. I'd just slept with a man from work and done things with him that I'd only seen in porno movies. And, to top it all off, he had a girlfriend.

"I gotta go. I—I can't stay," I stammered, and yanked open the door.

"Erin! Wait!"

I ignored Mark's pleas and rushed out of the room. When I got home, I took a long, hot shower and made myself a big pot of coffee. What should I do now? I wondered. I was torn. The night before had been fantastic, but it was wrong. The guilt I felt about acting like Santa's little slut was bad enough, but if anyone from work ever found out . . .

I was ashamed of myself. I spent the day lying on the couch fretting and reviewing my options in my head. I can call in sick tomorrow and avoid Mark altogether, I thought.

If word got out that we'd slept together, I'd just have to find a new job. I couldn't face everyone day after day if they knew what had happened. Visions of the night's escapades flashed through my mind. How could I have done and said some of those things? Mark had been a wild stallion in bed, too. I remembered him muttering something about it having "been a long time." Hadn't Val satisfied him?

Monday morning came sooner than I wanted it to. I left for work as late as possible and actually came in a few minutes after nine. Mark was standing by the time clock, sipping a cup of coffee.

I looked down; I couldn't face him. After the things we'd done to each other, I was embarrassed to see him in the light of day.

"We need to talk about this," he said.

138

"I can't." I kept walking toward my department. To my horror, Mark followed me all the way back to my desk. I put my purse down and turned away.

"Erin, please."

"Let's just forget it." I heard Libby's voice from around the corner and cringed. "Just go," I whispered. Mark took a manila folder off my desk and glanced over my shoulder. "Okay, Erin. Don't worry. I'll take care of this and get back to you later. Hi, Libby," he said as he turned and left.

"So, how was the party after we left?" Libby asked. "You didn't come to Milo's. You should've come out and had some fun."

I felt like telling her that I'd had all kinds of fun, but I didn't dare. "That's okay. I had a nice time, anyway." I stood up. "Excuse me, I have to go get some coffee."

I spent the morning hiding at my desk. Mark didn't call me or stop over again. I had to admit that I felt relieved; as much as Mark was a sexy guy, I couldn't face the consequences of what we'd done. I wouldn't have felt like such a slut if I hadn't known about Val, but he'd cheated on her with me. When I came back from lunch, I found my manila folder and a candy cane on my desk. I didn't think too much of it—everyone was always handing out candy canes. I unwrapped it and stuck it in my mouth on my way to the computer room. Of course, I ran right into Mark.

"We have to talk," he said.

I felt my heart thunder in my chest. I knew I had no choice; I had to face him. I twirled the candy cane in my mouth and nodded. "Fine, but in here." I opened the computer-room door and we went inside. I turned and locked the door behind us. The last thing I needed was for someone to walk in on us in there.

I kept my gaze focused on the floor. "Just don't tell anyone here," I muttered. "That's all I ask. If they ever knew—"

Mark chuckled and I glanced up. "I would never do that. Are you crazy? They'll never know anything happened at all." He rested his hands on my shoulders. "Erin, there's no need to be so upset. What happened was—"

"Was not like me." I pulled the candy cane out of my mouth. "I'm not a slut, and—"

He scowled. "Of course you're not. I didn't think you were. You were wild; I like that."

I stuck the candy cane back in my mouth and twisted it around. My heart was pounding a mile a minute, and I prayed that nobody had seen us go in there. "Well, what about Val? You cheated on her with me and that's—"

"Val? Cheated?" Mark shook his head. "No, no, no—it's not like that." He grinned. "Val's my sister."

I frowned. "Your sister? But then who's that blonde woman in the picture on your desk? Isn't that your girlfriend?"

He laughed. "No. That's Val. We took that photo when we went on vacation last year." Mark squeezed my shoulders and leaned close. "You've got it all wrong, and that's what I wanted to tell you over breakfast on Sunday morning, but you ran off too fast. I made up all that stuff so that Libby and her friends would have something to talk about."

Mark shrugged his wide shoulders. "I wanted to keep them occupied so they would leave me alone. The truth is, I lead a very boring life, and I don't have a girlfriend. So, you have nothing to be upset about."

My heart hammered in my chest. This was too good to be true. "You mean that everything's okay?" I breathed a sigh of relief. "You have no idea how upset I was," I admitted.

"But you did like your Christmas present, didn't you?"

I twirled the candy cane faster as I had a flashback of me clutching Mark's back and arching my hips to meet his. I grinned. "Oh, yeah, every second. You were the best present I ever got."

Mark pulled the candy cane out of my mouth. "That is a very lucky piece of candy." He smirked and arched an eyebrow. "I'm glad that I bought it for you."

"You did?" I asked playfully. I trailed my tongue along the length of the candy cane and stared at Mark. "It sure tastes good."

"So did you." Mark bent his head and covered my mouth with his. Our lips hungrily sought each other's as our tongues entwined. I thought about Mark's words for a minute. After we'd run out of condoms that night, Mark had said that Santa likes to eat something besides cookies. My body quivered as I recalled thrashing around on the bed in a fit of ecstasy.

Remembering that night got me all riled up again and I found myself losing control. Maybe I wanted to prove to myself that I could be a wild woman when I wanted to, or maybe I was still hormonally charged from Saturday. Whatever the reason was, I wanted him. "I did promise to return the favor, didn't I?" I whispered. I slid my hands down Mark's chest and toyed with the waistband of his gray slacks.

Mark groaned and leaned against the wall. "You can't be serious. In here?" he asked, his voice cracking.

I glanced up at him. "Why not? Nobody in this office would believe it for a second." I grinned and unfastened his belt. "Now hold still and be my candy cane."

After Mark and I left the computer room, I went to the bathroom and took a few minutes to compose myself. I was elated. Mark was available and I was the only one who knew it. For once, things were going just right. Everything was perfect.

My elation quickly faded when I got a call to report to Mr. Bartlett

140

at three. I got up from my desk and headed toward Mr. Bartlett's office. My knees wobbled and I felt guilt wash over me again. What if someone had heard us in the computer room? Had anyone seen us coming out? What if Libby had come looking for me while I was missing?

I knocked on Mr. Bartlett's door and stepped into his office. My heart skipped a beat when I saw Mark standing next to his desk.

"Come on in, Erin," Mr. Bartlett said sitting at his desk. "I want to talk to the two of you about what's going on around here."

My knees nearly buckled. I looked at Mark. This couldn't be good. How much trouble were we in?

"You both are dedicated, serious workers, and I know this is going to sound a little strange, but I've never had to deal with this kind of a complaint before."

I closed my eyes and folded my shaking hands behind my back. If this were what I thought it was, I'd resign and start looking for work at a temp agency. I couldn't face the humiliation of staying.

Mr. Bartlett continued, "Libby came to me on Friday complaining that the two of you are party poopers."

Mark burst out laughing. "What?"

Mr. Bartlett grinned and nodded. "I know, but she's all excited about that party tomorrow. She told me that you two are not working with everyone else to make it fun."

I stared at Mr. Bartlett in disbelief. I was so relieved that this was his big concern that I had no idea what to say.

Mr. Bartlett shook his head. "I think the term 'working' is the key here. You two do more work around here than anyone else in the office, and don't think I haven't noticed. That bunch is too busy using this place as a social meeting hall. But don't worry—come January, all that will change."

"I'm not sure I understand. Why are we in here?" I asked.

"I told Libby that I'd give you each something to do at the party to get you more involved. Mark, I'll have you hand out the grab bag gifts. Erin, you can give out the bonuses."

"Okay," I agreed.

"There's just one catch. You made a good Santa at the hotel, Mark." Mr. Bartlett turned to me. "And you, Erin, well, you can be Santa's little helper." Mr. Bartlett stood and opened his office closet. He gestured at the Santa suits hanging inside. "I rented them this morning. Just for tomorrow, please wear them at the party." He gave me an apologetic look. "To make it up to you, I've added a little bit extra to your bonuses."

I managed to stifle a giggle and looked at Mark.

He grinned. "Do you think you'd like to be Santa's little helper?" he asked.

"That sounds like fun," I replied.

I got in to work early on Tuesday morning and found a small box on my desk. The gift tag read: From Santa. I opened it up and gasped. "Santa" had bought me a pair of black-lace, crotchless panties. A card inside read, Wear these with your costume.

My stomach did flip-flops. What was Mark planning to do at the party? Somehow, I managed to get through the morning without losing my mind. All I could think about was being with Mark. He'd lit a fire deep inside of me, and I found myself squirming in my seat. Finally, it was time for me to change into my costume. I took my gift and the short, red dress into the bathroom and changed.

Everyone was already gathered in the conference room when I made my appearance. Mark was standing near the gift table, sorting through the presents. Libby's group of friends whistled at me, and Mark turned around.

I felt a little awkward. The panties were nothing like the ones I was used to wearing, and I was afraid to bend over or move around too much. Mark winked and stepped to my side. He handed me the Christmas bonus envelopes. "Do you like them?" he asked.

I pressed my legs together and swallowed hard. "Yes, I think they're quite interesting."

"Good. I told Mr. Bartlett that we'd stay late and help clean all this up as part of our helping." He nudged me. "You don't mind, do you?"

I smiled. "No. I'm happy to stay, Santa."

My body burned and ached for Mark all throughout the party. It seemed like we couldn't hand out the grab bag gifts and get rid of everyone fast enough. At one, the usual group left for Milo's.

Libby came up to me. "Are you going to stop by?" she asked.

"No," I answered. "I have to stay here and help clean up."

Libby shook her head and gestured at Mark. "I don't know why you're even bothering—the man's taken." I shrugged and pretended to be sad. "I know. But that's okay. He's nice to talk to."

Libby rolled her eyes and shook her head. "If you change your mind, you know where to find me."

I was clearing off the table when Mr. Bartlett stopped by. "Great party! You two are really excellent sports. Here are the keys, Erin. You know how to lock up?"

I nodded. I'd spent many hours working late at the office and knew the building like the back of my hand. "Yes. Everything will be fine. We'll manage."

About ten minutes later, Mr. Bartlett finally left, and Mark and I were alone. He tossed out a dirty paper plate and leaned against the table next to me. "He leaves you the keys?"

"All the time. What did you get for your grab bag gift?" I asked.

He grinned. "A book called 101 Places to Do 'It' at the Office. What about you?"

I laughed. Libby was something else. "I got a daily calendar of 'Hot Hunks.' It's not the greatest calendar, though."

"Why not?"

"You're not in there," I replied.

Mark slipped an arm around my waist and pulled off his fake beard. "That's okay. According to my book, we already did what's on page eighteen. That leaves us an even hundred." Mark nuzzled the side of my neck and my pulse flared. "So, little helper, are you a good girl?"

I looked into his eyes and smiled. "No, Santa. I've been really naughty."

Mark ran his hand up my short dress and gave me a light slap on my backside. It sent my senses reeling. "How naughty were you?"

I quivered and swallowed hard. "Not as naughty as I want to be."

Mark took me by the hand and led me over to an office chair. He sat down and patted his upper thighs. "Why don't you sit on Santa's lap and tell me all about it?"

I straddled the chair and positioned myself on Mark's lap. My dress rode up and I shivered as Mark's fur-trimmed suit touched places my panties didn't cover. "Do I get a candy cane for sitting on your lap?" I whispered in his ear.

"Definitely," he answered.

Even though the office party ended at one, we stayed behind and "celebrated" on our own until five.

Mark and I are keeping our secret from everyone. At work, we keep up the charade that he's dating another woman and I'm constantly pining for him. We've found that our little secret adds a lot more spice to our relationship. We both stay late at work at least twice a week, though we never seem to get much work done. I have no complaints; it's only January and we've already gotten through half of the places listed in his book.

THE END

Epic, Sweeping, Star-Crossed Romance!
CHRISTMAS IN ALASKA
Despite our hardships, the long winter is warm
and cozy for my mountain man and me!

When two people fall in love it is mysterious, usually occurring when it's least expected. With Ken and I, it happened because we agreed it wouldn't. I wish we'd followed our instincts, though; as Mom would say, it simply was not meant to be.

But I'm getting ahead of myself.

I was born and raised on a large, isolated South Dakota Indian reservation. My American Indian-and-Irish father taught me that love between two worlds is often hard, but possible. Dad shrugged off his sister-in-law who didn't welcome Mom and us kids at her house, saying, "If my family isn't good enough for her, then neither am I."

As the oldest of eight children, college wasn't possible. "Honey, you'll have to make your own way now," Dad told me after my high school graduation. I decided to try for beauty school and ended up landing a factory job, gluing beads on fake Indian jewelry, to save money, never thinking to leave South Dakota. I was dating a cowboy; if things worked out, we'd marry and I'd forget about school.

If things had gone that way, I would never have met Ken. But life doesn't always accommodate our "happily ever after" dreams. At least my life didn't.

The affirmative action movement changed my life. Fate came to me in the form of a recruiter from UCLA who was searching for Native students. He offered me a sweet deal: books, tuition, and a monthly stipend. "That's more than I make at the factory!" I confessed in astonishment.

"With a degree, you'll make a lot of money," the man predicted.

It was enticing, but I was afraid. Dad encouraged me. "You need to go, honey. You'll be the first in our family to go to college. And anyway, you can always come back if it doesn't work out for you. You just be careful, precious; the big city is a whole different world."

Soon I found myself in Los Angeles. In the crowded airport, I alone wore cowboy boots and my prized Stetson drew curious stares. The last thing a teenager wants to be is different, so I ducked into the ladies' restroom and squashed the cowboy hat into my backpack. I took off my boots and stuffed them into the trashcan, substituting them for a pair of flip-flops.

Enrolling 30,000 students takes forever. Long lines of bored students filled the huge college gym as I settled into a folding chair and began studying my freshman orientation packet. A dark-skinned guy sat down next to me; his wrinkled shirt looked like it'd been pulled out of a dirty clothes hamper and a heavy growth of beard shadowed his handsome face. He looked poor, like me.

He read a heavy textbook, but I timidly interrupted, "Excuse me, but what does this mean?"

He kindly explained and then asked, "First registration day?"

I blushed and smiled a little. "Isn't it obvious?"

"Not too bad. Where're you from?"

"South Dakota. Would you believe this school has more people than my whole rez?"

He laughed and we started chatting. I was the first American Indian he'd ever met. He was a premed student; his father was a doctor and he was a native Californian. "Third-generation American, but pure Lebanese," he clarified.

What is a Lebanese? I wondered, but did not reveal my ignorance.

"I need a hot dog," he decided. "Want one?"

"Thanks. I'm starving."

"How about dinner tonight? Want to see some of the town?" he offered as we devoured the tasty dogs from the student union snack bar.

I was thrilled; he was handsome and I hadn't explored on my own. I gave him directions to my studio apartment in Culver City, a blue-collar area.

When he arrived to pick me up he looked much different. Clean-shaven, he wore khakis, glossy loafers, a blazer and tie, and he had flowers in hand. I was touched; guys back home didn't buy yellow roses, as there were no florist shops on the rez.

I worried about my tank top and Levis—my stock wardrobe—but he laughed and said, "You're fine," taking off his coat and tie.

He opened the door of a shiny, chocolate-colored sedan for me and we sped to the freeway. As we barreled along in air-conditioned comfort, an elegant, black Cadillac passed.

"Wow! Check that out," I said in awe.

He smiled. "Pretty cool, huh?"

I later learned that his car—a gift from his parents—was a 450 SL Mercedes Benz. I didn't know then that it cost more than my parents earned in over two years of working.

In the beginning we were honest. I told him that I would return to the reservation, marry a member of my Tribe, have a large brood of children, and live on a cattle ranch. "I want an outdoorsman—a guy like my dad," I confessed.

He smiled. "I'm sure you can have whomever you want."

His family expected him to go to medical school, enter into

practice with his father, marry a proper Lebanese girl, and produce grandchildren. "It's not so bad," he surmised, shrugging. "Heck, it worked for my folks."

In the meantime, we would have fun. Ken escorted me to exotic restaurants, movies, concerts and plays—all novelties to me. We spent hours at the beach and he even tried to teach me to surf. He bought me jewelry and clothes; soon I was California chic, cowboy boots and Indian beads forgotten. I met his friends, many of them international students with blonde girlfriends. Ken preferred my looks, introducing me as "Jamila," which means beautiful.

But we did more than play. Determined to be a great physician, Ken, a straight-A student, hit the books for hours at a time. He challenged my passing grades. "I believe in you, sweetie. You're naturally intelligent, but you need to apply that intelligence. Look at me—I'm not much smarter than the average premed student; I just work harder."

It was the first time anyone had ever expressed confidence in my intellect. I didn't think that I was smart, but I soon made the dean's list.

"I knew you could do it!" Ken praised. "Now try for straight A's."

I threw a little sofa pillow at him. "You're never satisfied."

"That's right, baby. Only the best for me. That's why I want you, Jamila."

Soon we were spending every night at his spacious apartment. If we weren't going out to eat, I'd cook. "I really love your goulash," he'd say.

Our nights were pure passion. Ken bought a sex manual and he wanted me to please him. Afterward, we would talk for hours, sharing memories, fears, and dreams. I told him about the Lakota and he explained the Middle East and Arabs. He was passionate about the Palestinian cause and he helped me see that Native Americans aren't the only victims of history. It was the talking, more than the sex, which really drew us together.

But a shadow drifted across my happiness. Ken's family lived nearby and he visited them often but never invited me. Furthermore, whenever his phone rang, I couldn't answer it because it might be his mother calling. On Wednesdays, a maid—paid for by his parents—came to clean. Beforehand, I would have to remove all my clothing and other telltale "evidence" from the apartment. Ken feared she would blab.

I pretended not to care. After all, we'd agreed only to share a brief slice of youthful paradise.

After two years Ken graduated, but I was still a junior. Accepted by several medical schools, he opted for San Francisco. "It's close to you, baby," he said.

The next quarter was tolerable for me only because of nightly phone calls and passionate letters. "I can't stand this anymore," he finally urged. "Transfer to Berkeley. Live with me."

I moved, only to find life in Berkeley very different from our carefree days at UCLA. Medical school is demanding; we saw each other only at night, sharing brief dinners before Ken dedicated himself to long hours of intensive study. He hit the books diligently on weekends, too.

I joined the Native American Club for diversion. Ken was jealous, not seeing that the fellowship eased the loneliness we Natives felt, separated as we were from our close-knit families back on the rez.

At Christmas, Ken spent the holidays with his family, but showered me with expensive gifts before leaving. "I'm sorry, baby, but they won't understand. If I tell them about us, I'll be disowned. When I'm making my own money, we'll get married. Until then, though, I need their support."

"How long?" I asked him.

"Five years, baby. Seven, max. Don't worry; it'll go fast."

On Christmas day I played a Bob Dylan record over and over again. It spoke to me:

. . . It ain't no use in calling out my name, gal

I can't hear you anymore . . .

I'm not saying you treated me unkind

You could have done better but I don't mind

You just kinda wasted my precious time . . .

I went to The Play Inn, a Native bar, and passed the long day with other lonely souls. Walking home, I looked through windows of houses at the happy families inside. The hand-in-hand couples strolling down the street seemed to mock me.

Back at the apartment, the phone rang incessantly. I ignored it. A cold wind was blowing and the lonely wail seeped into my heart. The next day I packed my bags. Back home, I'd have to admit that I wasn't good enough for a rich non-Indian. Everyone would say, "I told you so."

A Yupik Eskimo told me about Alaska, the Last Frontier. It sounded like a good place to start over. After the airline ticket I had three hundred dollars left to my name. Within hours, I was northbound.

I found a cheap room in the friendly city of Fairbanks and took the first job offered, tending bar in a seedy joint frequented by Natives.

"What's your name?" the owner asked.

"Babe," I replied, falling back on my childhood nickname. No one knew my real name but that wasn't unusual: I wasn't the only one in Alaska who was running from the past.

Back with Natives, though, I didn't fit in anymore. Uneducated men bored me and I worried about rejection from non-Natives. I wondered if I'd been rash, but I realized that if Ken would not stand up for our love, it wasn't worth much. He wasn't like Dad.

Still, I yearned for the country. After five years I finally saved enough to buy a piece of land in the bush. The small plot was miles from the nearest road; summer access was by walking or four-wheeler—snowmobile, cross-country skis, or dogsled in winter. Alaska bush land is raw and undeveloped, but cheap. The tradeoff is an enormous expenditure of work to make it habitable. There would be no running water, electricity, or phone service, but I didn't care.

After building a cabin, I planned to work seasonally at the fish canneries and hunting camps. In the winter, I'd do beadwork. Hunting, berry picking, and cutting firewood would reduce my expenses; the living would be cheap, but more importantly, the wilderness would heal my ailing spirit.

It took two months of weekend labor for me to clear the dense brush and trees for a cabin spot. I saved the logs, peeled them, and laid them out to cure for a one-room cabin. Then the problem was manpower; I couldn't raise the heavy logs alone, so I advertised: Seeking carpenter to build remote bush cabin. Top wages for top hand. Two weeks later, I arranged to meet the two men who responded at a local café.

The first, a dirty rascal with tremors in his hands and whiskey breath, was a wash. As I waited for the second, I wondered what I'd do if I couldn't find help.

The next man drew appreciative glances from the waitresses. Tall and lean, his long, jet-black hair, brown eyes, dark skin, and even features almost made him look Native. He wore Carhartt pants, a flannel shirt, a wool vest, and boots.

He walked up to my table. "Are you Babe?"

"Yep. You called about an ad?"

"Yep." His smile revealed white, even teeth. "I'm Tug."

"Tug?"

"Babe?" he rejoined with a twinkle in his eye.

"Gotcha. Nice to meet you, Tug. Please, sit down."

He ordered coffee and I explained my project. He asked lots of questions, apparently considered details, and knew what he was doing.

"Why do you want to help me, Tug?"

"Ma'am, I'm a master craftsman, but I work for big companies." He shrugged. "It'd be satisfying to me to build a home for a real person—something that will be appreciated—a labor of love, you might say."

"I can't pay the wages you normally get."

He smiled. "I know that. But a chance like this doesn't come around every day. It'd be a vacation for me."

I grinned. "Okay, then; it's a deal."

"Deal," he agreed as we shook hands.

148

We drank two pots of coffee while studying my rough sketches. I saw the merit of his suggestions. "You know about log cabins, Tug."

"I'd like to build one for myself one day," he admitted. "Oh, and by the way—I can get a contractor's discount," he added. "Save you about twenty-five percent."

I decided to trust him, handing over money for material, and he kindly offered the use of his tools to save me even more. The very next weekend, we traveled to my home site on four-wheelers heavily laden with camping gear, raw lumber, and building materials. When we arrived, Tug was impressed.

"Beautiful location. You picked a level area and left trees standing in good spots."

It took a week to erect the walls and roof. Tug was easy to work with, endlessly patient. I was also relieved to find him a perfect gentleman. Each evening, I cooked a simple campfire dinner as we enjoyed the Land of the Midnight Sun. We talked, but he didn't press for personal information and neither did I. Afterward, he crawled into his tent and I into mine. His presence was comforting.

"I could stay here forever," he said one night.

I laughed. "I'm going to, but you're welcome to visit anytime. This cabin has your stamp on it."

"Do you mean it?"

"Sure, Tug. I'll appreciate visitors."

"I'd like that," he replied thoughtfully.

At the end of the week, he had to go. Then I moved into the bare-bones cabin, glad to have solid walls between me and the bears that might be attracted by the scent of food.

Tug came back for several weekends, hauling more material with him. After a month, the cabin was finally finished. We admired our handiwork.

"I don't know how to thank you, Tug," I said with happy tears shimmering in my eyes. "Because of you, it's more than I dreamed."

"Shucks, ma'am," he said in a perfect John Wayne imitation, "it's what any pilgrim would do."

I laughed. It was something Dad would say.

We celebrated the cabin with a bottle of wine and thick T-bone steaks. Tug took pictures of the small dwelling and insisted on one of me. I also snapped one of him—only to remember the master craftsman who made my new home possible, I told myself.

When he left, the sound of his four-wheeler dwindling in the distance made me feel lonely. I would miss him, but I knew I had to prepare for winter.

Still, from then on, every Saturday, I half-expected to hear the roar of an engine announcing Tug. But then the long fall passed without word or a visit, and soon the deep snow arrived. From then on, travel was possible, but difficult. Fortunately, I was well stocked, so there was no need for me to go to town.

I considered Christmas in Fairbanks with friends, but the dogs couldn't be left alone. Jinks, Joe, Jim, and Boss, Alaskan husky sled dogs, were my companions. Most Alaskans tether their dogs outside, but I let them stay in the cabin with me. Boss, the lead dog, slept curled at my feet.

I mailed cards and money to my family, set up a little tree, and hung stockings for my "boys." Moose bones would be their holiday treat. Otherwise, another lonely holiday lay ahead of me.

It was twenty below on Christmas morning and a fierce northern wind deepened the chill; it was a good day to be lazy. I snuggled under thick quilts, book in hand. Then suddenly, Boss sat up and growled.

"Settle down," I soothed, "it's only the wind. The bears are all fast asleep."

When he kept whining, the other dogs ran to the door and barked. I finally rose to investigate, peering out the frost-covered window at the gloomy arctic morning. A figure, clad in red complete with a tasseled cap, trudged toward the cabin through the deep snow.

"Ho! Ho! Ho!" it boomed merrily.

Tug!

I opened the door to him, laughing jubilantly. "Oh, you crazy man! Come in! Come in! You must be frozen solid! What are you doing here?"

He chuckled, trying to stamp the snow off his deerskin mukluks without much success. "Helping Santa deliver gifts to good little girls."

He'd brought me a beautiful, snow-white, deerskin Eskimo parka. Native-made, of high quality and exceptionally functional, it was absolutely perfect. He even pulled a smoked turkey and the makings for a pumpkin pie from his pack.

"Think you can chef this up?"

I laughed, hefting the big turkey in my arms. "No doubt. But I feel bad; I don't have a gift for you. I've only got moose bones! I wish I'd known you were coming."

"I can think of a gift," he replied with an impish grin. "A kiss would be perfect."

How could I refuse? Still, when he drew me into his arms, I shivered. Why had we waited so long? His strong heart thudded and mine beat in tandem.

"You didn't get my letter? I wrote, asking if I could come."

"I haven't been to town in a month."

"That figures. Well, I guess I'll have to tell you what the letter said."

We sat at the table. He stroked my hand and gazed into my eyes. "I've been thinking of you constantly, Babe. I know it sounds odd after such a short time, but I'm a man who knows my mind. You're the woman I've searched for all my life and I want to be with you always."

Tears filled my eyes.

150

"It's not that bad, is it?" he asked anxiously. "I mean, do you feel anything at all for me, Babe?"

A simple feeling of joy filled me; it was right. "Tug, I feel good when I'm with you and I think of you all the time. Is that love?"

His dark eyes twinkled in the firelight. "If it's not, it's a good start. I knew you'd be a good girl, Babe."

"There's just one problem."

"What's that?"

"I don't know your last name."

We laughed.

"It's Black."

"Then someday, I'll be Babe Black."

Tug wanted to get married right away. He also planned to quit his job, become an outfitter, and guide fall hunters and summer fishermen. He figured I'd be the ideal cook and assistant; he wondered if we could live in the cabin.

"You'd have a hard time getting me out of here," I told him.

He grinned. "That's what I figured. But we'll have to build an addition, because I want lots of babies. A healthy Native girl like you should be able to help me out with that."

"Mom says they're cheaper by the dozen," I giggled. "Oh, my family will be so happy, Tug."

A scowl passed over his face. "That's good, honey, but don't expect me to tell mine."

His comment, like a sledgehammer to my midriff, knocked the breath out of me. Was he ashamed of me? Was this a replay of Ken? I went to the sink, fiddled with the turkey.

"Why not, Tug?"

"Babe, I haven't spoken to them in years. It's a long story, but as far as they're concerned, I might as well be dead."

"It's not me, then?"

He shook his head, clearly puzzled. "Don't be a goof. It's me, Babe—all me."

I didn't understand, but I let it go for the evening. While the turkey roasted in the oven, we talked about our future. After gorging on our Christmas feast, we went to bed. I was needlessly nervous; it turned out to be the most glorious night of my life, sweeter than all the nights with Ken. Tug was mature, a thoughtful lover who wanted to please me in every way.

The next morning I thanked the Creator for him. Yet I knew we could not start our life together under a cloud. Over breakfast, I explained.

"Honey, I can't marry you without your family's blessing. Our children need to be accepted by both our families."

He sipped his coffee, still seated at the table; I busied myself with the dishes as deathly quiet gripped the cabin. Finally, he sighed.

151

"Babe, you're right; I've been stubborn for too long. I'll take you to meet them, but—parental blessing or not—we're getting married. Deal?"

I grinned. "Deal."

True to his word, he didn't waste time. Within the week we were flying south.

"You didn't tell me you're from Los Angeles."

"You didn't ask," he countered.

He had a point.

Besides, California is a big state. A doctor now, Ken could be anywhere.

The balmy sunshine was a welcome change. As our cab sped through the busy streets, I soaked up the once-familiar sights of palm trees and the ocean. "Where exactly do they live, Tug?"

"In a snooty part—Bel Air. Don't let it impress you; lots of idiots live there."

I compared the huge mansions on either side of the street to our cozy cabin back up in wildest Alaska. What did people do with so much inside space? The crowds and congestion made me queasy; I was accustomed to vast, open expanses.

Pulling into a long, circular driveway, the taxi crunched alabaster cobblestones and stopped in front of a mansion. Two massive, white columns flanked double mahogany doors and large urns filled with bright blossoms graced the marble steps.

We paused for a minute. "Just remember, honey—they're only people," Tug said, gently squeezing my hand. "If you don't feel at ease, we'll head right back to the bush."

"It's important for us to do this, Tug," I chided.

"You're right, but I'm a little nervous, too," he admitted. "Our last parting was ugly."

A maid in a black uniform, white starched apron, and perky white hat answered the chiming doorbell. "You must be Mr. Black and Miss Babe. I'm Hazel. The Doctor and Madam are expecting you."

"Thank you," Tug replied. He wasn't impressed, but I was.

Hazel ushered us across a shining foyer. Wide doors led to a sitting room where two elderly people, seated in front of a massive, stone fireplace, turned to us when we entered. The distinguished man with silver hair looked faintly familiar; she was short and pudgy, but immaculately dressed, her hair perfectly coiffed.

"Hello Mother, Doctor . . ."

"Tug!" his mother cried, tears streaming down her wrinkled cheeks. "Oh, darling—I've been so worried! No word—no letters—no phone calls—how could you treat us so?"

Before Tug could respond, her husband interrupted. "Dear, that's all in the past now. We're just happy to have our boy back with us where he belongs."

"Oh, yes—yes! You're right, Father," she agreed in a trembling voice. Then Tug went to her and as they embraced, she sobbed with quiet joy. Then Tug turned, extending his hand to the older gentleman.

"Sir," he began.

The old man smiled, gripping Tug's shoulder. "There's no need to say anything. All is forgotten, my son. We have prayed for this day to arrive."

Suddenly, they remembered me. Tug drew me to his side. "This is Babe, the woman I love—the woman I'm going to marry. She refused to have me without the blessings of family; I guess it's an Indian thing." He winked at me, grinning.

"No, it's a wise thing," his mother pronounced, regally extending a jewel-encrusted hand to me. "Welcome to our family, Babe dear. Thank you for bringing my son home to me."

We sat and chatted about the flight for a few minutes. Then when an awkward silence fell, Tug's father suggested that we rest before dinner. Hazel promptly led us upstairs to a luxurious bedroom suite.

"I think they're very nice," I commented to Tug when we were finally alone together behind closed doors.

He shrugged. "We'll see. They have a way of wanting to control things. Especially the old man. Docs are like that."

"You didn't tell me that he was a doctor."

"Doctor, schmoctor. What does it matter?"

"Well, by now, they should at least know that you won't be bossed around."

"Yes; I can be led, but not pushed. Not like my brother, the golden boy. He's a doc, too—can do no wrong. You'll meet him tonight."

I thought briefly of Ken then, for his was a similar situation, but I quickly dismissed the memory. "And whose boy are you?" I teased.

"I guess I got captured by an ornery Indian gal."

"And don't you forget it," I reminded him with a kiss. In his arms, everything was fine.

"Honey, you mean more to me than all the money in the world," he whispered into my hair. "Don't you know that by now?"

"Yeah; I just didn't realize how much money you were talking about."

"Believe me, Babe—money can't make me happy. Only you can do that."

I was nervous when we descended the staircase that evening for dinner. But with Tug by my side, I felt like I could get through anything; after all, we certainly managed the bush in Alaska. What was a little dinner party compared to that?

His mother and father were already seated at the grand, mahogany table, sipping champagne from crystal flutes. She wore a long, shimmering gown and pearls, he a formal suit. Our chinos and flannel shirts were dowdy in comparison.

"I told you this was overkill," the Doctor said to his wife. "You two look far more comfortable," he declared with a friendly smile.

"I don't even own a suit anymore," Tug confessed. "And if I made Babe wear a dress, she'd skin me alive."

The men laughed and his mother faintly smiled. "You're still handsome, Tug," she observed proudly.

Lights against the windows announced the arrival of a car out front. "That must be Tiger and his family—right on time, as usual," the Doctor said, glancing at his elegant, gold watch. "And here is my daughter-in-law, Fatima," he announced as a dark-skinned woman entered the room. The beautiful creature wore a full-length mink and diamond earrings glistened through her lustrous, jet-black hair.

"And where is Tiger?" Tug's mother demanded.

"Locking the car, Mama," Fatima replied. "He'll be right in with the baby."

Footsteps echoed on the marble floor. "Here they are!" Tug's mother smiled in satisfaction.

But when I turned to the doorway, an electric shock coursed through my body. Blood rushed to my cheeks and I closed my eyes in horrible confusion. The man standing in the doorway holding a wiggly little girl—was Ken!

He stopped in midstride. His eyes widened and his mouth opened slightly in surprise, but his wife was in the process of retrieving the struggling child from his arms and no one else seemed to notice. Then, in the blink of an eye, he gathered his composure.

Elegantly dressed, he was still handsome, but the years had marred his youthful perfection: his hair was streaked with gray, worry lines creased his forehead, and a slight paunch bulged beneath his jacket. Tug looked more fit and youthful.

"Ken, darling. Say hello to your brother and his fiancée, Babe, from Alaska," his mother urged.

"Hello, it's very nice to meet you," he complied.

Somehow, I responded, but I don't know what I said.

"This is my wife, Fatima, and our daughter, Alexis," Ken continued. "Say hello, Fatima."

Taking my rough hand into her soft one, she said, "Welcome to California," speaking with a faint accent. I liked her shy smile.

She turned to Tug who said, "I want a hug." Then everyone laughed and the tension was broken. I went over and stood by the fireplace.

"Hey, old man! You look great," I heard Ken say heartily as the two brothers engulfed each other in a gigantic hug.

Tug chuckled. "Wish I could say the same for you!"

Somehow, I got through the long dinner; the rich food stuck in my throat and I couldn't look at anyone. Tug regaled them with anecdotes about life in Alaska, telling them all about how we met, making me sound like a feminine Paul Bunyan.

"You're so brave," Fatima remarked. "Like a real Indian in the movies."

"I'm sure she has many ladylike qualities, as well," Tug's mother added graciously.

"Yes, she most certainly does," Tug confirmed. "She can shoot a moose, skin it, butcher it, and make the best stew you ever ate."

Everyone laughed, thinking it was a joke. I finally escaped to the powder room for a few minutes to collect myself. When I emerged, Ken was standing in the hallway. I couldn't avoid him.

"We have to talk," he whispered urgently. "I'll find a way."

I knew it was wrong; God had finally granted my prayer to meet Ken's family, but I'd never imagined this nightmare. And yet, I couldn't refuse him.

I spent a sleepless night. Tug loved me, yet, how could he possibly understand that his brother and I had once had an affair—that we'd even lived together? My happiness was crumbling beneath a renegade avalanche that couldn't be stopped.

The next morning I was quiet, but when Tug gently asked me about it, I feigned a headache and jetlag.

"You can walk for hours in the bush, but a little airplane ride does you in!" he teased. "Why don't you rest?" he suggested. "The folks want to visit a bunch of old relatives; it'd be boring for you."

"Honey?"

"Hmm?"

"Why is your last name Black? Fatima told me last night that your parents' last name is actually Kasem."

"Long story. I'll tell you sometime," he promised, kissing my cheek. Then the sound of a honking car horn drifted up to us through the open window. "Got to run."

"Thank you, baby." I smiled, but when he hugged me good-bye I felt like a dark traitor.

Ken called shortly after they left. "I know you're alone," he said. "I'll be over in an hour."

I was seated at the dining room table, drinking tea, when he arrived. Hazel ushered him in and he sat across from me, looking wan and tired. Strained silence reigned as we waited for her to return with a fresh pot of Earl Gray. I dared not look at him.

When the maid discreetly retired behind closed doors, Ken took a careful sip of the steaming brew she'd poured for him. Then he looked at me with those darkly liquid eyes that had haunted my dreams and sighed.

"Babe?"

"Yeah. So what?"

"When did you change your name?"

"I didn't, really. It's a childhood nickname. I took it up again when I moved."

155

"When did you move to Alaska?"

"After I left California. It's a good place—my home now."

"That explains it."

"Explains what?"

"I tried to find you, but your family wouldn't tell me anything. Not that I blame them . . . after the way I treated you. But you disappeared without a trace!" he exclaimed.

I glared at him. "I don't want to go into that. I want to talk about now. I need answers. I was in love with you and now I'm engaged to your brother! You never even mentioned that you had one."

From there, Ken filled in the gaps: He and Tug were half-brothers. Their mother's first husband, a construction superintendent, had been killed in a freak job accident when Tug was only six years old. When she married Dr. Kasem, he adopted her firstborn son. A year later, Ken was born.

Tug was mechanically inclined, like his natural father, a hero in his memory. He could not accept his father's death and, as children often do, he deeply resented his stepfather, fiercely clinging to the childhood nickname his dad had given him: Tug. Tug, the boy who loved to build things.

Dr. Kasem, the second physician in his own family, was determined that both sons would follow in his footsteps. Tug adamantly refused, vowing to enter construction, and at eighteen, he resumed his real father's last name, a further offense. Dr. Kasem threatened to disinherit Tug if he didn't go to college and on to medical school; Tug left home after the bitter fight and the family hadn't heard from him since until he brought me home.

"That's why I behaved as I did with you when we were together," Ken confessed. "I knew it was wrong, but I couldn't bear to break their hearts again. I knew Dad couldn't take it.

"Then, once you were gone and I couldn't find you, I just went along with the program. Fatima is a lovely woman, a devoted mother. She's from the old country, the daughter of old family friends. We can never divorce," he concluded.

My heart ached. There had been needless pain in many lives—ironically, due to the very best intentions. Though I had suffered, I suddenly saw Ken in a whole, new light. Suddenly, he was guilty only of being a dutiful, pampered son. Unlike Tug, he couldn't conceive of a life without luxury.

"What can we do?" I finally asked him heavily.

"We must never mention our past. It would only eat away at everyone—destroy us like a cancer. I mean, what are the odds of this happening? A billion to one?" he asked sadly.

"I made a horrible mistake with you," he continued. "Can you ever forgive me? You were my first love and I will always cherish that, and yet, I know you deserve happiness with Tug. Of the two of us, he's the better man."

I privately agreed with him, but I did not say so. "No, Ken, he's just different. You were wonderful to me. You still are."

Then I rose, went to him, and gently kissed his cheek, a farewell to the long years I had wasted. The closure was healing, freeing me of a ghost.

Tug and I spent another two days with his family. Ken didn't come around again, pleading the demands of his practice. I was relieved.

Dr. and Mrs. Kasem insisted that we visit often. When Tug suggested that they come to Alaska, I giggled inwardly, imagining them in our cabin.

"We'll bring each new grandchild to see you. Visit regularly, if you know what I mean," he promised.

Mrs. Kasem giggled. "Sounds like I'll have lots of shopping to do!"

Before we left, Dr. Kasem presented Tug with a sizeable check to finance his new outfitting business. Tug protested, but his father quietly observed, "It's a lot less than I spent on Ken's education. What good is money if we can't help our loved ones with it?"

"Thank you, sir," Tug said tactfully. He knew it was the Doctor's way of making amends.

Days later, it was dark when we finally got back to our cabin in the Alaska wilderness. It was thirty below zero and everything was frozen, but it was wonderful to be home. I lit the Coleman lamps while Tug went out to chop wood. The clean crack of the axe echoed through the snow-covered forest; then suddenly, the noise stopped.

"Babe, come out here!"

My heart stopped. Had he cut himself? Grabbing my heavy parka, I raced outside to the woodpile.

"My God, Tug—what's wrong?"

"Wrong? Nothing, honey," he assured me. "I just want you to see this."

He pointed to the sky. The northern lights were dancing. Brilliant, breathtaking hues of green, purple, pink, and yellow lit up the evening in a powerful display of astral beauty.

Tug sighed and pulled me into his arms. "Let's enjoy this, Babe."

I cuddled against his muscular frame. "The Natives believe the lights are sacred spirits."

Tug rested his chin on top of my head, almost purring with contentment. "Maybe they're welcoming us home."

"Tug, do you think the Creator meant us to find each other?"

"Baby, I know he did," my wonderful man murmured as he bent his bristly face to mine.

Our kiss linked two worlds together forever.

THE END

HAUNTED BY
CHRISTMAS PAST
Will I be starting a new family
tradition this year?

Isn't it funny how the most unexpected little gift can make the biggest difference? It seemed like our first Christmas in Florida was going to be just awful! I had never been alone at Christmas. I had always spent it with my big family at our home in Montana, complete with skiing, sledding, and lots of snowballs fights. But during my last year of college, I met a really great man—Peter Zaret—with big gorgeous eyes and a fantastic sense of humor.

The following summer, Pete and I graduated from college, got married, and made plans to move to Florida. Pete had accepted an active duty commission in the military. He had gone to college on an ROTC scholarship. It always had been his dream to become an officer and serve his country. I loved Pete and supported his decision, but I wasn't too sure how I'd deal with the constant moving that was part of life in the military.

"I'm sure you'll enjoy it, Kathy," my mom said with a smile as she pushed a strand of my hair out of my eyes.

My parents and my two older brothers were helping us pack our van for the move. Since we were newly married, we didn't have a ton of stuff. Most of it was wedding gifts that we had received along with a few castoff pieces from our relatives. We would definitely have to buy some new furniture at some point.

"But what if I don't like it, Mom?" Doubt colored my voice.

"Consider it an adventure or—a new chapter of your life opening up before you," she advised. "You always knew that someday you'd grow up, get married, and leave home."

My mom had a talent for looking on the bright side of everything. Unfortunately, I had not inherited that quality. I was far more cautious in my personality. Pete often teased me that cautious was my middle name because I needed so much convincing to try new things.

"But it's so far away," I said with a frown.

"Relax," my dad said, overhearing me. "We're only a telephone call away. You know you can call us anytime."

So that's how my "new life chapter" began. New husband, new home, and a new future.

I had grown up in the mountains of Montana, had gone to college there, and I was very close with my family who all still lived there.

None of my three brothers or two sisters had ever lived that far away. Even now, none of them lived more than two hours' drive from my parents' comfortable ranch. It made me feel extremely nervous.

My first impression of Florida was that it was very scenic, but still somewhat strange. Florida conjured up images in my head of beaches, bikinis, and a languid lifestyle lived while sipping those tropical drinks with little umbrellas. I thought the ocean seemed too big, and ever changing. The view of the beaches and dunes took some getting used to. It was so odd not having solid, dependable mountains framing the horizon in the distance, as it had been every day for as long as I could remember.

It was September when we arrived, and the first two weeks were actually great. We found a cute little apartment nearby because the waiting list for base housing was impossibly long. Pete attended training during the day, and I found a nice part-time job working for a private adoption agency.

We spent those first two weekends exploring our little corner of Florida. At a nearby town filled with picturesque, quaint little shops, I found a gorgeous stained glass lamp for our bedroom. Pete loved the pastries he discovered.

The base was pretty, and in no time at all, I could find my way around to the commissary and the PX. Then I got an invitation in the mail to attend my first officers' wives club meeting.

"I'm not sure if I want to go to this," I told Pete in a worried voice.

"Well, you kind of have to," he said firmly, "you have nothing to be nervous about. It will probably be fun! You might even make a friend or two. You never know."

"Nervous is a complete understatement of how I feel," I told him, tensely. "I've heard horrible things about this whole officers' wives club idea."

"You shouldn't believe everything you hear," he joked.

"Easy for you to say. You're not the one who has to go," I replied. "Are you absolutely sure I have to be a member of the officers' wives club?"

Pete sighed and sat down on the couch beside me. "Look, Kathy, it's very important for my military career that you attend those meetings and become part of the officers' wives club. Guys whose wives don't participate have a harder time getting ahead in the military. I need you to do this for me—and for us."

"Since you put it that way . . ." I couldn't say no to his logic.

I think I stressed about it for the better part of the week about what to wear, but finally settled on a nice pair of khaki slacks and a pale pink shirt. I didn't want to be underdressed or overdressed. Pete was no help because he told me I looked beautiful in everything, even my old sweats and a ratty T-shirt I wore to clean the house. And while I appreciated the sentiment, it didn't solve the problem of what to wear.

The meeting was being held at the home of Pete's squadron colonel. His wife was in her late forties, with a chic hairstyle and perfect clothes to match. It didn't bode well, as far as I was concerned. I felt ill at ease already.

The house was tastefully decorated, with gorgeous furniture and designer curtains to die for. I thought miserably of the extra sheet that Pete and I were using for a temporary living room curtain and our shabby hand-me-down table and chairs from my sister. The smell of the tasty hors d'oeuvres, wafted from the table. Looking at them, I decided most of them were too pretty to eat. I couldn't imagine myself in a hundred years hosting something like this. I quickly found a spot to sit that was out of the way as the colonel's wife began to speak.

"I'd like to welcome all of the new wives as well as the ones who have been here for a while. What I wanted to do was give you new wives a sense of what to expect as military wives . . ."

Blah, blah blah. She continued to drone on, and though I was trying to pay attention, I was quickly getting very bored. I did my best to stifle a yawn. I noticed a girl with short red hair about my age across the room doing the same. She sent me a small guilty smile, which I answered.

The colonel's wife snared my attention. She was holding up two books. "These will be invaluable in helping you to become a good officer's wife."

Good grief! I thought. They have books on how to become an officer's wife?

The party broke up soon after that. I was headed to my car, when the redhead came up to me.

"I'm Mara Holden. Could you give me a ride? We only have one car right now, and my husband dropped me off. I don't want to wait around for him to pick me up."

"Kathy Zaret," I introduced myself, "and it's no problem at all. Where do you live?"

"Sunshine Avenue apartments."

"No kidding? That's where we live, too."

Since the base was about a twenty-minute drive from where we lived, we had plenty of time to get acquainted. Soon, we were getting along like a house on fire.

"Could you believe it when she brought out those books?" Mara said. "I thought I was going to die laughing right there! I mean, books to tell you how to behave? If I can't figure it out on my own, then I'm not very smart!"

"I know, I know!" I said, chuckling. "Like I would buy any book that wasn't pure fiction. I read so many textbooks in college that I made myself a promise that I was never going to read anything that wasn't for fun again!"

Mara and I discovered that she and her husband lived across the hall in the apartment complex, and we made plans to go out to dinner together the following weekend. I had made a friend! I was thrilled beyond belief. When I sailed into the apartment, Pete was watching a movie on TV.

"So how did the meeting go?" he asked, very cautiously.

"The meeting wasn't terrible, and I met a really nice girl. Do you know Roger Holden? I met his wife, Mara, and we made plans for the four of us to go out to dinner this weekend."

"Yeah, I know Roger. He's a really nice guy. I wouldn't mind going out to dinner with them at all." Pete said. He tried to be very nonchalant about it, but I could tell he was pleased that I was making friends.

Dinner with the Holdens was so much fun that we decided to do it again the next weekend. At the restaurant, another couple that was also new, joined us. Before we know it, we had a whole circle of friends. We went to the movies and took little day trips in the area.

Mara and I started going to step aerobics classes held on base at the physical recreation center. We braved the officers' wives club meeting together, and we actually had a good time. There were a lot of opportunities during the holidays to do service projects for others. Now that we knew a lot of the younger wives, it was fun.

"If it wasn't for the weather and missing my family, I would really be enjoying myself."

Autumn turned into winter, and soon, it was December. Then it began to rain. And it rained and rained and rained, until I thought the whole state of Florida would float away! Not that I would miss it. Puddles were everywhere. Nothing ever seemed to dry, and mold—something I had never thought much about before—grew anywhere it could. Clothes had to be dried thoroughly in the dryer, and we didn't have a clue how to keep that icky mold from appearing around the edges of our windows.

I think the thing that bothered me the most about the weather was the lack of snow! I was so used to having a December filled with fat snowflakes thickly covering the landscape, blanketing everything in a pristine white. To me, Christmas and winter meant snow, and I was missing that special part of the holidays by being in Florida. It seemed bitterly unfair.

When I talked to my family on the phone, they could hear the homesickness in my voice. We couldn't go home for the holidays because of Pete's work schedule.

"New guys always get the worst schedule in the beginning. Next year, I should have it off because there will be other guys who are new," Pete told me.

"As if that makes me feel any better, right now." I sobbed. "I want

161

a Christmas covered in snow. I want to go sledding in the meadows and ice-skating at the pond. I want to make snow ice cream and break icicles from the edge of the garage roof. I want a red nose from being outside too long and fingers that hunger for the warmth of a mug of hot chocolate! I want the kind of Christmas I usually have!"

Pete tried his best to make me feel better, but nothing worked. I went to sleep dreaming of fluffy snowflakes falling against my windows and waking up to the unmistakable sound of rain sleeting against them, instead.

Just when I thought my spirits couldn't get any lower, I began to notice something funny that cheered me up, if only for a little while. We were on our way to an early holiday party with some of our newfound friends. That's when I noticed that people were putting up decorations of snowmen and Santa's sleigh with eight tiny reindeer on their bright green lawns and thinking nothing of it. The sight of houses and palm trees draped in Christmas lights was something to behold. It provided me with continuing amusement to drive past houses with immaculate, lush green lawns covered with all kinds of Christmas decorations. Didn't they know it all looked eerily out of place?

"Look at that, Pete!" I laughed as I pointed to a particularly festive yard in which several plastic snowmen appeared to be getting ready for a nonexistent snowball fight.

"They can't be serious, can they?" Pete asked, grinning.

"I guess they don't know that it looks weird," I replied.

"It really does," Pete said. "I never really thought about it before, but I guess they have to make do without the traditional look, don't they?"

On Christmas Eve, I woke up with the too familiar sound of rain falling. I walked around all day with a huge lump in my throat that I couldn't seem to swallow. I knew my family back home was getting ready for the traditional dinner of chicken and dumplings that we always had on Christmas Eve. I missed them so much! I also missed my mountains—especially the snow.

Of course, I had too much time to think about it, because we weren't doing much at work that day. The office had a Christmas party that afternoon, but I found I couldn't have much of a good time. I tried to put on a good face, though. I didn't want to talk about what was upsetting me or ruin anyone's Christmas spirit. I was really dreading coming home to our apartment later that evening.

As I was coming up the puddled walkway, I noticed Pete had switched on the Christmas lights that were strung around the inside of the front window. I smiled, knowing it was in an effort to cheer me up when I came home. I put the key in the lock and opened the door. As I came in, the light on the Christmas tree blazed forth. A delicious smell filled the air, and I followed it to the kitchen, where my mom's recipe for chicken and dumplings was bubbling merrily away in the electronic cooking pot. Laughter bubbled up in my throat. Usually the limit of Pete's culinary expertise was bacon, lettuce, and tomato sandwiches. He had really outdone himself! His thoughtfulness brought the tears I had been holding back all day to the surface. Then I heard something rustling behind me and turned. There was Pete, standing in the living room holding a brightly wrapped package with too much tape and a lopsided bow.

"What's this?" I asked with a bewildered smile. We hadn't planned to open our gifts until the morning.

"It's an early Christmas present for you," he said as he handed it to me.

"You don't have to give me anything early," I protested.

"Yes, I do. Now open it, because I've been waiting for over a week to give it to you," Pete commanded. On the gift was a note in Pete's familiar sloppy handwriting: To Kathy, from Pete with lots of love. I wondered what it could be.

I managed to unstick the bow and tear off the paper. Inside was a cream-colored square box with golden decorations. I paused for a moment, looking at Pete quizzically. What could it be?

Then I opened the box. Inside it was a snow globe. As I took it out of the box, I saw that it depicted a wintry scene of a family ice-skating on a frozen lake in front of snow-covered mountains. Tears ran down my face as I gently shook it to watch the snowfall inside. There was a wind-up knob on the bottom. I wound it, and the tinkling sounds of "White Christmas" filled the room. Pete had found me the perfect gift. I threw my arms around his neck and covered his face with enthusiastic kisses.

"I guess that means you like it," he said with a smile.

"You knew I would love it," I replied, choked with tears.

Pete wrapped his arms around my waist and pulled me close. "Does this mean I've earned a few brownie points?" he murmured in my ear.

"You'd better believe it," I whispered back as I turned toward our bedroom, pulling him with me.

"Good thing I turned down the electronic cooking pot when you came in," he said with a laugh.

"I always knew you were the perfect husband!"

I don't even remember what else I got for Christmas that year. We survived that first one by ourselves, and that was all that mattered. It turned out to be one of my best Christmases ever, and I was so sure it was going to be the worst.

Not only did Pete's gift mean more than I can say, but I also learned an important lesson. I learned that home is wherever you want it to be, and it has nothing to do with your location. You have to make the place you are feel like home. You have to build new traditions with your husband and friends because you can't always be with your other loved ones. Now, no matter where the military sends us, that snow globe is the first thing I unpack. It reminds me of where I came from, and also that because of my husband's love, I can look forward to where we are going in the future.

THE END

SANTA'S SECRET
Why I lived a lie and pretended
to be something I wasn't.

Father Michael finished reading the story of the first Christmas, led the children in a short prayer, and then, he just stood back and smiled as each child took a turn on Santa's lap.

After years of practice, I'd perfected the voice—deep and booming enough to be convincing—but not scary to the little ones. The snow white, bushy beard was securely glued on, so it couldn't be tugged off no matter how hard a child tried. I didn't even need much padding this year, because Santa was due to deliver twins just before Valentine's Day.

Everything was under control at home. The turkey and ham were in the oven. Freshly baked pies were on the counter. Mashed potatoes, sweet potatoes, and so much more was in the refrigerator ready to be reheated at the last minute. The long table was set with a bright holly patterned tablecloth, and green and red napkins. So was the kids' table.

I loved playing Santa. Every time I put on the red velvet suit, I remembered the wonderful day I'd met Dave.

It took hours to whittle down the long lines waiting in the St. Vincent's Church Hall for a real Christmas dinner. I'd lost count of how many times I'd scooped precise mounds of mashed potatoes onto trays, and made a gentle dent so the gravy wouldn't spill all over. Carefully ladling gravy over the potatoes, I asked if the honored guests wanted some on their turkey and dressing, too.

The guy who relieved the exhausted volunteer next to me, wasn't being careful at all. His green beans didn't just look sloppy on the trays; most of them would just go to waste. I leaned over and whispered that it was better to let folks come back for seconds, and I showed him how to easily serve a perfect portion.

"Thanks. I'm Dave."

"My friends call me Matti."

He didn't ask how he'd missed meeting me at some other church sponsored event. I didn't tell him that I was just pitching in for my roommate who'd gotten a real Christmas miracle: a last-minute invitation to go home with the love of her life.

"If I don't go, he'll probably never work up his nerve to ask me again. Besides, it's not like you have any plans for Christmas."

When we'd scraped the last bite of food into containers to be delivered to those too old or disabled to brave the snow and come to the church, Dave asked if I'd give him a hand with something in the storeroom.

"I made the mistake of missing the last volunteer meeting, so they decided I should play Santa. Could you at least help me put on this awful thing?"

"I can do better than that. Help me strap on the padding. My Uncle Eli always played Santa on Christmas so his best friend could spend the day with his family. When my uncle got sick, I took over. I just love being Santa."

"But you're a girl!"

"Thought you'd never notice. Trust me. That will be Santa's little secret."

I demonstrated my very best Santa voice while Dave helped me get ready.

"Guess I'd better just wait for you here so nobody catches on. Thanks, Matti."

"My pleasure."

When Santa came back, Dave wasn't alone. There was a gorgeous blonde perched on one of the boxes; and a cute redhead of about four sat on his lap. Sucking on his thumb while he talked, didn't make it easy to understand what the little boy wanted Santa to bring him for Christmas.

Dave introduced me to his sister, and his son, translated for Sam.

"He'd like you to bring him a mommy for Christmas."

I'd played Santa enough times to know better than to promise something like that.

"Santa knows you've been a very good boy for your daddy, but the elves and I might need more time to bring that special present. I promise you'll get some special surprises, instead."

"Sam, I saw some extra cookies in the kitchen. Do you want to take Aunt Susan and sample a couple?"

"Please."

"I'll come get you when we're ready to go home."

Dave helped me out of the Santa suit, and told me Sam's mother was a girl from his high school class.

"When she told me she was pregnant, I offered to marry her. She refused: said she was too young to be tied down by a husband or a baby, and she wouldn't even consider adoption. Said she'd rather have an abortion than give her kid to strangers to raise. I finally persuaded her to have the baby and let me raise him."

"I'm impressed. Most guys wouldn't step up like that."

"Most guys weren't raised by my mother. She's the world's best cook, and she always makes enough to feed an army. Please come have Christmas dinner with us."

"I wouldn't dream of crashing your family's celebration."

"Rumor has it she made her special 'Death by Chocolate' cake this year."

Something about Dave's deep green eyes and his gentle touch made me say yes.

Before I knew what hit me, his huge wonderful family surrounded me. Nobody asked why he'd brought a total stranger. Nobody asked why I didn't have Christmas plans with my family.

I enjoyed every bite of the feast, and I stood up to help clear the table when the last of Dave's family finally put down their forks—declaring that they couldn't possibly stuff in one more bite.

"Sit down, Matti. I can manage just fine." Dave's mother glared at me, but I just kept carefully scraping dishes and stacking them.

"My grandmother always used to say that an extra pair of hands made any job go faster."

I learned all too quickly why nobody else had volunteered to help. Before we'd started washing the first dish, Dave's mother made it abundantly clear that everything I did was too slow, too sloppy, or just not the way she wanted it done. Still, it seemed wrong to just walk away and leave her with all the mess.

"What are you boiling water for? Nobody wants tea!"

"It's a trick my grandmother taught me. I'm going to put boiling water and some soap in the roasting pan with the sweet potato casserole, and those pots with food stuck on the bottom. By the time we're finished the dishes and the silverware, all that guck will be dissolved enough to just sponge away—instead of having to scrub."

What I remembered most about pitching in to clean up after the holidays when I was growing up, was the conversation. Generations of women talking, laughing, sharing memories, and dreams. There was barely a word out of Dave's mother that wasn't criticism or directions of where to put something away.

I must have done something right. Dave's mother invited me to Sunday dinner, and she didn't protest when I offered to help clean up.

Dave and I started going out for pizza with Sam, or a grown-up movie and dinner alone, a couple of times a week. His mother kept inviting me for Sunday dinner. After a couple of months, Dave's mother didn't hover over me anymore, criticizing my every move. One Sunday, she shocked me by sitting down and taking her shoes off while I finished wiping off the counter and scrubbing the sink.

She started talking, rambling on and on about something. I wasn't listening all that carefully. So long as she wasn't criticizing me, she could say whatever she wanted. All of a sudden, I couldn't help catching bits and pieces.

"Damn Jews think they own the world!" "Should have let them all die in the Nazi camps!"

Tell her, Mathia. Tell her, I thought. My long dead grandmother's voice was every bit as loud and clear as if she were standing next to me. No. I didn't have the words to erase that kind of hatred. Speaking up would just slam the door in my face, shutting me out of this huge, wonderful family I'd come to love as if it were my own.

Biting my cheek bloody to keep quiet was a small price to pay for a chance at a lifetime of happiness with Dave and Sam. It wasn't the same as lying. Not really.

Deep down, I knew I should have told Dave Santa's biggest secret long before he surprised me with a tiny diamond and big promises of happily ever after.

I almost told him dozens of times, but something always kept me from sharing the truth.

Praying that God would forgive my deception, I exchanged marriage vows at St. Vincent's, settled into a comfortable routine of building a life with Dave and Sam.

Year after year, Dave and I stood side-by-side, dishing up Christmas dinner for the homeless.

Year after year, nobody at St. Vincent's guessed which member of the Riley household really played Santa. Dave never suspected Santa had another secret.

Dave's mother moved in with us just after Easter. She'd started having fainting spells, and finally had to agree that it wasn't safe for her to live alone anymore.

None of her daughters or other daughters-in-law volunteered to host the small army that shared Dave's name, so they would all be turning up at our house after we finished the other Riley family Christmas tradition.

Santa doled out inexpensive presents to the children who'd have plenty of presents to open on Christmas, and made sure the others got a carefully wrapped, brand-new toy. Church volunteers helped parents with vehicles load boxes of food, gently used clothing, and toys. They also jotted down addresses for those who'd walked or taken the bus to make deliveries to later. I hurried to the storeroom to shed the Santa suit, and I headed home. There was so much to do before Dave's family arrived.

The doorbell rang much too soon. I wasn't nearly ready. Dave's family wasn't usually on time, much less early, so I wasn't all that surprised to see a silver-haired stranger at the door. She had my mother's eyes, and my grandmother's trembling hands.

"Aunt Rivka? It's been a long time."

"Too long. I almost didn't find you at all. If I hadn't run into your old roommate at the supermarket, I wouldn't have known to look for Matti Rose-Riley."

"Please, stay for dinner."

She wrinkled her nose in disapproval.

"Is that ham I smell?"

"Yes, but there's turkey, too."

"I just came to give you this."

Aunt Rivka unwrapped the soft cloth as though there were a baby protected inside. It revealed our family's treasured menorah. The special candleholder designed to celebrate Hanukkah had room for nine candles—one to commemorate each of the eight nights of the Festival of Lights. The tallest one—the Shamash—served to light the others.

Praying she hadn't already seen it, I quickly tucked the gold cross necklace inside my T-shirt. Most of my mother's family had been exterminated in the German death camps during World War II. My great-grandmother spent her childhood in attics and cellars, one step ahead of the Nazis. She'd managed to hang onto the menorah through all the middle of the night miraculous escapes, and she brought it all the way to America where she met and married my great-grandfather.

Suddenly, I realized my silence was so much more than just a lie. It was a slap in the face to the memory of all those who had been killed because they were Jewish.

It was only right for Dave to be the first to hear the truth: to learn that Matti Rose was really Mathia Rose Goldberg. Mathia meant "God's gift" in Hebrew. Rose was in honor of my great-grandmother. I was born two months early; the doctors weren't sure I'd survive. Following Jewish tradition, I'd been given the name of a dead relative to fool the angel of death, and keep me safe.

My husband listened patiently while I tried to explain that I hadn't been inside a temple since my mother's funeral. It was almost impossible to admit how easy it had been to turn my back on my religion, and make St. Vincent's the center of my universe—just like it was for the rest of his family.

Aunt Rivka and Dave's mother will probably never forgive me for what I did, but the rest of the family seems to understand . . .

I'll put on the Santa suit next year, cook Christmas dinner for the small army that shares Dave's name, but I'll also tell the Hanukkah story, and light the candles in my family heirloom menorah. No more secrets for this Santa!

THE END

169

SANTA'S LITTLEST HELPER
My daughter is jollier than he is!

I paid the cashier for the doll, relieved that my shopping was almost finished. Emily had penned a long wish list, but she also knew that Mommy's budget is limited.

I glanced at my watch. Just as I suspected, it was already time to rush off to her school to attend the Christmas program. So much for a relaxing day off from work!

I was greeted by a few flakes of falling snow as I stowed my shopping bags in the trunk. There wasn't time for me to change clothes, so jeans and my favorite green sweater would just have to do. Time management has never been my strong suit and in the years since Alan's death I'd been trying to be all things to Emily and I sometimes needed more than twenty-four hours in a day.

By the time I arrived in the Prairie Regional School's parking lot, there was no question in my mind that we were going to have a white Christmas and I had no jacket on. The wintry weather apparently hadn't kept anybody away because I had to hunt for a place to park.

When I walked inside, I spotted Emily, a red ribbon in her hair, as she lined up with the girls' choir. They were ready to go on stage. I slipped into one of the few empty seats and shivered as I waited. After a few brief announcements and some dancing elves and snowflakes, Santa made a brief appearance in the spotlight. He welcomed us to the program, told us to sit back and enjoy ourselves, and introduced the star singers.

A few stifled giggles could be heard as the girls filed in nervously. Emily was in the front row and she remembered all of the words to the Christmas carols. It was too bad that one very proud mom in a sweater had forgotten to buy batteries for the camera when she bought the film.

The applause was sincere after the final song, "Rudolph the Red-Nosed Reindeer." The girls had given a flawless performance.

Next up was Santa himself. He seemed to have endless patience as each child took a turn speaking with him. He accepted lists from those who had them and smiled and handed out picture books for almost two hours. I watched as it was Emily's turn. She whispered in his ear. Santa nodded and listened some more. Then Emily accepted the big picture book and kissed him on the cheek.

Afterward, Emily came over, hugged me, and tossed a surprise my way. "Santa said I could probably have the doll, but no promises yet. Plus, I told him that you need another hero."

"Emily? You told him what?"

"I told Santa how Daddy was a soldier and died," she said. "I explained to him that it's time we had a daddy around the house again."

I could feel myself blushing and I avoided looking over at the man playing Mr. Claus. Emily and I exchanged small talk all the way to the car while I tried my best to fend off my embarrassment.

During dinner and throughout that evening, I couldn't erase Emily's words from my mind. She was right. We needed someone special to make our family feel complete again. I longed for Emily to have brothers and sisters, but I doubted that Mr. Right was out there waiting for me. Even if he were, between my job at the driving school and Emily, when did I have time to look for him?

Not long after school started up again early in the New Year, Emily brought home a neatly folded note. "I'm supposed to tell you this is from Santa's helper."

I laughed as I thanked her and accepted it with a mock bow. I thought surely it was nothing but a joke. I put the paper on the kitchen counter and continued making the meatloaf for that night's dinner. After we ate and Emily had finished her bubble bath, she was busy dressing her new doll. It was then that I remembered the note. Feeling silly, I opened it and read,

Emily tells me there's a void in your household and I think it might be time to get on with your life. If you'll allow me, I can recommend a very nice candidate. He's intelligent, punctual, reliable, and maybe even a bit magical. He's a whiz at repairing broken toys and he's a skilled driver, too. Call this number if you'd like to meet him.

The note was unsigned. Is one of the teachers playing a trick on me? I wondered. My best friend, Christine, is the school nurse, so I impulsively dialed her number to ask her opinion.

There was no answer. Then I remembered that she had a new relationship. Of course she's out on a Friday night! I thought. She has a life. When was the last time I'd had a date for a movie or a pizza? It was longer than I cared to think about.

Oh, what do I have to lose? I dialed the number mentioned in the mystery message. When a man answered, I identified myself, but he didn't seem to know me. "I'm Emily's mom," I added, suddenly feeling timid.

"Oh, great! You had on the light green sweater. That's my favorite color. I hope my little note didn't upset you. Emily's request touched me. Anyway, I guess I should explain to you that I'm Santa Claus. Well, not the real Santa Claus. It's only a part-time job, you know. My name is Ben and I'm a house painter. But not in this freezing weather, mind you." He laughed. "So, what's your story?"

I liked the sound of his voice, so I gave him an abbreviated version of things. I talked about fixing up the old house and how I came to work at a local driving school. I was honest about my grief at unexpectedly losing my husband. I even told him about Emily's ballet lessons and my attempts at learning to play tennis. When I mentioned the novel I was reading, he told me that he'd just started the very same book. Already we shared a favorite author!

"I'm on page forty-one," he said. "I'm a pretty avid reader. Look, when I finish it, how about we meet for coffee? We can compare book reviews."

He sounded safe enough. He'd painted the principal's house, after all. I gave Ben my number and hung up, wondering if anything would ever come of it.

By that time, Emily was fast asleep. I couldn't get through the final chapter of the novel, not that night. Just as I was about to turn off my bedside lamp and go to sleep, the phone rang.

It was Ben. "I just wanted to let you know that I'm on chapter fourteen. I might stay up all night reading, so be thinking about that latte."

We shared eight more extended phone conversations before we met in person, so it wasn't at all intimidating to sit down together with steaming mugs of coffee. We met at a book shop. Where else?

Ben was the first man I met who could talk more than I could. He had so many interests and playing Santa wasn't his only side gig. He filled up his free hours by volunteering as a magician at a children's hospital and an orphanage. In between his painting jobs in the summer, he coached a youth soccer team. He seemed to have endless energy.

"I've always wanted kids," he said. "I come from a large family. They all expected me to be happily married and have about a dozen children by now. Somehow, I just haven't found the right mother."

We laughed and exchanged details about our lives for hours. Ben listened without showing any signs of boredom. Christine was babysitting for Emily and I'd promised that I wouldn't be out too late, so I cut the date short even though I didn't want to leave.

For Valentine's Day, Ben presented me with tulips and a kiss, but somehow I felt that he was holding back on me. We're close friends, but can we ever be lovers? I wondered. He gave Emily a music box with a twirling ballerina inside and she loved it.

Ben was full of surprises. Springtime is his busy season and I hardly saw him without a paintbrush in his hand, but he still surprised me on my birthday. I came home from work and found he'd painted my house lime green! "To match your favorite sweater!" he told me.

As the days rolled into summer, Ben and I grew more intimate. He seemed more ready for a serious relationship and we were hardly ever apart. We went out to the movies alone, took Emily roller skating, watched soccer games together, played tennis, and swam in his pool. He even did magic tricks at Emily's birthday party, much to her delight.

One night, over pizza, he told me that his parents were about to celebrate a wedding anniversary. They lived in another state and he invited me on a long weekend trip to attend the celebration. His whole family would be there, he warned. It sounded a little daunting to me, but I was curious about the family of the man I loved and so I gladly went along.

I met so many people at that party—from his cousins to his grandparents. People had flown in or driven in from five states. He wasn't kidding one bit about his large family. His parents were wonderful, though—very welcoming and friendly to me. I didn't feel at all like a stranger in their midst. Instead, everyone in the family made me feel right at home.

"I'm so glad to finally meet Ben's future wife," one of his sisters told me.

I must've looked shocked because she whispered, "Our Ben is taking things at a slow pace, I know, but we're sure he'll get you to the altar sooner or later. All he ever talks about is you and Emily."

Winning the unofficial approval of his family seemed to be the charm. Overnight, Ben turned into a romantic. He wrote me love poems and painted my toenails. He baked heart-shaped cinnamon cakes and planted flowers in my garden. I marveled at the sudden change in him!

Meanwhile, Christine's Mr. Right had turned into Mr. Wrong and she kept calling me to go out with her, but I just didn't have the time. Ben and Emily were my only priorities.

Soon I was anticipating our first Thanksgiving together and I asked Ben what size turkey I should buy. "You don't remember that I can cook up a storm?" he asked. "I want you to sit back and relax on that day. I'll take care of everything—the bird, the yams, and I'll even make mashed potatoes from scratch. What kind of stuffing do you and Emily like?"

I was convinced that there was no better man on the whole planet!

We decided to hold our Thanksgiving feast at Ben's apartment because his dining room is so large. Ben did let me set the table and Emily helped. As we folded the napkins together, she asked me, "Mommy, why don't you two just get married? What are you waiting for?"

I looked up right as Ben walked in carrying a basket of rolls to put on the table. Did he overhear her rather pointed suggestion? I wondered.

Thankfully, he gave no hint that he had and only smiled at us before quickly disappearing into the kitchen. Next he emerged with serving bowls full of vegetables, and after that came the roasted turkey and more bowls. He gestured for us to sit down.

On my placemat was something red. How'd that get there? I wondered. I examined it as Ben placed slices of turkey onto our plates. Without missing a beat, he spooned out mashed potatoes and told me it was something for me.

"A Santa cap? What am I going to do with this?" I asked.

Emily giggled, amused by the new game.

Ben handed out our plates. "Go ahead, try the cap on," he urged. "See if it fits."

Puzzled, I unfolded the cap. Suddenly, a diamond solitaire ring appeared within its folds. Ben came over to me, got down on one knee, and said, "I want to do this right because I only plan to do it once in my life. Will you be my Mrs. Claus?"

Needless to say, I accepted!

THE END

Sweet Holiday Story:

A GIFT FOR MEEMAW

A present from a child always means the most.

"Meemaw, what's your favorite color?"

"Green. Why?"

"Just wondered," my oldest grandson said.

"I told you it was green, Drake," said Emory, the younger one.

"Sssh. We had to make sure."

I smiled to myself as they went on out to the porch still whispering between themselves.

Kids, I thought. They get such a big kick out of the season.

They were spending the day with me so I went on about the business of getting supper ready for two always-hungry boys. As I worked in my country kitchen, my thoughts were on the hectic holiday season—and, more important—the fact that my Christmas shopping wasn't done.

Then I thought suddenly of another child, many years ago, with the same thing on her mind, asking about favorite colors, etc. I was probably ten or eleven years old that year and I was at a total loss as to what to give my mother for Christmas . . .

We were just a little better off that year than we had been the year before.

Daddy had given me a little money and told me to choose a gift for my mother by myself.

I worried and pondered about it and drove Mama crazy with my "subtle" questions about colors, what did she want, need, etc. She evaded the questions and told me that anything would do and not to worry about it.

But I did worry. And then suddenly, I knew: Mama would be thrilled with a new dress. But just as suddenly, it hit me: How can I get her a dress? And what size? And where?

We had no stores that sold ready-made dresses in our small country town at that time. Everyone bought material and patterns and made their own clothing or had Mrs. Letts, the town seamstress, sew whatever they needed.

I didn't know a thing about patterns—nor material—and I sure couldn't sew. Not even a stitch. But I did know that Mama's favorite color was blue and I figured that maybe, just maybe, I could sneak one of Mama's dresses out of the house for Mrs. Letts to go by. After all, she made all of Mama's dresses—and all of mine, too.

So that's what I decided I would do.

It took a little effort, but I got a dress out of Mama's closet while she was out feeding the chickens and wrapped it in a sack. Then I called out to her that I was going into town for an ice cream cone and to get my uncle, who lived with us, a bottle of root beer. I had let Uncle Bob in on my secret. We didn't live but about a mile from town, but we were still very rural back in those days.

"This will thrill your mama," said Mrs. Johnstone, the general store owner. She had just measured and cut several yards of lovely, sky-blue material, cut me a dab of lace for the collar, and given me pearly white buttons to match wrapped up in a brown paper sack.

Mrs. Letts said the very same thing when I delivered the materials to her shop and she assured me that she would have the dress finished in time.

Another tale of some sort got me back into town and back to Mrs. Letts' shop to pick up the finished dress and bring it home to wrap it up a few days later.

My mind floated back to the voices of my grandsons still conspiring on the front porch.

I'd told them the story of the dress at one time or another, but at the time, it was to instill in them that the price of the gift itself is never important.

Now, outside, I saw them grin, shake hands, and holler, "Okay! Done!"

I laughed. I guessed that the dilemma of Meemaw's present had been settled.

Christmas morning came and after the boys had opened all of their presents from Santa Claus back at home, they came to my house and raced in the door, their arms full of presents. We always have dinner as a family on Christmas Day.

My husband and I greeted them and then we all gathered around the tree, the boys whooping and hollering and ripping open their presents from us just as fast as they could.

Then I saw them catch each other's eye and they grew suddenly solemn as together, they brought me a beautifully wrapped present resplendent with the signature ribbon and label of our ladies' wear store in town. (We had come a long way from Johnstone's General Store and Mrs. Letts.)

"Now, what can this be?" I eased the tape loose slowly.

Of course, both boys were bouncing up and down in front of me and shuffling and saying, "Hurry up, Meemaw!"

I finally pulled out a lovely, green, velour pantsuit.

"Oh, boys—it's beautiful! And just what I needed! But, how did you know I needed a new pantsuit? And just the right color!"

They grinned like Cheshire cats and hung on my chair, infinitely pleased with themselves.

"They picked it out all by themselves, Mom," their mother—my daughter—said proudly with tears shimmering in her green eyes.

I looked at the lovely pantsuit, hugged the boys, and thought about my own mother and that Christmas Day long ago . . .

Her sky-blue dress was wrapped in tissue paper and tied with a red yarn bow. There was no store name on it at all but, oh—how she loved that dress and my successful effort to surprise her.

I know my grandsons gave me the exact same wonderful feeling on that extra-special Christmas morning many years later.

A gift from a child is always precious, but the thought behind it more so—whether it be a green velour pantsuit from a fancy ladies' store, or a blue cotton dress from the general store.

Some things never change.

THE END